Crowns of Courage

To Aven &
Isaac,

Take Courage
& trust Him

Karen Hinkley

Crowns of Courage

Karen Kleinberg

Contact Karen Kleinberg:
www.couragekeeper.com

CROWNS OF COURAGE

© 2011 Karen Kleinberg

Published by
Deep River Books
Sisters, Oregon
http://www.deepriverbooks.com

ISBN 13: 978-1-935265-82-5
ISBN 10: 1-935265-82-2

Library of Congress:

Printed in the USA 2011941546

Cover design by Rebecca Barbier

Table of Contents

Acknowledgments

John, Ryan, and Kelly, my amazing grandchildren, inspired this story during a pancake breakfast when they expressed a desire to know more about the heroes of the Bible. Their faces have stayed before me as the narrative evolved. I pray they will remember the courage of these heroes and choose to follow their footsteps throughout their lives.

This book could never have been written without the encouragement and support of my family, friends, and writers group. My wholehearted thanks to my husband Jerry, my biggest cheerleader, for the hours he spent editing the many revised pages set before him.

Crowns of Courage was written to inspire young readers to look at life through a different lens and discover the amazing adventure that comes our way when we look for God in our everyday circumstances. He says that when we seek him with all our hearts, we will find him, and if we choose his ways, we will be blessed. Our choices in life shape our futures and bring with them benefits or consequences. God leaves the decisions in our hands. May we choose wisely.

So, Who Is the Real Hero?

—◆—

Pajamas, pancakes, and Cocoa Puffs," announced Nana. She smiled at her three grandchildren, who were parading into the kitchen with their eyes half-closed. "What could be better on this cold, blustery morning?"

Grampa poured batter onto the sizzling griddle with the family's infamous pancake spoon. Smiles stretched across sleepy faces as the sweet aroma of stacked cakes mingled with the scent of sizzling bacon.

Kelly, the youngest of the three, pulled her stool to the counter. "Mmm, let's go with the pancakes, definitely!"

John and Ryan ignored her enthusiasm. Without a word they settled themselves at the counter and bent their favorite action figures into fighting positions.

"Shoo…mmm…pow!" John mumbled.

"Well, boys," said Nana, "as amazing as those action heroes are, do you know there were *real* men, who actually lived in the past, who performed some incredible heroic acts during their lifetimes? In fact, true stories have been written about them."

Seeing their eyes flash in her direction, she smiled and continued, "Stories about superheroes are certainly fun to hear. It takes a good storyteller to create those brave characters for us to enjoy." She leaned over the counter and poured juice into their empty glasses. "We do have fun with their adventures, don't we? Even when we know they're only tales from the storyteller's imagination?"

Grampa flipped the pancakes on the griddle. "So, who are

these real heroes you're talking about?" he asked.

Nana scooted plates and napkins in front of the kids. "They were real-life superheroes who lived a long time ago and experienced miraculous events. God wants everyone to know about them, so he helped men who knew their stories write about them in the Bible."

Ryan looked up. "Did they have powers like Superman and Batman?"

"Yes, God gave them special strength when they needed it, or sometimes the ability to do miraculous things. But even better, their stories really happened." Nana smiled at Kelly. "No one made these stories up in their minds. Instead, the writers recorded what *really* happened."

The sweet aroma filled the kitchen when Grampa poured more batter on the hot griddle. Nana took the piled-high plate of steaming pancakes from the counter and served the boys. Pausing, she said, "Grampa and I just read about one of God's superheroes—Elijah. You'll never believe the surprising courage God gave him. It was incredible! In fact, his story could be called one of the most *super* stories in the Bible."

John peered over his juice glass and narrowed his eyes. "What did he do that was so great?"

Offering Kelly hot pancakes, Nana answered, "He proved to a selfish king and a very wicked queen that when God is with you, nothing is impossible. God is more powerful than anyone or anything in the world. Would you like to hear the story?"

"Yes," Ryan blurted. "Tell us!" He straightened up and leaned forward.

"Okay," Nana said, leaning over the counter with a sparkle in her eyes. "Think back with me to a time long ago, when cities and countries were ruled by kings and queens. One country, Israel, was in deep trouble. Cruel warriors wanted to take their land, their treasures, and even their people. Sometimes the kings of Israel would ask God for help and advice. But most of them ignored him and his directions and found themselves in big battles they couldn't handle. Without God's protection, they really suffered."

Pulling out a stool, she joined them at the counter. "This is the story of one of the most famous kings of old Israel, and it deserves our best storytellers. So let's hear the story from Seth and Michael. They'll tell us the story while it is happening."

"Who are Seth and Michael?" quizzed Ryan.

"Another good question. Think of Seth as a time traveler who was invited to go into the future—his future, not ours. He had the privilege of watching some amazing events that occurred with kings and prophets."

John picked up his fork and dug into his stack of hot pancakes. Nana handed him the syrup. "Well," she said, "when Seth was a young child, he lived in a troubled family. You may remember some of his story. His parents were Adam and Eve, who had to move away from their beautiful garden home."

"Why?" Kelly looked surprised.

"I'm afraid they made a choice that changed their lives…and not for good!" Nana shrugged. "Because they decided to ignore God's rule about a certain tree in the garden, they had to leave their home in Eden, and they could never return to their perfect paradise. Seth's parents had to work very hard to feed and care for their family. There was very little time to play or relax. But they loved God and taught their children about him. And they had lots of children. However, Cain, Seth's oldest brother, didn't learn from his father and mother's mistakes. He chose to ignore his family's lesson. Cain had a sad life when he walked away from God and his family. He was lonely and angry, and often his temper got the best of him. He even killed his younger brother, Abel. But that's a story for another time."

Pausing to pour coffee for herself and Grampa, Nana continued. "Back to Seth. Because of what had happened to his family, he was determined to listen to God and follow his ways. So God encouraged him and invited him into the future to see miraculous events that could change his life. The first would take place when Elijah, a *real* hero, challenged a king named Ahab. He was a king who was about to make a dangerous decision for himself and his people. Seth would watch the great contest that Elijah had called King Ahab to observe. The contest was between the God of heaven and the god of this world. But Seth wouldn't go into the future alone. God sent his mighty angel, Michael, to stay close and protect Seth in the great battles that would come."

Nana gave everyone more pancakes and put the empty plate on the counter. "Does anyone remember Michael from Bible stories?"

The children shook their heads. John stopped moving his action figure and watched Nana with big eyes.

"Michael is a very special angel of God. He is the mighty archangel who fought against God's greatest enemy, Satan. At one time, Satan led many angels into a great war against God. But God gave Michael awesome strength to throw Satan and his followers out of God's heaven."

Nana eyed the children one by one. "Sadly, kids, even as a fallen angel, Satan has never stopped trying to capture God's throne in heaven and hurt God's people on earth. But God's plans can't be stopped by anyone. Even angels and demons can't stop God, because he is the greatest ruler over everyone and everything."

"So what about Michael? When does he use his power?" Ryan asked.

"Oh, many times," Nana said. "God has used his archangel Michael many times to fight for his people and defend them from their enemies. He is an amazing angel! Michael was even there when God promised that one day the King of the Universe would come to earth. God said that this king, the mightiest of all kings, would come and rescue God's people once and for all! He would make a way for them to live forever with him in heaven." She smiled and pointed upward. "And that's even a better place to live than the garden home God made for Seth's parents!"

Nana pushed aside her stool, went over to the children, and pulled them together with a big hug. Their eyes widened in surprise, and smiles spread across their sticky, syrup-filled faces. Releasing them after a final squeeze, she stepped back and asked,

"Well, are you ready to meet some of God's real heroes?"

Smiling and wide-eyed, John swept his hand toward Nana and declared, "Let the adventure begin!"

The king's heart is in the hand of the Lord;
He turns it like the river,
Wherever he wills.

PROVERBS 21:1, PARAPHRASED

BOOK ONE

Battle of the Gods

—◆—

CHAPTER 1
The Challenge of Faith

⸻✦⸻

Seth felt his muscles tense and his head pound with excitement. He watched the angelic army mobilize into position behind their heavenly commanders. Their faces radiated with the lustrous countenance of another world. He listened to the hum and clatter of their weapons as they adjusted their stances and waited for the battle command. Searching the crowd for the archangel Michael, his escort and mentor, Seth fidgeted with his belt and the small hunting knife that hung there. His heart pounded with anticipation.

Am I really here? he wondered.

He had heard the calming voice call his name in the field that very morning. *"Seth, do not be afraid. I am taking you to another time and place. Observe carefully all you see and hear. Be especially mindful of the choices men make, both good and bad."*

He remembered dropping his plow handle like a hot piece of coal when warm light and the sound of rushing water surrounded him. It had all happened so fast. When the incredible being appeared before him, he'd felt dizzy. The man's flowing white robe glistened with white, dancing lights that faded away when he spoke his first words.

"Do not be afraid, Seth," he said. "You are going to a place where you will see events which God Almighty will use to complete his plans and purposes for the people of future generations. When you arrive, wait for your escort and mentor. His name is Michael. He is the archangel of Almighty God. He will protect you and guide you through the events that take place."

Before Seth could utter a sound, the visitor had disappeared, and Seth found himself standing with thousands of angels. The air was fresh and sweet. His senses jumped, and his mind filled with questions. Everywhere his eyes roamed, spectacular heavenly sights flooded his vision. He watched sparkling streams of light burst from the stars. Jeweled colors shot like lightning through hundreds of breathtaking rainbows. Seth couldn't take his eyes off the sky. A foggy white light surrounded the moon and reflected the sun's heat. He could feel its fingers of crystal light warm the space around him until it was near enough to touch his face. In the distance he heard singing, and the melodic sounds of stringed instruments mingled with the music of bells.

Magnificent warrior angels were all around him, gathered in squads. Some wore breastplates and sheathed swords. Beyond the host preparing for battle were angels with mighty wings extending from flowing robes. They moved freely from one group to another.

Taking a deep breath, Seth bowed his head and whispered into the air, "O God, thank you for this unbelievable honor. Why did you bring me here? I don't understand. I am not strong like my father, nor smart like my sister." Seth glanced at his calloused hands and dirty fingernails and quickly brushed them on the folds of his tunic, hoping to hide evidence of his simple life. He was a young man, and strong, but he knew he didn't fit in with these spotless beings. He felt totally outclassed in their presence. But the angels seemed to ignore his insecurity, and they passed him by with nods and smiles.

Sensing a powerful presence beside him, he turned and looked up into the steady eyes of a towering angel who stood erect with folded arms and a slight smile.

Seth caught his breath and felt his heart pound. His legs tensed. The great angel wore a pleated tunic with a form-fitted breastplate of brownish-gold metal, scarred but sound. From his belt hung a tremendous sword encased in a gold sheath. His shoulders and arms were protected in the folds of heavy, leather-like sleeves. But it was the angel's size that overwhelmed Seth.

"Do not be afraid," the angel instructed. "I am Michael. I will be with you and guide you through the events God has planned for you to watch. We will face the enemy of Almighty God today, an enemy who wants to destroy God's people in the nation of Israel. But I am called to protect them…and you. You will not be harmed."

The confident strength of past victories rested on Michael's face. The angel's calmness relaxed Seth's nerves, and he felt his shoulders drop, loosening the tension in his neck. He flexed his fingers and uncurled his fists but never took his eyes off Michael. Drawing a deep breath, Seth asked, "What do you want me to do?"

"Observe carefully and remember what you see," answered Michael. He placed a strong hand on Seth's bony shoulder, then pointed to the earth below.

From their vantage point in the heavens, they had a clear view of a shaggy-haired man making his way up the rocky path of a mountain. "Look, Seth, here he comes!" Michael declared. "It's Elijah, the prophet, climbing Mount Carmel even as we watch! Pay special attention to him today. He is God's man. He will orchestrate the contest we are soon to watch."

Seth brushed wispy hair from his face and gazed at the scene below. The mountain was bustling with people. His mind filled with questions. *What is all this about? What contest will happen here today? It must be important if God wants me to watch.* Seth thought about his father, Adam, and all that he knew about God and his angels. *Father said that God spoke to him in the garden, that he knows God's voice. He says God will always be with us, no matter what happens. What is going to happen?* Seth realized he had been holding his breath. He looked at the huge angel standing next to him and let out a deep, relaxing sigh. *God, will I hear your voice today like my father hears you speak to him?*

"Elijah's conflict with King Ahab has gone on for many years," said Michael. "But today the king will tolerate Elijah because he thinks this contest may bring him a good result with his people."

Seth steadied his gaze on Elijah.

"The events you are witnessing here will take place thousands of years after your lifetime," Michael continued. "Many generations of men and women from your father's family will be born and die before this historic event occurs. You are the third son of your father and mother, and they have put their hope in you for the good future of their family. Watch and listen, and take the truths you gain into your heart, and you will not disappoint them…or Almighty God."

Seth nodded but thought, *He sounds like Father. He is always serious, and he expects me to hear everything he says and then remember it. Well, this is different. How could I forget all of this? I won't forget the angels, that's for sure!*

Elijah, the legendary maverick, stopped at the foot of Mount Carmel and looked toward the top of the mountain. He was roughly clothed in an old camel-skin cloak, and he wore a large leather belt around his waist. His rugged sandals kicked up explosions of dust with each step. In the little nation of Israel, this solitary man embodied power and suspense. God had sent him today to end a three-year drought. This contest would prove the awesome power of the Almighty, Israel's forgotten God.

Michael pointed at Elijah. "They call him 'The Lone Wolf of the Lord.' And here he comes again, to defy King Ahab and Queen Jezebel, the rulers of Israel. They both encourage the people to follow the queen's god, Baal."

Michael's voice dropped and filled with disappointment. "She brought *the idol* with her to Israel when she married King Ahab. After he built her a special palace, he also built a temple for her gods. The people think Baal controls the rains and storms that affect their crops. But Elijah denies Baal's power. He continues to declare that God Almighty is the true god, and the only god they should follow."

Seth listened to Michael's explanations, but his eyes kept coming back to the amazing sights around him. Angels were everywhere, and they glistened in rainbows of light. Then Seth looked up at Michael, who stood erect with his arms folded across his middle. He was focused on Elijah. The prophet looked terribly alone as he climbed the mountain. He gave no sign that he could see the angels.

Michael relaxed his stance, softened his voice a bit, and said, "Elijah wasn't always so brave, Seth. For years, people ridiculed his belief in God Almighty. They laughed at him when he would not join them at their temple or participate in the celebrations and festivals for Baal."

Seth understood the need for courage. His long legs and lean, lanky body made it easy for him to run from his enemies rather than face them. He was becoming an able hunter, but he shied away from confrontations with the neighboring kinsmen—the descendants of his exiled brother, Cain. He felt anxious when they shouted insults and bragged about their strength. Their loud bravado and teasing made Seth feel stupid and alone. He preferred the familiar protection of his family and stayed close to home. Despite the angelic wonders all around him, a familiar fear suddenly came to mind. *What would I do if Cain came home? Would he be the same angry man who left our family before I was born? Why was he so hostile? If he comes back, he might hurt us or even kill us, like he did our brother Abel.* Seth shuddered at the thought and looked down at Elijah. *I wonder if Elijah was ever afraid of his own family?*

Seth snapped back from his thoughts when Michael waved his hand toward the growing crowds on Mount Carmel. "It didn't take long for the Israelites to accept Baal as their god. Even some of Elijah's friends joined in Baal worship. They indulged themselves with exotic foods and got drunk on intoxicating beverages and wines.

And to make things worse, they engaged in all styles of physical immorality, thinking it would please their gods."

Seth furrowed his brow and looked inquisitively at Michael. *That sounds like some of our neighbors, who have made statues for themselves. They treat the statues like gods too. How can they think a statue they've made with their own hands can protect them?*

Again, Seth's thoughts were interrupted when Michael said, "Elijah watched the disturbing practices of the Israelites when they ignored the Almighty and gave the idols a place of importance and power." Michael's face darkened. "It's hard to think about, but they thought they could encourage Baal to give them a good harvest if they threw their babies into raging fire pits and rushing waters."

Shock spread across Seth's face. "What!" he stuttered.

"It's true."

"How could they do that? Don't they love their children?"

"Yes, but they believed the lies about Baal. They decided it would please the gods and that it was the best thing for the welfare of their families," replied Michael. "But Elijah hasn't given up on these people. He prays that God will stop the powerful forces of evil that entice them and rescue his people from the evil lies they spread."

With renewed interest, Seth watched Elijah approach the mountain. He was a big man, and his steps seemed to thunder up the rugged trail. A crowd began to gather at different places along the path. Others continued to climb to the top of Mount Carmel. Seth studied the stream of people making their way out of the valley. *Something important is going to happen. I wonder what they expect to see? Elijah doesn't look concerned, but I sure wouldn't want to be in his sandals today!*

Michael seemed to understand his questions, even though they remained unspoken. "Elijah has been hiding for the last three years. The people think he was hiding from King Ahab and Jezebel. But actually, God had much to teach him, so he kept him safe and out of sight during this time. His friends missed him, and some of the people will be glad to see Elijah today. But most of the Israelites are just here to see what Elijah is going to do. They fear the wrath of Queen Jezebel and will turn their backs on God's prophet. I'm sure even those who support Elijah will be quiet today."

A dry, hot wind moved through the heavens. The changing air whipped up dusty whirlwinds on the mountain below. Elijah looked over his shoulder and ducked his head when loud laughter and shouting erupted behind him.

Turning to Michael, Seth asked, "Surely his friends will stand with him. He shouldn't have to face the queen's men alone." Seth motioned toward the other angels. "What about all these angels? Won't they protect him from her prophets?"

"Yes, we are preparing to face the enemy if God Almighty sends us out. But Elijah is not aware of our presence. He comes to the mountain alone, and as God's prophet, he will speak the truths of God to these people. But the queen is very ambitious for Baal and has given her prophets instructions to do all they can to oppose Elijah. They will try to prove him wrong and humiliate him in front of the people. They may even call on powerful demons to stop Elijah and weaken what little faith the people have in God Almighty."

Michael reached out and put his hand on Seth's shoulder. "Seth, you may see Satan's demon spirits today. But do not be afraid. Almighty God is more powerful than Satan and his minions. Though they have some power to hurt the people of God and to do great evil—even to win battles, at times—they are not stronger than the Lord Almighty. With God's favor, we will be victorious against these strong warriors of Satan."

Seth felt his stomach sway. He choked down the terrible taste that spiked in his throat. He wondered if the demons would be as terrifying as the nightmares he sometimes had about Cain, or as grotesque as some of the statues his neighbors worshiped.

Michael gripped the handle of the heavy sword hanging from

his waist and flexed the muscles in his hand. "Elijah has finally pushed King Ahab to his limits. Queen Jezebel is enraged and is always looking for a good reason to kill Elijah. She discourages the worship of God in the land. Already, she has killed many of God's prophets. The rest, she has driven into the caves to hide. But not Elijah! Here he is. And he's not afraid to speak to these people about God."

"Why not?" puzzled Seth. "If Queen Jezebel is killing God's prophets, Elijah must be afraid of her. He is one of God's prophets." Seth cocked his brow. *She sounds like she is trying to be God and decide who is to live and who is to die. My brother made decisions like that, and it broke our family apart.*

Michael replied, "Most men would be afraid. But the Most High has trained Elijah well for this contest. The battle will be for the minds and hearts of the Israelites. You're right: Queen Jezebel is greatly feared by the people. She rewards those who follow the ways of her gods, and she punishes those who refuse them. But Elijah decided to trust God long before today. He has already learned that God is faithful and will do what he says he will do."

Michael paused to scan the heavens and survey the holy army. Angelic commanders, gathered near Michael, returned his attention, and slapped their right hands across their chests to acknowledge the readiness of their armies.

A slight smile broke Michael's furrowed brow. He crossed his own chest before returning his attention to Seth. "Elijah's trust in the true God will be his shield of protection against the king and queen's prophets. He knows Almighty God has a purpose for this challenge and that God will never leave him alone or defenseless. But his real battle is not against the prophets of Baal. Sure, they are his visible enemy." Michael opened his stance and stretched his right arm toward the clouds in the distance. "But his unseen battle is against evil powers and rulers who fight in the heavenly realm and follow another master, Satan. That's why God has called his holy army to this mountain today. Satan doesn't want Elijah to encourage the people to trust Almighty God. He will send his warriors to stop Elijah and confuse God's plan. It is our job to stop him."

Seth swallowed hard. *Satan! You were in the garden with Father and Mother. Were your demons there too? This angelic army appears very powerful—but won't your demons be powerful also?* He looked back at the prophet, still laboring up the mountainside. Elijah walked with such confidence.

"Elijah may not be able to see the angelic army around him, but he is trusting God to prevail," Michael said. "He will not be standing alone against God's enemy."

Seth's head swam as he remembered returning home from a hunting trip last year. He had run into the neighboring boys on the other side of the river, and their threats had left him shaking. *All I had to defend myself was my bow and arrow and a small knife. Father said everything changes when you know God is on your side. I guess I didn't believe it, because I sure felt alone. What would I have done if they hadn't stopped their insults to chase after the deer? They might have come after me like they did my brothers last spring.* Two brothers from Nod had ganged up on them, held them down, kicked dirt in their faces, and pummeled them with their fists. When Seth's little brothers broke away, they could hear the insults and threats of the brothers of Nod all the way to the clearing near their home. It had taken days for the swelling and bruising to go away. Seth bowed his head at the memories. *Mother was so distressed. I'm sure she thought about the day Cain killed Abel. Where were God's angels on that day?*

Michael raised his head again and studied the angelic army he would soon lead into battle. Their squads surrounded the mountain, and they knew their enemy well. Satan would use all the evil at his disposal to defeat Elijah and Elijah's God. The heavenly angels were attentive, armed, and waiting for Michael's command.

Comfortable that things were calm, Michael relaxed and returned his attention to Seth. He sighed. "All the people of the northern kingdom of Israel suffer under King Ahab's rule. They have lost their homes and fields. Some have even lost their families and lives because they wouldn't accept the idols of Jezebel as God. She is ruthless and unpredictable. King Ahab agrees with her ideas and will do nothing to stop her."

Their eyes darted to a noisy scene below. "Move aside, move aside quickly!" A wave of people turned to see Elijah following them up the trail to the top of Mount Carmel. They scurried aside, out of his path. A few mocked him as he passed. Someone shouted, "Let the prophet pass in peace!"

Looking over at Michael, Seth said, "At least there seem to be a few people who like Elijah. Maybe he won't be alone after all. Maybe someone will stand with him." His eyes scanned the crowds, picking out the lavishly dressed priests of Baal. They were like a small army. "He's sure outnumbered. It looks like there are hundreds of the queen's prophets here who want to prove him wrong," Seth mumbled under his breath. "Elijah would feel safer if he could see you, Michael, and the angels who are here!"

The archangel was the chief warrior of God Almighty. His job was to guard Israel with diligence. Seth watched him scan the horizons of heaven, standing alert to the dangers of the coming battle. This was certainly not the first time Michael had faced the strength of the enemy's army. Satan's demons had surely attacked God's people before.

Seth pulled his robe around his chest and held it tight against his body. A shiver went down his spine, and he hunched his shoulders. *But I've never seen it. This is my first time to see this kind of warfare…angels and demons in conflict. Father might have experienced it when he and Mother had to start their lives over outside of Eden. But he hasn't talked about it. Maybe he is afraid to. Maybe the demons were stronger than the angels. Is that why my brother is dead?*

Maybe the demons inflamed Cain's temper and incited him to turn against Abel...

He realized his anxiety was obvious when Michael touched his shoulder and commanded, "Do not be afraid, Seth! Be strong now! You are positioned in God's cloud of witnesses. Elijah will feel your courage as he faces the enemy's force of evil. God is leading him to act in strength. This is a dangerous time for the Israelites. They call themselves God's people, but they are trying to serve two masters, Baal and God Almighty."

Michael shook his head in frustration. "The Israelites are not loyal to Almighty God. They have forgotten his great love for them. They have forgotten the miracles he accomplished to make them a great nation. They have set the Almighty aside for these worthless gods of Baal."

The anguish in Michael's face was clear. "I've watched their faith fail so many times. Accepting these idols diminishes their memory of Almighty God. The people are infected with a blindness of heart and mind. Clearly, they have lost their zeal for the Lord and replaced it with fear of Queen Jezebel." Michael shook his head and stood in front of the young man whom God had put in his care. "And Seth," he said, "they fear her so much because they fear God so little."

Seth was hesitant to ask, but he could hardly help it. "What will happen to them?"

"That is largely up to them," Michael rumbled. "This is their time of truth. They will see God's majesty and power today. They must decide whether to live in fear or in faith. The real question is, will they trust Almighty God for their blessings, or will they trust the demonic spirits that hover around their wooden statues? Today, Elijah will prove to the people that Baal is powerless against Almighty God. He is the true and living God."

Seth focused his attention on the elaborate performance happening on earth. Hundreds of priests and prophets of Baal, in pointed headpieces and colorful robes, strutted before the regal platform of King Ahab. *What are the other angels thinking as they watch all of this?*

King Ahab ignored the pretentious exhibitions by the mystics of Baal. The king brushed aside his attendants and took his seat in the prepared place of honor, his royal traveling throne. Then he reached up to adjust his ornate crown. It rested on an embroidered linen cloth that protected his long, tight ringlets from the hot sun. He dropped one side of his blue cloak from his shoulder, exposing the royal necklace and medallion. The large ruby in its center was surrounded by aqua-blue gemstones.

Seth noticed that Queen Jezebel was not with Ahab. He watched the attendants lead the king's team of decorated horses and the royal chariot behind a large pile of boulders, separating them from the noisy crowds. The animals snorted and pawed the ground for water after the long, hot pull up the mountain. A military aide quickly unstrapped leather bags from a wagon nearby and poured warm water into a large wooden trough. The horses slurped it up. The aide went back for more.

Beyond the camp of watching angels and heavenly witnesses, a brood of deformed, ghoulish shapes circled in layers of the distant sky. Impatient demons growled at each other and snarled as they waited for instructions from their leader. Several squads loosely squared off against each other, shoving and jabbing. Their caws and squeals sounded like wounded ravens trapped and tossed in a windy cage.

Hiding in the depth of the shadows, Deceiver, Satan's chief warrior, sharpened the blade of his sword with a crystal stone. He groaned and hissed while watching the activities on the mountain. A hideous odor penetrated the stale air around him. His lip curled up on one side, and he breathed, "Elijah, you are a foolish little man. Your day has come, but King Ahab is surely in *my* hands."

Not far away, a shiver shot through Seth. *What happened? Something is different.* His eyes darted toward Michael.

Michael sensed the interference and stared at the changing sky. "Soon the heavenly battle will begin," he whispered to himself. He adjusted his breastplate and reached for his sword. Michael motioned for Seth to step beside him. He slid his mighty sword from its cover and held it above his head, alerting his commanders to be ready.

Seth could hear the angelic hosts of God stirring in the sky as they positioned themselves for battle.

Cautious, Michael kept his sword ready.

"Do you know what's going to happen?" Seth quavered.

Michael kept his eyes on the troubled sky. "I know some things. God Almighty will give King Ahab another chance today. The king may choose to listen and do what is right. But it will be hard for him to make the right decision. I've watched him agree with the lies of the enemy so many times. Maybe this time it will be different. He will have a choice to make. Maybe he will choose Almighty God and his ways instead of the ways of Baal."

Seth protested, "But if he wants to please Jezebel…what then?"

"That I cannot say," Michael responded. "I know Satan well. He sees the king's selfishness and pride. He will use those cracks in the king's character to encourage thoughts of greatness and feelings of superiority. Satan has convinced the king that his royal position allows him to do whatever he pleases, no matter how many people it will harm. The king refuses to consider the consequences of his decisions, so his people suffer along with him."

Michael leaned closer to Seth. "I've been instructed to help you understand the contest that will take place here today, between the God of Elijah and King Ahab's Baal. You will understand more as the day unfolds. But it will help you to know more about King

Ahab. Look at him, Seth. What do you notice when you look at him?"

Seth focused his eyes on the king, with his ringlets and rich clothing. "Well, he is very fancy, like one of the priests. He is wearing beautiful clothes and that jeweled crown. But he stands alone and seems to be a little cranky. Is he angry at someone besides Elijah?"

"Anger resides in his heart, and you are right—he is lonely. It is hard for a king to have friends. His high position is impressive, but it keeps him away from people except his advisers and attendants. Ahab enjoys the attention people give him when he is in public. But I wonder if he realizes that he and Queen Jezebel have become puppets for Satan."

Seth felt another chill radiate through his body at the familiar name. *Satan deceived my parents and enticed them to disobey God. He told them they could be like God if they ate fruit from the forbidden tree. He convinced them to do it! Look what happened to them because they decided to believe Satan's lies: We have to struggle and sweat for our food, and—well, look at what happened to our family because of Cain.*

Tears pricked Seth's eyes as his memories and fears collided. *What will my brothers and sisters become? They may decide to follow Cain's ways and let their frustrations and anger overcome wisdom. Already they strike out at each other if Father is not around. Sometimes I wonder where my own bitterness comes from. I get so annoyed when I have to do all the tilling and then Mother has more for me to do when I get home. I just want to play with my brothers and do the extra work tomorrow—or never.*

Michael's voice interrupted his thoughts. "The Prince of Evil is the enemy of God Almighty and of man," Michael continued. "He finds a weakness, like pride or fear, and uses it to stir up selfish choices. If Ahab and Jezebel only knew what good they could do for themselves and their people by following the ways of Almighty God! But their hearts are self-centered. The king ignores God's truths and has forgotten his miraculous acts for Israel. Ahab is easy prey for the enemy of man."

Seth stood somber and still. He knew he should be trying to remember all Michael was saying, but he couldn't help wishing he was at home and safe. He didn't want to be here, watching demons and angels clash. *Why am I here?* Seth felt his fists tighten at his side as the familiar fear spun in his head. *Someone is going to get hurt, and all I can do is watch…as usual.*

Seth let out a deep sigh. *Michael has done this before. He is not afraid. But how will this all turn out?*

Michael saw his concern, and his features softened. "The history of their nation has much to teach them, but most of the people refuse to learn its lessons. King Ahab refuses to consider the rebellion of his own father, Omri, who forgot the great acts of God Almighty on behalf of Israel. You would think there was no God of Israel while he was king! Maybe God will use his prophet Elijah to remind King Ahab today. Maybe the king will listen and return to the only true God. We will soon see. Be alert, Seth. The day has just begun, but the battle is at hand."

CHAPTER 2
The King's Choice

Soldiers shouted orders to the crowds who continually blocked their climb up the mountain. "Clear the path! Out of the way!" But more people made their way up the trail to be a part of the day's activities. Scurrying up the stony trails, men scrambled to join those gathering at the top. They hurried to secure a good vantage point to watch Elijah's challenge of the gods.

The morning air was thick and hot as the face-off between the army of God and the minions of Satan neared. Seth and Michael stood like statues and watched Elijah boldly approach the royal grandstand.

Even now, Seth sensed the impending battle lines being drawn.

Israel's enemy was bitterly determined to weaken and destroy God's followers, whoever they might be—king or pauper. But the crowds on Mount Carmel were unaware of the angelic army standing ready to do battle for their hearts. Seth felt small in their presence, but now, somehow, next to Michael he felt safe.

"Stand alert, forces!" commanded Michael. "We go to battle today for those on earth, those who trust in God's truths and power. God Almighty promised their ancestors that he would defend and protect them if they follow his ways and choose him alone as their God. And we fight for them today. Stay ready!"

Michael turned and looked down at Seth. "There is another reason for this confrontation today, Seth. The forces of nature are in God's hands, and he uses them to either bless or judge the people. Three years ago, Elijah surprised Ahab at his magnificent palace with a prophetic announcement from Almighty God: he told the king that God was sending a drought, and why. He said, 'There will be no rain, not even dew in the morning for you and your people, except at my word. I serve the God of Israel who holds your life in his hands. You have rejected his promises. You have chosen to trust these worthless wooden idols for your security and prosperity. You have even killed his prophets who came to help you as you rule over his people.' God's judgment for their rebellion was coming."

Seth took a deep breath and watched Elijah kneel on the dry ground. *What is he doing? Is he bowing to someone? Or maybe he is tying his sandal. No, I think he is praying!*

A sudden bolt of energy exploded through the sky, shaking the atmosphere. The angels spread their wings but held their guard. The heavens hushed above Elijah as he silently spoke to his God. His graying beard folded on his chest as he lowered his head and silently prayed.

After a few moments, Elijah stood tall and calmly walked toward the rebellious king. He appeared confident and sure of himself, like a man who had recently heard from God.

Elijah stared at the king until Ahab twitched with nervousness, and then the old prophet turned to face the people. "God Almighty is going to break the drought and bring rain to this parched land. Israel will see God's unshakable power and provision for those who trust him. Be sure of this. He will indeed reward those who sincerely look to him!"

King Ahab stepped out of his royal box. He paced back and forth over the dusty terrain. He repositioned his crown, rubbed his temples, and glanced toward Elijah as though he didn't know what to do with him. He stood in silence for a moment longer. Then, puffing out his chest, he growled, "Is that you, you troublemaker of Israel?"

Michael spoke softly to Seth. "The king agreed to this face-off because he thought it would prove the power of his gods. But now he wonders if it is still a good idea."

King Ahab looked toward the eight hundred and fifty royal prophets he had summoned for today's contest. They were milling around on the mountain while they waited for their high priest to call them to work.

"Perhaps these prophets of Baal will give the king confidence and assure him of success." Michael straightened his shoulders.

"There are so many of them!" Seth responded.

"Queen Jezebel appointed them to run her temples for Baal. Ahab called them from all over Israel to answer Elijah's challenge," said Michael. "The king believes there are enough of them to stir up some rain from Baal. But look at him. He is nervous and fidgety."

"Ha!" laughed the king. He looked at his attendants with all the bravado he could muster. "Who does Elijah think he is to challenge Baal this way? Does he really think Baal, the lord and master of the harvest, the god of rain and storms, can't make it rain?" Without waiting for their response, Ahab smiled and turned his attention to the hundreds of busy prophets preparing for the contest.

The Israelites and the other people of Ahab's kingdom surrounded the area, anxiously waiting for the contest of the gods to begin. They filled the craggy spaces and climbed jagged rocks to better position themselves for the event. No one wanted to miss this.

King Ahab shot a glaring look at the lone prophet. Elijah remained calm and stood tall. His piercing eyes returned the king's stare. The king shivered as he extended his scepter toward the crowds, expecting silence. He cleared his throat, turned to Elijah, and demanded, "Speak! Say what you have to say."

The king curled his fingers into fists when his hands began to quiver. His legs were heavy, and his feet felt frozen to the ground as he forced himself to stare back at Elijah, waiting for him to respond to his command.

Seth felt his own body stiffen when distorted, ugly creatures with hollow faces bolted through the skies, unheard and unseen by the crowds below. Terror filled him at the sight. Some resembled ghoulish scorpions with long black tails. Others were like giant locusts with black metal legs and sharp talons under their thundering wings. Some of them had faces like humans and stringy, long hair to protect their bodies. Their long, wispy wings and screeching voices invaded the atmosphere over Jezebel's prophets. But their noisy display of strength didn't seem to rattle God's army of angels. His heart pounding, Seth watched the demons soar higher in unpredictable motions and formations. Hundreds of dark creatures flew back and forth over the prophets of Baal, targeting some of them and whispering in their ears. Several hovered over the shoulders of the high priest.

Seth couldn't look away. So this was the kind of evil his parents had unleashed when they listened to Satan! No wonder it had been powerful enough to tear his family apart.

Michael didn't take his eyes off the creatures. He stood ready to command his own forces to attack. The demons kept their distance from the angelic warriors, who hovered around the people of Israel. Three mighty angels stood in position around Elijah with swords drawn.

Without warning, Seth felt a sharp, murderous pain in his shoulder blade. "Agh!" he cried, crumbling to his knees in agony. Before he could see what had hit him, he heard Michael's booming voice shout, "Halt!"

Turning, Seth saw a silver blur of swords slashing around him. He crouched and covered his head with both arms. He peeked through the open space near his elbow to watch Michael battle a demon soldier twice his size. The incredible strength of the opposing warriors shook the air. They struggled until Michael suddenly landed a crushing blow to the demon's side and yelled, "In the name of God Almighty!"

The ugly creature reared back. It growled, and then, with a whimpering squeal, it stepped back and shriveled to its knees. Seth froze in place, watching Michael plant his foot at the neck of the fallen creature and thrust his sword into its side. The dark demon disappeared from sight like water being poured into dry sand.

Michael lifted Seth to his feet. "You are safe, Seth. He tried to scare you, but trust God, and the demon spirits cannot harm you. They search for those who open their hearts to Satan's lies. Remember, there is no enemy weapon that can gain ground in your heart when you follow the Almighty. He protects his children with his strong right hand, and his plans will not be thwarted."

Seth rose from his knees and rubbed his shoulder blade. He took several deep breaths. "I'm not hurt. I don't feel any pain now." *But I was sure my shoulder had been stabbed through!*

Comfortable that Seth was secure, Michael turned his attention to the angels flanking Elijah. The mighty creatures moved from left to right to deter the satanic warriors. He watched the demonic creatures fly in wild patterns and confusing circles over Elijah. His protective angels maneuvered into new positions to thwart their aggressive actions.

In what seemed like seconds, the scene changed again. The sky over Elijah turned into a dull haze. The demon warriors flew haphazardly, almost out of control. They flailed and flew in rapid, chaotic movements, dashing into each other and colliding through the sky in turmoil. Loud squeals and curses followed their frustrated attacks. The angelic army held their positions and hurled their swords against demonic warriors who moved into their space.

Seth was relieved that the skirmish had ended so soon. *It looks like the Almighty is intervening for Israel already and has turned Satan's warriors against each other. Maybe this won't be much of a contest after all.*

Before he could finish his thought, he felt a somber stillness settle around him. The demon warriors had vanished. The angelic army returned to their ranks and positions of rest. Michael's eyes were on Elijah.

Seth's terror at the demons' coming seemed almost silly now. He replayed Michael's earlier words in his mind. *They fear Jezebel so much because they fear God so little.* When the demons had appeared, Seth had not even thought about God—nor had he done so when running from the brothers of Nod.

Slowly, Seth was beginning to see why he had needed to come here.

On the mountain, Elijah shook his shaggy head at King Ahab and frowned. "I did not make trouble for Israel," he thundered. "But *you* and your father's family have made big trouble for Israel! You abandoned the Lord's promises and commands! You have encouraged the people to follow the idols of Baal!"

He stretched his arm toward the crowds and gazed at their expectant faces. "You see how they have suffered for believing these wooden idols have power! Satan's spirits persecute your people when they open their hearts to your shrewd, lying prophets of Baal. You keep them and yourself in great danger."

King Ahab scowled and stood in silent paralysis.

Elijah's booming voice declared to the crowds, "So, it is time to be wise. It is time to acknowledge the truth. It is time to stand up for God Almighty and follow him!"

The prophet struck his staff on the ground with a gesture that was almost angry. His eyes were alight with passion. "Let us see whose god is the true God of Israel! Let us see which god you will

choose to follow!" He looked over the crowd sternly. "Will it be
God Almighty…or will it be these idols of Baal?"

Not waiting for an answer, Elijah turned back to the priests
and prophets of Baal, his sandal stirring up a dust cloud. Raising
both arms toward them, he thundered, "Let the battle of the gods
begin! Get two bulls. Choose one for yourselves and one for me.
Cut them into pieces and put yours on the wood above the altar.
But do not set fire to it. I will prepare the other bull for Almighty
God. But I will not put it on the altar or set fire to it until you call
on the name of your god to send fire first."

Elijah turned to face the crowds behind him. He shouted, "The
god who answers by bringing fire to the sacrifice—he is God!" His
face relaxed and softened, and his huge body shrank into a sad
slump as he looked at his people. Long, wispy hair blew across his
face. Shaking his head, he brushed it aside and pleaded with the
Israelites, "How long will you waver between two choices? If the
Almighty is God, follow him! But if Baal is your god, follow him—
and perish."

Surrounded by watching angels, Seth placed his hands on his
knees and leaned forward. He strained to hear the people's
response to the challenge. But he heard nothing! *What are they
waiting for? Why won't they answer the question and proclaim God
Almighty as the only true and living God? Maybe it's true that they don't
remember God, like Michael said.*

Sadness stirred his heart. *Just like I have forgotten him, so many
times,* he thought.

Instead of a reply from the people, he heard the rattle of armor
behind him in the heavens. Turning slowly, Seth was shaken by
what he saw. Advancing armies of grotesque fallen angels appeared
in the distant skies, their manlike faces and black limbs a sea of

horror. A dreadful silence encircled him. Looking over his shoulder, he saw the heavenly army raise their swords and close their ranks for battle. He felt weightless, but his heart pounded in his throat.

The warriors of the Prince of Evil slowed their advance toward Elijah and the people. A chilling hum echoed off their armor, and they froze in place. Seth watched as they sank into the shadows. *Are they gone or just waiting?* Seth backed away, retreating safely behind Michael.

"Don't be afraid, Seth!" said Michael. "Remember, Almighty God has invited you to watch what is about to happen, and *he* is your great strength in times of need. This vision of God's power will live forever in your memory."

Seth knew his face looked panicked. *Will I have to face the forces of Satan someday, like Elijah?* Seth wondered. *Will I have the courage to stand for God like he does?*

Michael put his strong hand on Seth's back. "Someday you will have your own family. What you remember today will help you to be strong for your children and for God. What you believe is true about God will influence your offspring and help secure a line of people who will trust in Almighty God. What you learn today will keep you from following in the path of your brother Cain."

Michael paused. "Seth, part of my job is to help you understand the amazing strength God gives to those who choose to follow him. So watch Elijah, stand tall, and do not be afraid. Take my hand. We are going down to Mount Carmel."

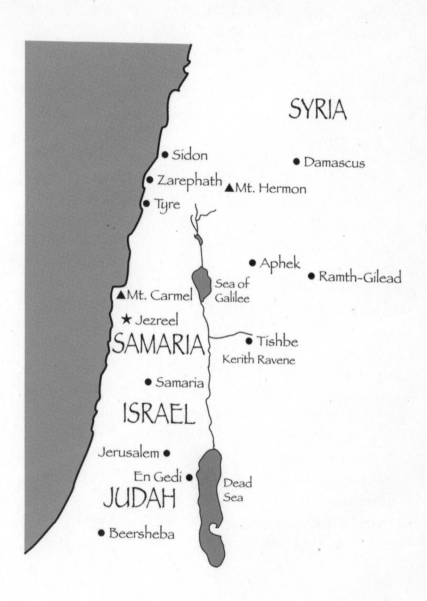

CHAPTER 3
The Cry for Courage

Seth caught himself chewing on his lip when his feet touched the solid ground of Mount Carmel. He looked around the knoll and realized they were not far from the Israelites and had a perfect view of Elijah and the prophets. Somehow, he knew that no one could see him or Michael.

Elijah stood before the crowds of Israelites and raised his hands to the heavens. When they quieted, he pleaded with a booming voice, "Make a choice today. Follow the God of your fathers. He is the only true and living God. He will never ignore you or drop you from his hand. He hears your heart cries and sees your distress. Return, O Israel, to the God of your fathers!" Elijah inhaled a deep breath, surveyed the people, and sighed. Then he clutched his walking stick and made his way into the crowds of Jezebel's priests and prophets.

Seth didn't take his eyes off Elijah. *He is bold standing up for God that way, in front of the priests and prophets of Baal. And he doesn't even know that Michael and the angels are fighting for him. Where did he get his courage?*

Michael noted Seth's attention to Elijah and raised an eyebrow. "Some of the people of Israel are nervous for him," he said. "They probably think he's been hiding from Queen Jezebel during the drought. It was common knowledge that she wanted to kill him after he announced to the king that God would stop the rains."

Michael's hair glistened in the sun as he looked across the horizon for trouble. He stepped to Seth's side and continued. "But God didn't send Elijah into the desert to hide from Jezebel. He sent him there to depend on God and learn to trust him no matter his circumstances. Most of the people don't know how he was miraculously cared for during those dry years."

"Was he alone there too? How did he survive?" asked Seth.

Michael smiled. "In various ways. Once, when he hid by the ravine, God sent ravens to feed Elijah. The people know he is God's prophet and speaks what God instructs him to speak. Only a few have heard the stories of how he was protected. Elijah had to depend on God Almighty or die. But learning to trust God, as he does now, was not always easy. He went through some hard times."

"Like what?" Seth asked. "Could you tell me about some of those times? I'll help you watch for enemy warriors."

Michael's eyes sparkled, and his strong face broke into a slight smile. "We may have time for a quick story." Seemingly comfortable with the peace of the moment, he continued. "One time during the drought, the Lord told him to go to the countryside near the city of Zarephath, where Jezebel's father ruled. That city is the very heartland of Baal worship. The people depend on figurines, idols made of wood and clay. You've seen such behavior, even in your own day. Some of your kinsmen have bowed down to snake and animal carvings, and they wear bone jewelry thinking it will help them as hunters."

"Yes, they even build altars in the woods and talk to the statues they carve. But I think they only sacrifice animals on their altars, not children," Seth murmured.

Michael nodded. "The people of Jezebel's land pray to statues of Baal to bring rain and a good harvest. And often, they treasure their idols more than their children. Yes, as I told you, sometimes the mothers will kill their babies on the altar as a sacrifice to Baal. Others will throw them into the mouths of raging rivers. They think it will encourage the idolatrous gods to bring rain for the crops and secure a good harvest. But Almighty God is greatly dishonored! The people practice witchcraft and sorcery instead of trusting his strong right hand. Israel is now a dangerous place for God's people to live. As I told you earlier, hundreds of his prophets have been murdered at Jezebel's orders. And of course, Elijah himself is a walking target. He's risking his life to be here today."

With Seth's full attention, he continued, "It was not easy for Elijah. He may have been afraid, but he obeyed God nonetheless. As a prophet to Israel, he went into Jezebel's homeland to proclaim the promises of Almighty God. He was bold and called the people back to their faith, back to the only God who could rescue them from the detestable practices of Baal worship."

Seth scratched his head and frowned. "The people must have thought Elijah was crazy for standing up against Jezebel and refusing to honor her gods. Didn't he worry about what they would think?"

"No, he only cared about what God thought about him." Michael opened his hand toward Elijah. "In fact, Elijah learned to trust Almighty God even more while he was in their land. He met a widow there and asked her to feed him her last bit of bread. He knew that she and her son would starve if she gave him their food. It was astonishing to see Elijah's faith in action! He seemed to know that God would provide for all three of them if she would act in kindness, and she did. Elijah knew God Almighty had sent the ravens to feed him. So, he reasoned, why would he not also care about them now?"

Seth felt a jolt like an earthquake under his feet. Wind whipped at the hem of his robe. He raised his head to see the sky fill with iridescent speckles gliding from above and landing on the heavenly army that hovered in the heavens. The angels raised their wings and bowed their bodies in sweeping gestures of worship. It was clear to Seth that hearing the truth about Elijah's faith had released electrifying surges of power and strength to the angelic warriors.

Hearing about God's faithfulness to Elijah was enabling them to stand with new force against the dark and taunting warriors of Satan.

Michael watched a band of evil forces dart toward Mount Carmel. They began to surround the prophets of Baal and irritate the crowds with quick finger jabs at their bodies and hissing in their ears. "Trouble—they're trying to stir the people into attacking Elijah, or at the very least hardening their hearts against him. Stay right here!" Michael shouted at Seth.

Racing away, Michael led the angelic army toward the enemy. The angels swung blazing swords above their heads, breaking the forces of Satan. They zigzagged back and forth, attacking the demons with full force and splitting their line of defense. Strengthened in victory, God's army began to pound back the dark army of Satan.

Seth watched the battle and felt the familiar fear churn in his stomach. He didn't take his eyes off the enemy, expecting to see them overcome Michael and the angels of God at any moment. His heart was pounding, and sweat poured down his back. *Why do I think this way? Michael isn't afraid, and he told me not to be afraid. And it's so obvious that God's forces are as strong as Satan's—maybe even much stronger!*

Even as Seth pondered the abilities of God's army, the dark warriors turned and fled into the shadowed creases of the deep heavens. Michael and his angels chased them until they too almost disappeared in the distance.

When Michael returned, his face broke into a broad smile. His story of Elijah's faith had filled his warriors with vigor. He drew in a deep, husky breath and sheathed his sword. Energized, he picked up his story as if he had never left Seth's side. "I wish you could have seen us celebrate in heaven when the widow went back each day to her flour jar! Every day, Almighty God filled it with just enough flour, and her jug with just enough oil, to make a fresh loaf of bread for herself, her son, *and* Elijah."

Seth pondered the story, recalling hungry years when the ground had not cooperated with his father's efforts to sow and reap a good crop. "Hmm! Bread during a famine—that's an amazing miracle!"

Thinking out loud, Michael continued, "There is more to this story, Seth. Because God provided bread for the widow, she had the courage to ask for another miracle, a bigger miracle. But now we must pay close attention to the preparations below. I need to be ready to defend God's people and his prophet, Elijah."

Activity increased on Mount Carmel. Crowds were still gathering to watch the priests of Baal perform their preparations for the contest. Their dramatic gestures and curious facial expressions captivated the crowds who watched the ambitious display. Several priests debated about who would slaughter the large black bull, draped with a colorful blanket and jangling trinkets. Six men led the somber animal by the ring in its nose to the altar area. Some of the priests standing nearby argued that the rules of their temple must be observed. But others insisted that they were not at the temple, so new rules could apply to the slaying and sacrifice of the bull.

The discussion went back and forth until someone in the crowd cried, "What are you waiting for? Put the animal out of its misery!" Finally, several priests were chosen, the bull was butchered, and the meat was prepared for sacrifice to Baal. After laboring through the process, they began to lay large pieces of meat on the wooden fire pit, as Elijah had required. But arguments erupted again between several orders of priests. They debated about who had the higher authority to arrange the sacrificial meat on the altar. Finally, it was decided to cast lots to determine which

order would have this honor. The onlookers sneered and snickered at their contentious behavior. Israelites huddled with their
friends, waiting for the contest to begin.

Michael and Seth watched the debacle without comment.

Suddenly, Michael swung his head around and thrust his right
arm into the air, again alerting the angelic army to action. They
moved into new positions, preparing for another attack. Michael
nodded to direct Seth's attention toward the angels who were gathering around the drama below.

Seth watched the holy warriors circling around Elijah, protecting him from a sudden show of force by the demons heading
in his direction. One after another, Satan's minions charged the
holy warriors, attempting to penetrate their wall of protection
around Elijah. Seth could feel the demons' malevolent purposes
in the air around him. They intended to distract Elijah from his
mission with their physical disturbances and hoped to instill fear
in him and cause him to give up on this holy challenge. Surely Elijah felt their presence, but he was not moved.

One by one, the demon warriors were overcome by the might
of God's army and pushed back to their stronghold in the heavens.
Seth was relieved. He felt safe and thankful to be in Michael's care.
It is an honor to be here to see these supernatural battles take place. He
raised his eyes and quietly prayed, "Thank you, Almighty God, for
bringing me here to watch this amazing event. Help me remember
all I see."

"Look at Elijah now," directed Michael. "He is truly God's ser-
vant-warrior. His name, *Elijah,* has become his calling card. It
means, *My God is Lord.* Each time it is spoken, the power of Satan's
evil warriors is shaken. Elijah is bold today because he knows without a doubt that God is able! He has learned valuable lessons
through his hard times. Elijah knows now that he can depend on
the strong right arm of God Almighty for every circumstance in
life. His strong faith will lead the way to God's miracle today."

Changing his stance, Michael said, "In another time, a great man of faith proclaimed, 'Some will trust in chariots and some will trust in horses, but we trust in the name of the Lord our God. They are brought to their knees and fall, but we rise up and stand firm.' That is the faith you see in Elijah today. He knows he can only trust God to achieve this miracle."

Once again, with these forceful words of faith, God's angelic army was emboldened to fight the dark soldiers of Satan. It didn't take long to see their strength in action.

Below, the priests of Baal stopped their work and stood erect. Skin tightened on their foreheads, and many priests looked to the sky in anxious anticipation of danger. Some shivered and nervously looked to each other for direction. Others crouched in fear.

The sky turned gray with thick, heavy air. Seth spread his palm on his chest, wishing he could calm his labored breathing. Again the screeching sounds of battle filled his ears. Wild cries and roars of rage mingled with hateful howls and mockery. Seth stayed behind Michael's bulky body and moved with his protector, who shouted battle commands to his soldiers. He watched the furious contest between the brood of demons and the mighty angelic forces. Roaring in anger, the dark soldiers of Satan attacked the angels of God. Swords swept through the air, crashing and clashing together in discordant melodies until the army of God forcefully drove the satanic warriors out of sight.

Seth exhaled and considered what he had already experienced today. *God brought me here, and his angel told me not to be afraid of the things I would see. Surely God will keep me safe. This is not my battle. It is the Lord's, and he is going to win this battle against his enemy.*

A slow smile came to Seth's face as he realized that the battle he was thinking about was not only the one playing out before him—it was also one for his heart. Somehow, God could help him overcome his own fears as he learned to trust him. He would not fall like Cain had fallen. He would follow God.

This great angel, Michael, is my guide and teacher. I am in the place God wants me to be, and I'm here to watch and remember what I see. With his next breath, Seth realized he wasn't afraid. His body was loose, no longer tight and rigid as it had been earlier in the day. His eyes danced from sight to sight, not fearing the heavenly battle this time.

Relaxing his stance, Michael rested his hand on the knob of his sword. Returning angels gathered in squads and waited for instructions. Michael narrowed his eyes and acknowledged God's work in Elijah.

"Seth, Elijah's faith and confidence are evident to all who watch him today. He is bold now because he followed God's instructions concerning the widow's dead son. You see, there is more to the story of his time in Zarephath. As I told you before, the widow had the courage to ask for a bigger miracle."

The demons were staying away for the moment, so Michael motioned for Seth to sit down. "Her son became very sick, stopped breathing, and died. But it wasn't until Elijah took the dead boy from his desperate mother's arms that he felt truly helpless. He carried him upstairs to his own room, crying out to the Lord, 'Why, O Lord, have you brought this tragedy to the widow? She has just begun to see the truth of your ability!'"

Michael glanced toward the listening angels. "Even we wondered what would happen to her small faith. What would God do? Three times Elijah cried out to the Lord, 'O Lord, my God, let this boy's life return to him!' Three times he prayed for God to have mercy on the fragile widow and return life to her child.

"I remember that all the hosts of heaven watched and waited when Elijah threw his body over the dead child. We held our breath as he finally stood and relinquished the outcome to the

Lord. Elijah had prayed for what he thought best. Now he would trust God's decision. His mind and heart let go of the boy's fate. He surrendered the boy's life to the will of God."

Michael looked directly into the anxious eyes of his young charge. "We watched as Elijah took that long breath. It looked like his heart would burst out of his chest as he filled himself with God's peace. Elijah knew that the boy and his mother were in the mighty hand of Jehovah. He knew that somehow, God would use the widow's unbearable situation for good. No matter what, God would show her his unwavering love. She would know, whatever her situation, that God Almighty could be trusted."

Michael softened his voice. "Do you understand that sometimes God uses severe situations to show you that you can't make it on your own? Sometimes you have no resources to escape a crisis. It's only when you depend on Jehovah, like Elijah did, that you can let God be God and trust the outcome to him."

"I think I understand what you are saying," Seth responded. He looked down at his side as he remembered how helpless he had felt before the brothers of Nod, and how much his mother still mourned Abel. Still eyeing the scene below, he hesitated and asked, "So, what did God do about her son?"

Michael smiled a broad smile. "God Almighty brought the widow's dead son back to life! He righted the world for her with his miracle and caused the hosts of heaven to cheer." The archangel laughed aloud. "And once again, the Almighty God, the Lord of Life and Death, taught Elijah to trust him, even in discouraging times. Those hard times became God's training camp for Elijah's new courage."

Smiling, Seth understood. "So that's why Elijah is not afraid of King Ahab and Jezebel today."

Michael paused for a long, thoughtful minute. "Seth, Elijah has the courage to stand before kings *now* because he first learned to kneel before Almighty God."

Seth took a deep breath, relishing the truth of that statement. He closed his eyes and enjoyed the reality of God's omnipotent strength. God was greater than fear. God was greater than demons, kings, and murderous brothers. He was greater than Seth's own weaknesses.

Seth took a deep breath. He had told himself the truth. Now the question was whether he would still believe it if he faced crisis again!

Michael returned his attention to the relaxed and confident prophet of God who stood with his arms folded comfortably and his chin up. Pointing toward Mount Carmel, Michael said, "Elijah knows he must trust Almighty God this time too. God's word will be the last word for Elijah. He must trust him completely to perform an amazing miracle today. It must be a miracle that will show God's people his unfailing power. He must show his complete control over everything, even the elements of nature. God has spoken to Elijah. Now Elijah must trust Almighty God for the altar fire as well as for the life-giving rain that the people and the land so desperately need."

Seth stared at the courageous prophet of God and nodded in agreement, echoing Michael's words. "Once again, God's word must be the last word for Elijah!"

CHAPTER 4
Crossroads of Chaos

P eople of Israel," roared Elijah. "You are in grave danger!" The booming voice reverberated through the tense activity on Mount Carmel. Conversations stopped and heads turned to see who had shouted the warning. Eyes flashed toward Elijah, the prophet of God.

Jumping onto a pile of stones, Elijah shouted, "Do not doubt the truths of Almighty God! He commanded, 'You will have no other gods before me.' Yet you hold him in one hand and Baal in the other."

He threw up his arm and moved his finger back and forth across the crowd. "You double-minded and unstable people! How can you expect to receive anything good from God?"

Elijah reached for a scraggly tree limb and pulled himself onto a large stone. He stood above the crowd and declared, "Choose this very day whom you will serve: God Almighty, who makes the earth his footstool, or the wooden and stone statues of Baal which litter your land."

Before they could respond, Elijah continued his rebuke. "You reduce God to the imagination of your minds. How small you have made him! He will not be mocked. You cannot pull him off a shelf to work for you. No! God uses his power for his will and for his purpose."

Watching their solemn faces, he paused. "Make up your minds. Whom will you follow? You of all people were chosen by God to be his treasured possession. He calls you his children. Why do you dishonor him with these worthless idols? I ask again, whom will you follow?"

Overhead in the highest heavens, far above the ongoing challenge on Mount Carmel and the angelic battles surrounding Elijah, God Most High, the Lord of all creation, listened to Elijah's strong proclamation of faith. Great bolts of lightning shot from his presence, framing him in blinding light.

Seth's legs wobbled, and he fell to his knees when the heavens rolled open like a scroll. In shock, he lifted his face, and his jaw dropped. There before his eyes appeared a sudden and awesome wonder. *I...I can't believe I'm seeing this*, he thought. He was filled with an overwhelming sense of awe—and, strangely, he felt secure. *Surely I am dreaming! I feel so safe. Nothing can hurt me now.*

Seth's eyes filled with the golden grandeur of heaven and the huge, majestic throne. A robe that looked like crystal satin cascaded down into the heavenly temple. A sparkling mist surrounded the throne with brilliant golden lights. Flashes of lightning continued to explode around it as a sweet, inviting fragrance danced through the wind and the clouds.

Then a great and powerful arm unfolded from the throne. The commanding right hand pointed directly to the earthly events, and a stream of crystal lights encased Elijah.

Seth didn't take his eyes off the sight while he stretched his own hand toward Michael, who was bowing on one knee beside him. Michael beamed and rested his hand on Seth's shoulder.

Michael and Seth watched two heavenly beings hover above the throne of God. They looked human in form but had six wings. One pair of wings shielded their faces, another covered their feet, and the third gave them flight. They chanted with joyous voices, "Holy, holy, holy is the Lord Almighty! His glory fills the earth."

Each happy cry sent ripples of warmth throughout the heavens, and the skies around them filled with golden smoke.

Then, the same glorious hand that had pointed to Elijah moved toward Michael. Streams of light followed until Michael was clothed in their glow. Immediately, he stood to receive his instructions. Michael nodded several times before bowing low. Then he backed away from the holy presence of the Almighty God.

Seth didn't hear the commands given to Michael from the heavenly throne, but he recognized what had happened. *What will he do now to protect God's people from the Prince of Darkness? What did God say to Michael?*

Michael stood tall and raised his mighty wings, filled now with fresh power to lead his faithful angelic army. But the fight for Elijah and for Israel would not be easy. Michael knew it would be difficult to hold back the strong forces of evil that Satan would send against them.

Immediately, the scene changed as the clouds closed upon the high heavenly presence. Phantom shapes began to appear in the distance, moving quickly toward their defensive stronghold. Conflict was imminent.

Darting above his angelic warriors, Michael spread his powerful arms, displaying his immense stature and strength. He turned his head and raised his sword toward the approaching enemy. Other angels followed his example and positioned themselves for the fight. The ominous demonic forces were again on their way to harm Israel, the people God had chosen for himself.

Michael fortified himself with truth. The enemy of God was strong. Satan would not allow the challenge at Mount Carmel to go easily for Elijah and the Israelites. But Michael knew that God's eternal plan would be successful and that his job was to protect Israel from the destructive tools in Satan's war chest.

A warrior from the Prince of Darkness bolted toward him. Michael watched Demander approach. He had faced this evil warrior many times. The strength and cunning of this taunting spirit could not be ignored. The sun broke through the eerie sky and showered the angels with light, which shot like lightning off their gleaming swords. They circled, eyes locked and faces tight. Demander lurched at Michael with his sword but was thrown off balance when Michael dodged his colossal force.

The clash and clang of iron drew more enemy warriors into combat. Ignoring the squealing rage of the horrid brood, the angelic army kept up their offensive.

Michael knew his orders were to hold back the enemy forces of Satan while the prophet Elijah spoke God's truth to the Israelites. Confident that the Almighty would not allow Satan victory, he eyed his target. Positioning his huge sword for attack, he rushed toward Demander. Emboldened with God-given strength, he swung his shield overhead, drawing the demon's attention to the flying object. Then he plunged his mighty sword into the belly of the foreboding spirit. A shrill screech escaped from the throat of the demon as it lunged forward. Its ghoulish form twisted and shriveled into a grayish mist before it disappeared.

Seth could feel his blood coursing through his veins. His heart pounded. He reminded himself, *I was chosen to observe Elijah's challenge on Mount Carmel today. But I can't take my eyes off these angels and the battle raging in front of me!* It struck him, suddenly, that such invisible battles might be raging around him all the time, just as they were for the Israelites today, who could not see the angelic clash being fought for them. His mind leaped back to his own family. *I'm sure God's angels have gone to battle for Father and Mother before. But I wonder if they've ever had to fight for me?*

The angels and demons were locked together in heated combat. Seth shuddered and flinched at the piercing wails and cries of the demonic warriors who tried to throw God's army into confusion and chaos. But their exhibition of strength did not stop Michael's forces. The angels of God Almighty were daring and strong. They outmaneuvered the enemy warriors and sent them squealing back to their dens.

Below, a warm wind stirred the air on the sun-baked mountain. The crowds watched Elijah march defiantly toward the ceremonial assembly where King Ahab and his religious leaders were gathered. Elijah's shabby robe hung unevenly as he moved, scattering pebbles and dirt with each deliberate step.

The racket of the crowd died down. Seth no longer heard the bangles and bracelets of the women or the husky voices of the men. A hush fell on the crowd as they watched Elijah. *Are they afraid of Elijah's accusations, or are they just anxious to see what will happen next?* He waited, glued to the scene.

Elijah turned to observe the mystics of Baal. Many were gathered around their sacrificial altar, chanting with soft voices. Some were bowed in prayer. Others were lighting incense lamps throughout the company of religious leaders. But most of them paraded among the royal officials in their fine robes and jeweled head-wraps, looking for something to do that would appear important. The green emeralds and blue sapphires embedded in their costumes sparkled in the hot sun. Long fringe hung from the ceremonial robes of those with high positions in the priesthood. Some covered their faces with garish paint. Others wore intricate animal masks of bulls and birds. Silver and bronze metals accented the masks designed to honor Baal.

Seth watched a horrid, eerie form move at will throughout the priestly gathering. Somehow he heard the soft voice whisper vulgar accusations against Elijah into the gullible ears of the arrogant prophets.

The demon snickered and hissed, "Elijah needs to be separated from the people of Israel. He is under the illusion that his god is more powerful than Baal. He may cause the people to question the abilities of Baal. Then, of course, they will question your position as his prophet, and things will not be good for you, especially if the queen isn't happy with your reputation and influence with the people."

"We need to get rid of this peasant-prophet, Elijah," stammered one of the priests. "He could sway the people of Israel away from Baal and put us out of a very good job with the queen."

"There will be time to have the soldiers kill him after Baal brings fire to our sacrifice today," answered his companion. "He is a big puff of wind. Baal will answer his challenge. Do not worry; we will rid ourselves of this vagrant soon."

The man's words were spoken with all the arrogance and venom that Seth had heard many times in the brothers of Nod. "Michael, they are listening to the lies of the demon! What will you do?" asked Seth.

"I will do whatever Almighty God tells me to do. But Elijah is safe today. The Lord knows everything Elijah needs and will never fail him."

Seth nodded and looked back at Elijah.

Elijah stood alone, observing the busy crowd of prophets. He lowered his bushy eyebrows and shouted to the Israelites, "Look! I am the only one of Jehovah's prophets here today. But the king and queen have gathered four hundred and fifty of Baal's prophets, and four hundred more who belong to your goddess, Asherah. Do you think this great number of prophets can overwhelm the hand of the Lord God Almighty?"

Mumbling broke out in the audience. "Hush, hush. Quiet!" shouted a bystander. "Elijah is speaking. Listen to what he is saying."

Elijah looked over the crowd at King Ahab. "Do you think the Lord's arm is too short for this challenge?" he questioned. "This is God Almighty's day, and it will be his victory."

Hanging on his words, the people caught their breaths and waited for the king's response.

Michael returned to Seth's side, slid his sword into its sheath, and zeroed in on the drama in front of them. "Our battle with Satan's army is over for the moment. They will not return in strength until they have new assignments from their commanders. Meanwhile, Elijah is provoking the people to think about God's truth. But they must listen with their hearts to understand."

The heavenly audience stood silent, watching and listening to God's messenger.

Pointing his finger toward their sacrificial altar, Elijah instructed, "You have chosen and prepared the bull for your fire pit. Now, go ahead. All of you call on the name of your god to light the fire on your altar. I will call on the name of the Lord Almighty to light the fire on my altar. The god who answers by fire—he is God!"

Voices hummed as the high priest of Baal considered Elijah's instructions. The excited crowd of Israelites froze in anticipation of their reply.

"What you say is good." The chief prophet nodded and shouted, "Baal will hear us and send his lightning and fire to our sacrifice!"

All eyes watched the prophets of Baal gather in their ceremonial circle around the sacrificial bull. Each prophet tried to make his way closer to the altar where the more important priests from the highest orders stood. They crowded together and tried to nudge their way to the front of the circle.

Seth watched a young priest try to stay in step with the others, but his mask slipped from his sweaty forehead and covered his eyes and face. He tried to adjust it and lift his bulky garment from the ground. But when he stepped aside too quickly, his foot landed on the fringe of his companion's cloak, causing him to stumble under the weight of his heavy robe. With arms flailing, both men tumbled to the rocky ground, tangled in a pile of cumbersome fabric. The young priest's mask was inadvertently kicked aside and lost in the crowd. He scrambled to his feet but was pushed off balance again as others fell against him. Arms and hands reached out to stop the avalanche of bodies falling around him.

Speechless, Seth jumped up to watch the chaos. "Ha!" he laughed and pointed toward the sight. All around the priestly circle, men were flailing and shuffling for a secure footing. "Look at them!"

A crowd of nearby Israelites laughed and watched the prophets struggle to stand and adjust their disheveled wardrobes and reclaim their important stations. The elder prophet frowned and stared at his colleagues. Then he turned and rearranged the sacrifice on their makeshift altar. When order was restored, he waved both arms above his head and bowed to the ground several times. A quiet hush came over the assembly. Hundreds of prophets followed his example and began to bow in worship and call out, "O Baal, answer us. O Baal, answer us. Set our sacrifice ablaze. Show us your power."

The noise of their chants filled the air. Many in the crowd waved small wooden idols in the air and joined in their cry.

Seth heard a chilling staccato of discordant squeals join the chorus of chants from the prophets and priests. The winged enemy darted among the pleading prophets and priests of Baal and landed among the religious leaders. Seth pinched his nose shut when the stirring of wings forced their foul odor into his face. Long black scorpion tails curled over the backs of the demons crouched on men's shoulders. But when they flew throughout the crowds, wisps of wiry hair loosened from their bodies like small antennae and amplified their irritating squeals, stinging any skin it happened to

touch. Seth noted that the Israelites didn't seem to notice the deafening noise or smell of the demons, but they began to slap their
arms and legs as if bothered by mosquitoes. Seth covered his own
ears to soften the deafening shrills.

Under the shade of his royal tent, King Ahab adjusted his position on his armchair to get a full view of the altar. Turning to his
military adviser, he whispered, "What is Baal waiting for? Where
is his fire for the sacrifice?" Avoiding the eyes of Elijah, Ahab shifted
his body to settle into his throne. He raised his chin and scanned
the scene. Adjusting his bulky robe, he took a long, calming sip
from his silver goblet and shivered.

An unseen, shrouded being leaned toward the king's ear and
whispered suggestions into his mind.

"I'm not about to let that ragamuffin prophet of Jehovah see
me worry about the outcome of this celestial contest," grumbled
Ahab. "Certainly Baal will not let his honor be questioned!"

The royal adviser rested his hand under his chin and
responded, "Have patience, Sovereign Ruler. Our gods are preparing now for their display of power, and Elijah will be humiliated.
After this demonstration, he will be forced to run in shame from
the people he has provoked."

"Humph! We will see, won't we?" King Ahab growled. Raising
his chin, he smiled at the crowds. Then he returned his attention
to the stale sacrifice and the anxious prophets. The smile faded,
and sweat beaded on his forehead. Squirming on his throne, he
lowered his voice and said, "I am afraid of what might happen
today if Baal does not respond." He shook his head and mumbled,
"What will the people of Israel think? Will they blame Queen
Jezebel and me?"

The king stood and paced before his seat. "Oh, why do I worry
about their opinions anyway?"

His adviser stepped toward the king. "Don't worry about what
they think, sir. Your word is law in Israel. You are their king! The

people will follow your example. They must honor you as their leader. Besides, Baal will show his power. We must be patient."

The archangel Michael stood beside Seth as they continued to watch the priests solicit Baal for their sacrificial fire. Squealing little demons planted themselves on the shoulders and headdresses of the religious leaders and continued to babble in their ears. Michael turned his attention to the king. "Seth, this contest may remind the king of when he was a boy. He tried very hard to make friends with other children of the court. But those he chose as friends were selfish and cocky. They teased him and laughed at him behind his back. Young Ahab wanted them to like him, but he knew they only accepted him because he was the son of Omri, the great and powerful king of Israel."

"Maybe he is afraid the people will laugh at him now too," chimed in Seth.

Michael bristled. "It is no real excuse. I remember how determined Ahab was to follow the easiest path in life. I watched him too many times as he turned away from his responsibilities. He was selfish and put his desires over the needs of others. His grandmother told him the great stories of his ancestors and how strong they were when they walked with God. But he ignored the ways of Almighty God and did not care about his promises for a good and happy life."

Seth studied the king's nervous pacing and asked, "What do you think King Ahab is going to do? He keeps rubbing his hands and talking to his advisers."

"We will see soon. The king has forgotten the words of his ancestors. Their writings tell about the mighty power of the Lord of Hosts. It appears Ahab disregards these truths, and instead expects to see the power of Baal. For now, Seth, look at Elijah resting on that big rock. He is peaceful, trusting the promise of God. His victory is near."

King Ahab studied the priests. He watched the uproar of the prophets performing their ceremonial rituals. They begged Baal to hear their plea for fire. The king shook his head and rolled his eyes. Scowling, he turned toward Elijah, who was resting against a boulder with his arms folded comfortably.

"What will this day bring?" King Ahab muttered. "I want to be rid of this man. I want to prove him wrong so the people will stop listening to his gibberish. Then he must be slain for his insidious rebellion."

A slight smile broke through the solemn expression of the unseen figure towering over the king. The demons standing by cackled and relayed their haunting promises of victory throughout the crowd of prophets.

Seth shifted his stance and glanced at the king again. "Ahab looks irritated. Maybe he'll consider the purpose of this challenge and remember that the idols of Baal are only carved from wood and stone. Maybe he'll think about the good ways of God Almighty."

Michael rested his palm on the handle of his sword. "If he chooses God and follows him, he will receive the strength he needs to lead the people with truth and wisdom. They will respect him and give him the honor he craves. And the Almighty promises to give him the desires of his heart…if only he will believe the Lord and acknowledge him as the true God, and as *his* God."

Their concentration was shattered as the crazed shouting of the prophets brought them back to the contest. Feverishly, the prophets of Baal accelerated their frenetic cries. Their annoying voices roared as they bellowed and bobbed for Baal's attention. They cried and wailed under the rising sun. Some locked arms together, swinging around in circles, calling, "Show us your might and strength! Show us you are god! Show us with fire, O Baal!"

Others raised their voices, bowed, and begged, "We are your servants and worship only you. Show the people your great and mighty power. Prove to everyone that you control the rain and fire, and make your name renowned on the earth! Receive our sacrifice, and strike your altar with fire!"

A quiet breeze from the throne of God Almighty calmed the angels above. The enemy's demons had retreated, leaving the prophets and priests to their own wailings. But Michael knew that Deceiver would not give up so quickly. He would issue new orders to his commanders, and they would resume their fight against the armies of the Almighty God and Elijah, his faithful prophet.

For the remainder of the morning, Seth and Michael relaxed along with the host of heavenly angels and concentrated their attention on the spectacle below. As the sun grew hotter overhead, Seth yawned as the deafening uproar continued and the ritual dances droned on and on.

Michael remained at Seth's side, serene and noble. He glanced upward and squinted when his eye caught the sun over-head. "It has been hours, Seth, and there is still no fire for the prophet's sacrifice. God's army has fought diligently. They with-stood the demonic attacks on Elijah and on the Israelites who follow Almighty God. Remember the evil warriors were sent to plant doubt and fear in the minds of the people, and now they will try to incite them to violence. But the courage and faith of Elijah have helped us minimize their efforts and secure our pres-ent victory."

As the scorching sun rose above their heads, the expectant Israelites realized it was almost noon. Impatiently they jostled and stretched, relieving stiff and sore muscles. A few reached into their sacks for bread and fruit.

Without warning, loud, wild cries and frantic dancing broke out among the prophets of Baal. They began to skip and jump around the altar of their god. They screamed at the top of their voices for his response.

The crowds jumped to their feet, expecting to see fire and smoke rising from the altar of Baal. But there was no such reward. They shook their heads and complained, "This is hopeless. Where is Baal's answer? Why can't you move the gods to light the fire?"

Baal was silent.

Again, beads of sweat glistened on the king's forehead. He lowered his eyebrows and groaned, "This is miserable! How long can I bear this contest?" He slumped into his chair and buried his head in his hands.

CHAPTER 5

The Command from heaven

"Shout louder!" Elijah taunted. "Is Baal really a god? Perhaps he is deep in thought, or off on a restful vacation. Oh—he could be sleeping, and you must wake him. He doesn't realize what time it is. Or maybe he's sitting on the toilet." The prophet reached into his cloak and held up a piece of bread. Waving it in the air, he suggested, "Perhaps your god is having lunch and doesn't want to be disturbed!"

Elijah paused to survey the crowds in front of him. His face saddened, and without warning, he shouted, "How can you allow yourselves to value these worthless idols over the almighty force and power of God?"

Shaking their fists at Elijah, the prophets of Baal raised their voices again to their god and begged, "Bring us fire! Bring us fire!" They pleaded with uplifted arms, "Avenge yourself, O Baal! This old man slanders your name and your honor!"

The chief prophet of Baal waved a purple scarf in the air and commanded, "Hush, everyone! Listen and watch for the great Baal to answer."

The priests and prophets grew silent. But still, no reply from Baal.

Seth was startled when a few angry prophets pulled small knives from their belts. Deliberately, they drew the sharp blades over their arms and legs until droplets of blood formed garish patterns down their extremities. The crowds began to clap their hands. Some shouted, "More, more!" Others turned their heads and looked away in shock.

"What are they doing? Have they gone mad?" Seth questioned.

Michael nodded. "Almost. This is their desperate attempt to move their god into action. They hope that shedding their own blood will remind Baal that they need his answer. They hope to excite him to pour down fire on their altar and show his power by bringing rain. But their acts of mutilation are foolhardy. Scarring their bodies won't arouse a response from the idol. They choose to believe the lies the queen's prophets tell about Baal, rather than the truths of Almighty God."

Michael planted his knuckles on his waist and studied the position of the sun. His lips curled into a sad smile. "The morning is over, and still they wait for a response from their god."

"I don't understand why they even try," Seth said. "What can a god made of wood and stone accomplish?"

Michael laughed. "Of course. There will not be a response when there is no one to answer their prayers. Wicked men can put up a bold face, full of confidence. But when they give no thought to their ways, they have no wisdom. They have no insight, and they have no plan that can succeed against the Lord."

Seth's mind flooded with images of the brash, turbulent brothers who lived in Nod and often taunted him, his sister, and his younger brothers. He remembered the words he had often thought about them: *I never want to face that brood of boys. They are too strong for me. I have to stay out of their way. I just want them to go away and leave my family and me alone.* But was it possible that the brothers, like these priests, had no real power?

Throughout the afternoon, Seth watched the priests and prophets of Baal continue their frantic chanting. A cloud of flies buzzed on the sacrificial carcass. A breeze pushed the foul stench of the rotting bull through the air, an idle reminder of their hopeless exercise. The sun sank lower in the afternoon sky. The prophets of Baal looked to their leaders for direction, but the leaders scowled at each other and argued about what to do next. Some sat to the side of the altar, slump-shouldered. They fidgeted with their hair and clothing, while others continued to moan and twist their necks and backs into strange positions. Still others dropped to their hands and knees and panted like dogs.

Everyone knew it was nearing time for the evening sacrifice. But still Baal had not responded. The mythical god of thunder and rain was silent. And the horrific attempts of the priests to motivate their god were laughable.

The people watched as Elijah, the man of iron, rested quietly under a scrawny cypress tree, a stark contrast to the weary priests and prophets of Baal. His faithful spirit seemed to strengthen as the day moved on, and he waited quietly for God to call him to action

The frustrated noises and frenzied activity continued until late afternoon. No fire appeared on the altar. The people looked weary and exhausted. The hum of their chatter angered King Ahab. He raised his hand to his brow to shield himself from the afternoon sun and the eyes of his people. Stepping back into his covered grandstand, he turned to his attendant and barked, "Draw the drapes behind me! I will not stand for this charade to continue. Call this demonstration to a halt. I am bored with all of this, and Baal is not moved today."

"O great king, think about what could happen if we call off the contest," protested the royal adviser. "We must not allow the people of Israel to think that Baal is incapable of lighting his altar. It would make them question his ability and his stature before the God of Israel." The adviser lowered his voice and leaned toward the king. "Baal *must* prevail today. Calling off the contest would weaken your throne and give the people more contempt for Queen Jezebel, who brought this god to Israel. Please give them more time."

"Fine!" roared the king as he threw up his hands in disgust. "We'll wait a while longer!"

Meanwhile, unseen by the officials and the crowds on the mountain, the outstretched arm of God continued to encourage and empower his holy army in battle. The army of God fought with renewed strength and purpose. Seth watched the desperate, vicious demons pound into Michael's companions. For several gruesome moments the air was spinning with swiping swords and clashing shields. Seth covered his ears when the piercing squeals intensified and a sudden horrible growl resounded through the heavens. In front of his eyes, demon forces stumbled in hasty retreat, limp and exhausted. Truth was calling for a choice, and there was no middle ground. Satan's dark army temporarily vanished in the face of God's authority. Michael and the angelic army regrouped but remained alert, waiting for Almighty God's command. Satan would not relent so quickly.

The time had come.

"Come here to me," Elijah called gently to the people of Israel. "Come here."

Many of the Israelite men approached and watched as Elijah began to repair an ancient altar that had been used to worship the Lord in times past. It had lain in ruins on the summit of the mountain for hundreds of years. Carefully, he selected twelve stones and piled them at its foot. "I build this altar in the name of the Lord God Almighty, the God of Israel. Each stone represents one of the sons of Jacob, who bore the families that became the twelve tribes of our nation."

Elijah swung his arms wide and looked to the heavens. "Long ago, God led the tribes out of captivity in Egypt to this place, the Promised Land. And remember—you, O people of Israel, are their children's children! You are their heritage."

He knelt and continued to carefully place each stone in place. When he finished the altar, he dug a deep trench around it. After arranging the wood on the stones, Elijah placed the butchered meat from the second bull on the altar. Then he turned to face the throngs of people and raised both arms. He pleaded, "O Israel! How long will you waver? If the Lord is God, worship him!"

The command did more than challenge the people on Mount Carmel. In the heavens, a loud, shrill noise alerted Michael to the enemy's presence once again. He jumped into action and again unsheathed his sword for battle. But before he could signal his troops, he cocked his head and smiled at the familiar, ancient sound of chariot wheels roaring through the distant skies like rushing waters pouring off the mountaintops. Seth ducked and again covered both ears with his hands, but he never took his eyes off Michael.

Michael shouted, "Almighty God is with us! Gird your weapons. The battle is upon us!"

The new wave of evil warriors approached the soldiers of God. The heavenly realms reeled with the clamor and clash of flashing swords and tumbling bodies. Angelic soldiers of Almighty God fought with fierce strength against the forces of Satan. If blood could splatter freely from demons, the sky would have been crimson red. Instead, greenish-blue fluid spewed from the ragged enemy forces. Swords and shields flew in bitter battle.

The angels of God faced a forceful counterattack from the demonic army when Satan's warriors surrounded a company of angels and overwhelmed them with crippling strength. The defiant demons were zealous in their attempts to destroy God's army and to undermine Elijah's influence with the people. Israel had accepted Baal as their god, and Satan wanted to keep it that way. His warriors fought with dogged determination to prevent Elijah's interference, wounding angels right and left as they forced their way toward earth.

Michael focused his advance on the second and third waves of fiendish spirits, who darted at them with agitated fury and wild screams. The deafening war cries of the hateful phantoms inflamed the skirmish, but the strength of the angelic force prevailed. Again and again, the angelic army was reenergized. Somehow, Seth realized that the faithful prayers of Elijah were flooding the heart of God, and it was God who refreshed his heavenly warriors with renewed strength by his strong right hand. The valiant angelic army warred against the demons of darkness until they forced the enemies of God away from Mount Carmel and the challenge from Elijah.

Looking back over his shoulder at Seth, who was shivering and on his knees, Michael shouted, "Don't be afraid! The enemy army will not intervene this time. Almighty God has not allowed it. He will not be moved in this battle for the hearts and minds of his people. He's once again offering them the choice to return to him, the only true God. How long will they waver before their hearts become stone? Only the Lord is God, but we will see if they choose to worship him alone."

Seth nodded miserably and chided himself for his own fear. *Why do I not believe that God is powerful enough to protect us?*

"Be strong in the Lord, Seth, and in his mighty power!" shouted Michael.

Seth watched wide-eyed. It was clear that Satan did not want the people of Israel to embrace Elijah's challenge. His lying demons had deceived them, and they had forgotten God's kindness. Seth could hear the hatred in their cries, and he knew that if the evil spirits could succeed, they would even kill Elijah to keep the people under the hard hand of Satan.

As bellowing screams and squeals intensified, Michael focused his attention on the surging army from the Prince of Darkness. But before Michael could order a strategic defense, a bright light burst into the eastern sky. Michael fell to his knees and bowed his head. Multitudes of angels followed Michael's posture of worship as the flash of the bright star soared across the heavens and filled the skies with intense light.

Deceiver's warriors scattered like roaches running for cover.

Seth forced himself to stand and look up at the blazing star. But he crumbled to his knees when Michael's face lit up and he shouted, "It is the Lord of Hosts, the King of the Ages, the Bright Morning Star!"

All around him, kneeling angels were singing, "Holy, holy, holy, Almighty God!"

The star blasted through the eastern atmosphere with power and majesty. Shock waves vibrated through the air, and suddenly, no one was standing. Every being in the heavens fell on its face in awe and fear. An awesome presence towered before them, clothed in blinding white light, looking like a man. Rings of multicolored rainbows radiated from his image like lightning. Glorious angelic voices surrounded him with music. Bolts of thunder rocked the skies and sent shivers through the angelic audience. His awesome presence filled the heavens.

And yet, tranquility fell at his gaze.

Seth, too, was on his knees with closed eyes. He inhaled the warm air and felt blankets of peace envelop him in weightless waves of joy. Sighs of relief resounded around him. He could almost smell the coming victory of God.

The angels rose, full of new resolve and strength. The strong arm of Almighty God had secured their victory. The air cooled as they waved their mighty wings to worship the God of heaven and earth. Seth joined their reverent praise, "Holy, holy God! You are strong and mighty, and you do hold the victory in your hand."

Time seemed to disappear as they applauded the glorious King of Kings. Then with a breath it was over, and he had vanished. The quiet angelic army moved freely, rejoining their squads and units.

"What just happened, Michael?" Seth exhaled.

"You were in the close presence of the King of Kings and Lord of Lords, Seth. He is God's Son, who comes to earth to offer forgiveness and restoration for man's rebellion and rejection of the Almighty. He will be called the Prince of Peace and *Emmanuel,* which means *God with us,* but most people will know him as Jesus. His coming has been long promised. Even your father and mother know that he will one day break Satan's power."

"Humm." Seth smiled and pondered the hopeful news.

Elijah stood quiet and still with his head bowed. Then he looked toward the skies and inhaled dry, dusty air. Confident, he commanded those near him, "Go, gather four large jars of water from the people, and pour it on the offering to Jehovah. Pour it also on the wood under the offering."

Watching intently, Seth shook his head and inquired, "What in the world is he doing that for, Michael? Why is he asking them to soak his offering and wood?"

Before Michael could answer, Elijah ordered his helpers, "Do it again." They hurried off to get more water to pour onto the offering and the wood. The water soaked into the meat and began to pool around the altar.

"Now, do it a third time," he instructed.

Surprised by his demand, the helpers hesitated. Nodding, Elijah said, "Do it again."

"Look at him," Michael said with a proud smile. "He is making it impossible for the wood to burn under natural circumstances. The water is running down the offering and wood, filling up the trench around the altar. He knows he is putting himself and Almighty God at a great disadvantage by this decision—or so the people will think. He knows it is impossible to start a fire with wet and soggy wood. Look at the puzzled faces of the people."

Michael lifted his foot onto a boulder and motioned for Seth to rest on a nearby stone. Unseen, but close to Elijah, they joined the crowds observing the prophet of God. Michael broke the silence. "Now everyone will see the impossible become possible. For what is impossible for man is wholly possible for God! Nothing is too difficult for Almighty God. Elijah knows this truth, and the people are about to experience the power of God."

Without exaggeration or ceremony, without frantic activity, Elijah took a step forward, raised his eyes, and with a gentle voice began to pray. "O Lord, God of Abraham, Isaac, and Jacob, let it be known today that you are God, and let it be known that I am your servant and have done all these things because of your commands."

Elijah raised his voice and continued, "Hear me, O Lord! Answer me, so these people will know that you alone are God. Because of your great love for them, and your faithfulness to your promise, turn their hearts back to you."

The brightness of the Star still blazed in the high heavens, but it was shrouded by the surrounding galaxies and encircled with stars. Sounds of awe shot though the crowds of men when an intense bolt of lightning flashed against the sparkling sky, shooting visible energy straight toward the altar of Elijah. A blazing fireball followed, with vivid streaks of blue, orange, and yellow light. The fireball struck the sacrifice, incinerating the wood and stones and blackening the dirt under Elijah's sacrifice. The blaze didn't stop until it licked up all the water in the trench around the altar. The blistering air from the fire popped and crackled, reflecting lights of sapphire, crimson, and amber. Florescent waves of color danced and wove themselves into ribbons of energy that became a powerful smoking cord, shooting upward and disappearing into the heavens.

The people of Israel fell to the ground in shocked, tear-streaked waves, facedown on the hard, dry dirt. They shouted, "Great is our God!" They wept and wailed, torn between joy and remorse, overwhelmed by God's miraculous deed. Many cried out, "The Lord, he is God! The Lord, he is God Almighty!"

Seeing the people's response, Elijah again raised his arms toward the sky in thankful praise. His body swelled with delight, and his face flooded with tears. Yet, he could hardly contain the jubilant smile that spread across his cheeks. Along with the crowds, he shouted, "Yes! The Lord Almighty is God! He alone is God! There is none like him! Who is God besides the Lord?"

Looking over the people, he paused, stood erect, and cried out to the crowds, "The Lord has shown you today that he is the only true God. But he will not share his glory and throne with another! He alone is worthy of our worship. The Almighty God will not be mocked!"

People rose and circled around Elijah. Some sat at his feet while others stood close, holding each other's hands. "Shush…shush!" went through the expectant crowd. They quieted themselves and waited for him to say more.

Elijah looked at King Ahab, who was standing on the edge of his platform in front of his advisers. The king cupped his hand over his forehead, protecting his eyes from the light and pushing away curls of hair that blocked his view of the burning altar. Elijah raised his voice and repeated, "No, God will not be mocked by any man or by those who worship foolish idols. If it is true that the Lord is God, then devote yourself to him alone!"

The great prophet hesitated only a moment before he drew in a large breath and commanded, "Therefore, seize the prophets of Baal! They have turned you and your children from the only true God, Creator of heaven and earth! They have tried to destroy your faith. Bring them down to the valley now for the judgment of God. His hand will not be light. Just as God told Moses, 'Leaders who incite his people to spiritual rebellion must not live.'"

There was stillness and silence in the heavens as Seth, Michael, and the hosts of angels witnessed the deaths of the prophets of Baal at the command of Elijah.

The heavenly army stood in awe as the people made their way down the mountain. Seth stood like a statue, his shoulders hunched. He held both hands over his mouth as he stared at the scene below.

"What a powerful reminder to all," whispered Michael as he looked over at his somber young companion. "There can be no middle ground for the people of God. They cannot divide their allegiance between Almighty God and Baal. When they don't commit themselves to Almighty God and his truths, they are drawn into the dangerous trap of idolatry. The people don't even realize how easily they replace the truths of God for Satan's lies."

Michael straightened his stance, raised his mighty sword to the heavens, and proclaimed with a commanding voice, "There is only one choice. There is only one God. Worship him!"

Seth swelled with understanding and nodded in agreement.

"Yes," Michael cried. "Truth demands a choice. Today the people have chosen God…but will they choose him tomorrow?"

CHAPTER 6

The Cloud of Promise

The death carts rattled over the rocky terrain of the Kishon Valley, piled high with the wilting bodies of the slain prophets. King Ahab turned away from the distressing sight. His aides and advisers stood before him like stone pillars. Agitated, he shouted, "Go away!"

He slumped against a jagged boulder, rested his teeth on the knuckles of his right hand, and began to chew on his signet ring. Brooding and sullen, he closed his eyes and slid his teeth over the stone of his ring several times while pushing dirt and pebbles around with the toe of his sandal.

Michael pointed to the king of the Israelites. "Look at King Ahab, Seth. Elijah's victory has shaken him."

Seth raised his eyebrows. "Do you think he is still committed to the queen's gods after seeing the power of the Almighty today?"

"We will see soon." Michael drew his hefty sword from its sheath and rested the flat blade on his palm. He surveyed the heavens for any further disturbance and raised his head, anticipating another order from the Almighty. When none came, he relaxed his pose but continued to keep a watchful stance. "He may even be questioning his wisdom as ruler of Israel. Think about it, Seth. If he accepts this awesome act of heavenly fire from God Almighty, then he should reject Baal. But if he rejects the pagan idols, how will he escape the wrath of Queen Jezebel? She calls herself a prophetess and misleads her people by worshiping these false gods made by the hands of men."

Agitation twisted Seth's stomach. "Yes, but King Ahab has seen the amazing power of the Lord today! How could he turn away from the truth of God and ignore the Maker of heaven and earth? How could he agree to Baal worship now?"

Seth was almost afraid to admit how familiar all this felt. *Whoa. This is what happened to Cain!... and to Father and Mother, who were with God in the garden. They received his breath of life and knew his love. They walked and talked with him, and he gave them everything they needed. Yet they turned away from God and ignored his command to not eat from the Tree of Good and Evil. God told them that if they did they would die. And their life, as they knew it with him, surely did die! They were put out of their garden home and couldn't go back.*

Seth hung his head and kicked his toe in the dirt. He knew how hard life had been for his family. He remembered his father weeping as he told the story to his children. *How can I question King Ahab's choices when my own family listened to a lie and rebelled against God? But God told Father that he has made a way for us to come back to him. And Ahab has heard all the stories of how God protected his ancestors. Why . . .?*

Michael interrupted Seth's concentration. "Life has been good for the king lately, Seth. So he has not encouraged the people to be faithful to Almighty God. And besides, the queen hardly tolerates the true God of Israel. She would be very angry with King Ahab if he tried to stop Baal worship. The king is a strong warrior in the battlefield, one of the best. With God's guidance, he has often protected Israel from her neighboring enemies. But Jezebel is a strong woman in her own ways. She has great influence and persuasion over him. Ahab will often relinquish his power in exchange for her approval and affection."

Seth shuffled uncomfortably. "What will he tell her has happened today? How will he explain the hundreds of prophets slain at Elijah's command? He certainly can't keep it from her, can he?"

The king sulked and swatted flies from his face. He dropped his shoulders and stared at the dirt. Dust gathered on his sandals and the bottom of his robe as he kicked the pebbles at his feet.

Elijah's husky voice broke the noise of rumbling carts and the humdrum sounds of the departing crowd: "King Ahab! King Ahab!"

The king jerked his head around to watch Elijah approaching his rocky hideaway. At the sight, he took a deep breath and swelled in annoyance.

"The rains are coming." Elijah stopped and stared at the king. "God Almighty is going to break the drought."

He stepped closer to the king and in a soft voice said, "So go, eat and drink, and prepare to cross the valley before the gullies overflow with the Lord's downpour."

The heavenly audience took in the earthly scene with great interest. Seth watched Elijah walk away from the irritable king. Then he looked at Michael and said, "It's late. The day is almost over. Does Elijah really believe the rain will come today?"

"Yes. The mighty God of heaven and earth has demonstrated his unlimited power beyond question. Now he will bring the needed rain. He has shown the people that he is the true God of Israel. His miracle of fire has devastated this pagan priesthood. He has proven that their idols are useless." Michael stood squarely on both feet. "Look at the king now, Seth. He is full of his own thoughts about God and what this will mean to the Israelites. And like King Ahab, Elijah is also thinking about God's faithfulness and what it could mean to the nation. Yes, the Almighty has shown his people what is true." He hesitated. "*And* what is a lie. They know he is God. But the question is, will they return to him and follow his ways?"

"And," continued Seth, "will they get rid of the worthless idols of Jezebel? Or will they keep them and go on rejecting God?" Thoughts of Cain's descendants with their carved idols flooded his mind. Cain knew about the true God—so did his descendants, the people of Nod and others. Yet, they crafted false gods and worshiped them.

Would I ever do the same? Seth quietly asked himself. *After all that I've seen—could I also be so faithless?*

"If they do, they will harden their hearts to his blessings as well," said Michael. "Elijah is afraid that the people will fear the anger of the queen more than they fear the wrath of God. But they can't continue to follow two masters. They will despise one and love the other." Michael pointed toward the straggly man of faith who was talking quietly to his helper. "Look at Elijah's face. Even though he is weary, his eyes are dancing with anticipation. You can see that his heart is full of hope. He wants the Lord to fulfill his promise today and bring the rains they desperately need. He wants the people to be overjoyed by God's provision and fully return to worship him alone."

They sat quietly watching the servants fuss over the king, offering him fruit and nuts off a gold platter. Nervous advisers whispered instructions to dismantle the awning as soon as the royal chariot arrived. Busy attendants bickered about how to keep the king calm and comfortable while they prepared for his departure to Jezreel. Soldiers stood near their horses, waiting for orders to depart with their king.

Noise from the last carts carrying the slain prophets began to fade. The dust clouds from their wheels grew smaller as they trudged away toward the royal city, Jezreel.

Michael pointed to the top of Mount Carmel, where Elijah had made his way back to the smoking altar of God. They watched as he bent down and put his face to his knees. His voice, quiet though it was, reverberated through the heavens.

"O holy God," prayed Elijah, "I have completed the task you asked of me. You told me to go and present myself to Ahab and you would bring rain on the land. You have let it be known today that *you* are the God of Israel and that I am your servant. Now, I am asking you to keep your word and bring us rain."

Elijah raised his head and turned to his assistant. "Go and look toward the sea. Tell me what you see."

The young servant went up and looked as Elijah had asked. "Everything is as it was, sir. There is nothing different. It is arid, and there isn't a cloud in the sky. The horizon still vibrates with heat."

"Go again."

The servant obeyed, running even further ahead this time. Returning, he panted, "Still there is nothing. The skies are blue and calm."

"Go again."

"Oh!" the servant sighed.

Seth smiled to himself—he could understand how the young man felt. But the servant turned and ran toward the sea again. Once again there was nothing to report. Seven times Elijah sent him to the edge of the mountain to look out toward the sea. Weary and discouraged, the servant trudged the seventh time to his vantage point. This time, a cool sea breeze tussled his hair. He put his hand over his eyebrows and looked harder at the horizon. Something bird-like appeared in the distant sky. Tensing, he stood like a statue, staring at the object. A broad smile crossed his face. Full of excitement, he shouted as he ran back to the prophet, "It's a cloud! It's a cloud, Elijah! It's a cloud!"

He could hardly get his words out clearly as he fluttered, "It's small, like a man's hand, but it's there, rising from the sea."

Elijah pulled himself up from his humble position, and a smile spread across his weathered face. His eyes sparkled in the folds of his cheeks and the bushy hair of his brows. "Now, go quickly and tell King Ahab to hitch up his chariot and get through the valley before the rain catches him and buries his wheels in mud."

The young servant hurried to deliver his message to the king.

In the heavens, Seth and Michael watched the gloomy sky begin to push away the light of day. They jumped to attention when the atmosphere filled with the power of Almighty God. Again a holy energy and authority exploded around them. In the distance, thunder rumbled and tore at the changing sky. Dazzling displays of lightning danced through the heavens. Seth's tunic flapped in the strong winds that pushed the heavy sky toward the Jezreel Valley. Finally, the massive clouds unleashed their pounding rain. The king's caravan jostled madly across the land as the downpour drenched the chariots and carts, which tried to stay upright as they maneuvered around the flooding ruts and waterholes.

"Watch now, Seth! See the incredible power of God in this storm," instructed Michael. "It looks like Elijah can feel it in his spirit. See how he is tucking his robe into his belt for the run." Michael laughed at the sight. "Elijah doesn't need to ride on a chariot or a wagon today. He rides on the wings of Almighty God, who always keeps his word and does what he says he will do!"

Elijah ran with ease through the heavy rain and overcame the king's chariot. Pounding droplets of cool water crashed against his flushed cheeks. Erratic winds loosened his cloak, and tangled fabric locked against his legs. He gathered his garments in his arms and again secured them in his belt. Shouting to all who could hear, he cried, "Today the Lord Almighty has turned the hearts of Israel back to himself! He parted the heavens with fire and walked on the dark clouds of rain to confront his people in their sin. He has rescued them from the enemy. Who is God besides the Lord?"

Elijah raised his voice even louder and roared, "Who is the mighty rock if not our God?"

Bolting ahead of the royal chariot, Elijah slowed his pace and came alongside the king. He stared at the water-soaked figure holding the crown on his head as he jostled through the storm. "What about you?" the prophet bellowed. "What do you say, O King of Israel? Who is your God? Who will you worship as Lord?"

Seth heard the rushing sound and felt the wind brush his cheeks. He turned to see Michael unfold his mighty wings and soar above the able army of God. Thousands of angels moved with him. Signaling for their attention, Michael raised both arms above his head and proclaimed in a bold shout, "Almighty God has won the victory today! He has enabled us to defeat the minions of Satan!"

The angels shouted, "God is good, and his kingdom will last forever!"

"The victory is ours," Michael declared. As his forces listened in rapt attention, he continued, "But you know this is not the end of the war. The demonic warriors are counting their losses and blaming each other for their defeat. They face the dark wrath of Satan, who hates all humankind, especially those who follow God Almighty. The Prince of Darkness will certainly send his demonic minions again and again to deceive those who reject the truth of God. They will continue to coerce the hearts of the Israelites away from God. One thing is certain: the battle continues for the minds and hearts of men. But remember, Satan roams like a lion, and he is always on the prowl for the next victim who will listen to his lies."

Commending the heavenly soldiers, he continued, "Return to your celestial assignments. We will wait for the Lord Almighty to direct our next task."

All together they shouted in praise, "Almighty God is merciful and just! His goodness will last forever!"

With a blink they were gone, leaving Michael alone with Seth. They stared into the clouds and listened to the rain hammering the earth.

"Wow!" exclaimed Seth. "Wow! What an awesome day this has been. I will always remember the courage of Elijah today. Surely now, the worship of Baal will end, and the people of Israel will follow Almighty God. They must see how good he is to them and that he keeps his promises!" He spoke the words as if to convince himself of their truths. He *would* remember. He *would* be faithful to fear and follow God alone! And God would help him, just as he had helped Elijah.

"Yes, God's promises are certainly available to the people, but they are not automatic, Seth," Michael reminded him. "His people must remember them. Life is hard. They must trust God to provide for their needs and help them through tough times. Their lives will not change unless they depend on the Almighty and acknowledge him as their God and the source of all blessings."

Seth raised his eyes and stared into the sky, letting Michael's words soak in. Was there any limit to God's power, really? *I wish Cain could have been here today. Surely he would have been impressed by these astounding miracles of fire and rain. Maybe he would give up his own idols and come back to God too. I wonder if it is too late? Cain is such a strong man, and he doesn't think he needs God. But if God would show his power to the Israelites, who rejected him, he could also show Cain that he still cares about him, and that it's not too late for him to return to the God of his father. It would be great to see him laugh and enjoy our family again, and bring his descendants back to worshiping God. Hmm. Maybe even the brothers of Nod would change their ways if they knew this awesome God.*

Seth smiled. *God must care about me, too, if he would do all of this for the Israelites, who don't even follow him. Truly, I won't forget this day.*

Michael motioned for Seth to walk with him toward the clear, bright sky beyond the storm. "As for Elijah," he continued, "he has done what God told him to do. He has given the people an opportunity to believe that Almighty God is the only true God. Now others can follow in Elijah's faith and continue what God has started today. And God will continue to lead Elijah. He is not finished with his servant. He is always at work in the hearts of those who choose his ways and follow him. No matter what desperate situations Elijah may face, the Almighty will take care of him, just as he always has."

Seth turned his head and looked back toward the storm. "So what will happen to King Ahab, Michael? Will he have the courage to stand before Queen Jezebel? Will he proclaim the Almighty as the only true God? Will he lead the people in the ways of the Lord?"

Before Michael could answer, Seth continued, "Do you think he will destroy the wooden idols of Baal?"

Smiling, Michael replied, "So many questions."

"Surely the king will honor God now," Seth responded without hesitation.

"We must wait and see. People make their own choices. Some will choose to follow God, but many will not."

The flooded chariot of King Ahab charged into the outer courtyard and stopped abruptly in front of Jezebel's beautiful palace. Guards opened the heavy wooden gate to the king's private patio and apartment.

Jezebel had commissioned craftsmen to adorn the smaller castle and to mimic the splendor of their lavish ivory palace in Samaria. Large pillars supported the cedar roof that extended into the patio. Each pillar was decorated with intricate, ivory carvings.

The smooth walls of the courtyard displayed massive ivory plaques, and each alcove hosted ivory statues of distorted human bodies and animal heads. A three-tiered ivory fountain filled the center of the courtyard and flooded the stone floors with its stormy overflow of rainwater.

The drenched horses panted and snorted in exhaustion. The king jumped from his chariot, splashing into a pool of muddy water. He grabbed a dry robe from the queen's handmaiden and stalked down the long hall to Jezebel's gathering room. Maids and attendants for the queen jumped to their feet and bowed their heads when he passed.

He wasted no time finding her room. His wet, squeaky sandals announced his homecoming to the queen. The king entered the gathering room and stiffened as he met her steely eyes and haughty stare.

"Well?" she questioned. "What happened on that mountain today?"

Michael shook his head in disbelief as he watched King Ahab strut around the room in front of Queen Jezebel.

The king gritted his teeth and buried his hands in his hair. "Ah! It did not go well for your prophets today!" He exhaled. The queen narrowed her eyes and waited. Ahab backed up against the wall and stared at the floor.

Michael and Seth watched in silence. King Ahab told her everything Elijah had done on Mount Carmel. He told her that Baal worship was futile; that the gods had been totally unresponsive to her prophets' pleading. He told her that they had chanted and performed rituals all day to encourage Baal's answer. But it had done no good.

"Only Elijah's God brought a fire to the altar. The people saw it all!" Ahab exclaimed. Then he told her how Elijah had called for the death of the prophets.

Before she could respond, King Ahab stepped forward. Their eyes locked. He threw up his arms and burst out in frustration, "What could I have done to stop it? Baal was powerless against Almighty God! His triumph today has shown the people that *he* is the only true God for Israel. Baal and the prophets were humiliated."

Drawing a deep breath, he shook his head and sighed, "Besides, the people remembered the law of God: 'If wicked men lead people astray and cause them to worship other gods, they must be killed.' I was afraid to lift my voice against them. They could have turned on me too."

Queen Jezebel relaxed her rigid frame and motioned for him to come to her. The king crumbled onto the cushions of her lounge, buried his face in her skirts, and wept. She stroked his tangled, wet hair. Then her body stiffened, and her mouth tightened in anger.

Saddened, Michael said, "It seems he has made his decision. Already he has chosen her approval instead of the approval of God."

Seth stood and shivered in unbelief. "No!" he squealed, looking up into Michael's piercing eyes. The archangel stood as still and as speechless as a statue. *Is it that easy to ignore the mighty works of God?*

Michael put his powerful hand on Seth's shoulder and said, "We must wait." After a long pause, he continued, "God is very patient with man, but he will not be mocked, and his plans will not be thwarted. Even so, the enemy of God Almighty is especially dangerous to those in powerful positions. But we will fight for everyone who trusts in the only true God, God Almighty."

Michael nudged Seth's shoulder and smiled. "We can be sure of one thing, Seth: God is not finished with this war for mankind. And he is certainly not finished with the Israelites, any more than he is finished with Elijah or King Ahab. Those who choose to follow him will not be disappointed."

CHAPTER 7

Road to Revolution

Seth kicked his foot at the pools of water in his path as he strolled alongside the mighty archangel Michael. Heavy clouds hung in the sky, promising more rain.

"I've been wondering about something, Michael. How did King Ahab become the ruler of Israel anyway? It doesn't look like he cares much about God or what God wants for the people. So why would God allow him to remain king when he encouraged the people to follow Baal rather than the God of Israel?"

Michael shook his head and smiled. "That's a question that is not easily answered. But the short answer is that God keeps his promises. Almighty God made a promise to a man named Abraham long before King Ahab was born. God promised Abraham that he would become the father of many nations. He promised that he would bless Abraham's children and that kings would come from his descendants. God also promised that he would never leave them or forget Abraham's family. He said he would always be with them, even when they chose not to be with him."

"Humph!" Seth threw out his arms and exclaimed, "He sure showed the king that he was here today on Mount Carmel! King Ahab couldn't miss the fire from heaven and all that rain afterward." Skipping a rock over a large pond of water ahead, he laughed. "Ha! He almost drowned going home during that downpour."

The powerful angel stopped and watched Seth leap across a large water hole. "Yes, Seth," he said. "And the Almighty always keeps his promises." Vaulting ahead, Michael moved into Seth's path.

Seth stopped abruptly when he saw the mighty angel towering over him with crossed arms and commanding stance. His piercing eyes demanded Seth's attention.

Releasing a deep breath, Michael continued, "Seth, King Ahab has an important history and comes from a particular family line. He is a descendant of Abraham, whom God chose to be the father of this mighty nation of Israel. The destiny of Abraham's family is crucial to God's eternal plan ...even for *you* and all of your descendants."

Seth froze in rapt attention. "What do you mean? Why are the lives of these Israelites important to my family? We don't even live in the same time. Besides, Father always tells us about God. I think he is worried that we might follow Cain into the land of Nod."

Michael motioned for Seth to join him near a rocky stream. They sat on the stony ground, crossed their legs, and faced each other. "Think about it, Seth. God has allowed you to see events that will take place many years in the future. You have just experienced a mighty battle for the people's loyalty to Almighty God."

Seth nodded his head, and Michael leaned on one elbow. "God showed them his power in the fire and the rain to prove his love for them. Most of them will choose independence from him anyway. Nonetheless, he knows that others will realize that he is the true God. They will know in their hearts that he is the only God to follow. They will call themselves 'his people' and pass his truths on to their children and to their children's children, because they trust him and love him, just like your father, Adam, does. He knows God better than anyone. But he also knows that he can't make you or his other children follow God. You must each choose him for yourselves."

They sat in silence. Seth looked away from Michael and gazed at the clouds.

"You're right. Father and Mother have told me many stories about God. He walked with them in the garden and even spoke to my brother Cain and showed him mercy. We've heard that God will never leave us. If I have any children in the future, I want to tell them about God too."

"Yes." Michael leaned back onto a boulder and continued. "And that is why God has brought you here. Your descendants— well, let's just say they play a very big role in all that is happening here. But do you see that the choice to believe him will be given to them, just as it is given to you and just as it was given to King Ahab? Your children will have to make their own decision whether to follow Almighty God or not."

Picking up a smooth stone, Seth tossed it across the murky creek. "I'll have to tell my future family my own stories about God, huh?"

"That is just what Abraham did with his family. God promised him that he would be the father of a great nation, so he told his family about the promise. And God kept his promise when he gave Abraham a son, Isaac."

Michael chuckled. "How happy Abraham was to tell Isaac that his children would be included in the promise too."

"Has King Ahab heard about the promise?" asked Seth. "You said he is a descendant of Abraham's family."

A bird screeched above their heads. Michael swung his head to watch a hawk settle on a scrawny tree limb not far from their resting place. Then he answered, "Yes, Ahab is from Abraham's family. He may have heard about Abraham's promise from God, but he chose to ignore it. You saw how he let his people practice idol worship with Baal."

"Looks like someone forgot to tell him," Seth sighed.

"It was not that simple, Seth. Remember how the demonic forces tried to confuse the people today on the mountain by whispering doubt about God into their minds? Satan wants to destroy the Almighty's plan any way that he can. He encourages men to think about themselves rather than the goodness of God. When they forget God, they also forget to pass on the great promise given to their ancestor, Abraham."

Michael watched Seth pick up a stone and toss it from hand to hand. "You should have seen Satan's warriors come after Abraham, Seth. The enemy of God did not want Abraham to believe the promise God gave him or act on it, so Satan brought many problems into Abraham's life. First, he tried to plant questions in Abraham's mind. Would he believe God's promise or not? If he did, he would have to leave the security of his homeland and move to a new and perhaps dangerous territory. Satan even caused Abraham's family to question his decision. They tried to discourage him and keep him from leaving."

Seth tugged on his ear. "I remember Mother telling me how much she wanted my brother, Cain, to stay nearby. She cried and cried when she heard he would leave. It was very hard on him to take his family and become a wanderer, a nomad. He left his fields and crops behind. But he had no choice after he killed Abel. Cain couldn't live near the family any longer. He had rejected God and didn't want to follow him. Father said he became an angry and dangerous man. I don't think he likes our family, and he surely doesn't like God."

"Abraham made a choice, too, Seth. He chose to believe what God said and what God promised him. But God's enemy was not happy with Abraham's decision. When he began to follow God's ways, things got really hard for him. All along the journey, Abraham encountered local tribes who fought to keep him from moving forward. He tried to be friendly with everyone he met, but often, he had to take up weapons to defend and protect his family. Satan would not give up. He tried to frighten Abraham with doubt and stories of giants. But Abraham was courageous and continued to trust that God would lead him to the land he had promised his family. The darts of the evil warriors followed him throughout the journey."

The darts of the evil warriors. Seth thought of the brothers of Nod and shivered. Would they always be a threat to him, like the tribes were to Abraham? Was following God worth so much trouble? Again, a crow screamed and cawed as it flew overhead. A chilling breeze broke the warmth of the sun on their necks. Michael propelled himself to his feet and unsheathed his sword. Seth jumped to his side. A foul odor permeated the air, growing intense.

Michael pushed Seth behind his powerful torso and flowing robe. "Don't be afraid, Seth. This is not unusual. The enemy always gathers when accounts of faith and dependence on the Almighty God are told. He hopes to confuse your thinking so that you will not hear the truths of heaven."

Michael's eyes darted from side to side, searching the skies for evidence of the enemy's presence. He lifted his sword to summon angelic warriors.

Seth stepped back from Michael and crouched behind a boulder. He watched the defending angels soar above and hover, ready for battle. Several angels encircled Seth. They turned their faces toward the horizon and waited for the enemy's assault.

In the distance, shadows began to move back and forth in the sky. The horizon changed from blue to dreary shades of gray. The colors churned and wavered before finally disappearing in a volatile puff of smoke. The satanic warriors had accomplished their immediate mission from a distance—to tease and taunt the army of God into useless action.

After a tense moment, a refreshing sweetness cleansed the atmosphere. Michael motioned to God's warrior angels to relax their stance. The enemy was nowhere in sight. And for the moment, Seth's fears of the brothers seemed to have evaporated.

"Whew!" Seth sighed when Michael turned his way.

Returning his sword to its sheath, Michael smiled at Seth. "The Almighty has instructed me to explain to you the line of ascendency for the kings. But his enemy does not want you to have this knowledge. He will try to strike you with fear and distract you so you will not understand the importance of God's plan for Israel and all of mankind."

"But I want to understand," Seth pleaded. "Tell me more. Did kings come from Abraham's children and grandchildren?"

"Oh yes, but not right away. Abraham's son, Isaac, grew to depend on Almighty God. He passed on the promises of God to his children. But again, Isaac's children had to make up their own minds about God." Michael paused. "We know that Almighty God always keeps his promises. But what we *didn't* know was what Isaac's children would believe about God. And would they pass on the promise to their own families?"

Seth and the towering archangel walked along the creek in silence. Michael cleared his throat and spoke again. "Isaac had twin boys. One of them, named Jacob, had twelve sons, and God Almighty changed his name to *Israel* the moment that Jacob believed God's promise was also for him and his family. Jacob's sons and their descendants became the twelve family tribes of this new nation. Named after Jacob, it's known as the nation of Israel."

"Oh, so that's how the Israelites got their name," Seth acknowledged with raised eyebrows.

"Yes, and this new family nation of Israel struggled for survival. But when they were loyal to God and followed his instructions, they became strong and courageous."

Bending down on one knee, Michael smoothed the dirt in front of them and picked up a stick. "But let me show you what happened before the first king came to power in Israel."

Seth sat down when Michael began to write large letters in the sand.

Revolution

Seth looked up at Michael, questioning. The angel pointed back to his writing in the sand. "Look at the family chart, Seth. It will help you understand how hard it was to keep God's promise to Abraham alive in the hearts of his descendants. And it will show you all God does to carry out his plan and promise for their future." Michael scratched three names in the sand, one under the other:

ABRAHAM
   ISAAC
      JACOB

Then he wrote:

(12 Sons / 12 Tribes)
KINGS

Pointing to the "12 Sons" on the chart, he said, "God was the king over the twelve tribes of Israel. But the custom was to choose the heads of the family or elders as the tribal authorities. Later, God would call special judges to save the people of Israel from oppressive invaders. This pattern continued for hundreds of years. But eventually, the people wanted to be like all the other nations—so they demanded a king like the nations around them, an earthly king of their own. And God gave them what they asked for."

Seth studied the chart in the sand. Slowly, two forms, like men, began to rise up from the dirt. The first man was smiling and looked like Seth's father, Adam. He was handing a bowl full of sparkling seeds to the second man. Seth knew immediately: *The second man is me!* He watched his figure turn and hold the glowing bowl to another man, who was rising up from the sandy dirt to take the treasure from him. This ritual continued, man after man, until one figure grew larger than the others. Across his head was a banner that read, "Father of many nations." *Abraham! Abraham is my descendant!*

Seth watched men continue to form and rise from the chart near their names. The Abraham figure passed the fiery bowl to Isaac, who passed it to Jacob, who passed it to his twelve sons, who passed it to others as the line of men faded into the distance. All Seth could see at the end of the line was bursts of light shooting high into the sky from the bowl.

"I get it, Michael!" said Seth. "The truths about God will not be forgotten. God will always find someone who will pass them on to the next generation, and when that happens—more and more people will know about God's plan to rescue us from the lies of his enemy."

Michael's face wrinkled into a broad smile. "You're on the right track, Seth. But when Israel asked for a king like the idolatrous nations around them, Satan's lies about God took root in their thinking and affected their choices. It didn't take long for the kings to forget the good and right ways of Almighty God."

"Who was the first king the people chose for Israel? And did he forget about God?" Seth questioned.

"The first king was Saul. They chose him from the tribe of Benjamin, the last son born to Jacob. The people wanted Saul, their new king, to make decisions for their nation, rather than God Almighty." Michael shook his head and grimaced. "But King Saul often ignored God's instructions and led his people into peril. After a while, God rejected Saul as king because he ignored God's commands. Saul even took the advice of a witch rather than trusting in God for success in battle. His disloyalty to God threw the country into civil war and even idolatry. But Saul enjoyed being their king, and he fought to keep his crown."

With sweeping strokes, Michael wrote another name in the sand.

David

"David was from the tribe of Judah, the fourth son born to Jacob. As a young shepherd boy, David trusted God, and God knew David would lead the people in his ways. The promise to Abraham would be fulfilled because David wanted to please Almighty God. David became the greatest king Israel would ever know. No others would seek after God like David."

Michael stood and put out his powerful hand to help Seth to his feet. They picked up their pace and continued their journey toward the hills. "God could not allow Saul to lead the people astray. So he chose David to replace Saul as king. David listened to God and led the people with God's wisdom and power. David called on Almighty God when he was in trouble, and he tried to follow God's ways."

The sun burst out of the clouds, and Seth looked up at the clearing sky. Enjoying the warmth on his face, he closed his eyes and raised both arms before returning to their conversation. "What kind of life did the Israelites have with David as their king? Were they happy? Did they know that the promise God gave to Abraham, Isaac, and Jacob was for them? Did they follow God's ways, or did they follow their own? Did they end up like King Ahab?" Seth jumped back in before Michael could answer. "I remember Father told me that because God loves us, he reveals himself and his ways to us even when we crave to be self-sufficient and free from him. He said God's rules offer us safety and help us know his love."

Beaming, Michael said, "Your father knew Almighty God better than anyone has known him. Adam told you the truth! God's eyes are always searching for those who seek after him like David. David trusted God for directions, and God answered his prayers."

Seth bit his bottom lip. *I only ask God for big things, like rescue from that mountain lion I saw at the edge of our field. As I backed away, I kept praying that the lion would stay where he was and not chase after me. Maybe I should ask God to show me how to follow his ways instead of always wanting to do it my own way. Usually, when I get stubborn and expect my brothers to do what I want them to do, I end up angry and frustrated, and we get into a tussle. Could it be that way with God too?*

"David surely didn't do everything right," Michael commented. "But he believed God would make Israel a strong nation, and he encouraged his people to follow their God. David showed them that he was serious about God. He spoke about God's ways with his advisers, and he worshiped the Almighty along with his people. But he knew his own strength came through prayer. David knew God's power had no limits and that the Almighty would not impose his will on anyone. So he boldly asked God to intervene for his needs and for the needs of his people in Israel. David helped to shape the new nation and strengthened the people's faith for generations. For eighty years, King David and his son Solomon ruled a peaceful and united kingdom, a brotherhood of twelve tribes."

They walked along the stream, listening to the water rush over the narrow channel. "If David's kingdom was so strong," asked Seth, "and God was with him, then how did the families and tribes break apart? Why was there a revolution?"

Before Michael could answer, Seth continued, "I bet Satan was behind their arguments. He seems to show up when God's people are in trouble."

Michael laughed out loud. "You are beginning to see Satan as what Almighty God calls the 'roaring lion.' He roams the earth, looking for fragile people to torment by distracting them from God and God's truths. He pounces like a roaring lion and sends his demons to deceive and confuse those who trust in anyone or anything more than God....even if the 'anyone' is himself. David knew he could fall into Satan's lying traps, so he reminded himself of God's truths and asked him to help him when he was weak, confused, and frightened."

Seth lowered his head and walked on in silence. *God, will you help me to trust you that way and to turn a deaf ear to Satan? I don't want to be led astray like my parents and brother were. I want to be as faithful as Abraham was so that I can pass down your truths to my children someday.*

Michael stopped abruptly. He pulled his imposing sword from its cover and pointed it above his head. "Seth, we are in battles all over the world against Satan's demonic forces. They never tire at diverting God's plans and separating his people from their faith in him. We must be ready to protect them. Whenever people call on God for help, we are sent into action."

He paused and lowered his sword. "From the time David was a young boy until he breathed his last breath, he asked God to lead him and help him in times of trouble. We fought many battles against Satan's warriors for David's sake, just like we have fought battles for you! Do you remember when the brothers of Nod passed you by in the woods near the clearing? Satan's demons could almost smell your fear. They kept screaming doubts into your mind, telling you that you would be beaten and laughed at, and that you couldn't do anything to defend yourself. We attacked the evil warriors on God's instructions and fought until they fled. The deer was sent by God to distract the brothers so you would know your prayer had been answered."

Seth watched Michael slip his sword back into its protective sheath. "Wow!" he breathed. "You were there to protect me!"

Michael smiled. "Yes, just like we are there for anyone who calls to God for help." He paused. "Even so, things were not always good in Israel, Seth. David chose his son Solomon to succeed him on the throne. King Solomon knew it was a difficult job and asked Almighty God for wisdom. And God granted him greater wisdom than any other man has ever had. Under his rule, Israel prospered. But as his riches and power increased, he often ignored the needs of God's people and squandered the wisdom he'd received."

Michael motioned for them to cross the stream ahead, where

larger stones provided a bridge. They stepped cautiously on the slippery rocks until they reached the other side.

"David's son, King Solomon, was not as faithful to God as David had been. He did not resist the temptations and pleasures offered by the roaring lion. As he grew older, King Solomon made his own decisions as he saw fit rather than seeking God for directions. As a result, his kingdom began to unravel like an old blanket. Unrest and contention infected the growing family of Israel. They began to separate from God and compromise their relationship with him. Arguments and fights broke out. Families even split apart. The kingdom fell into great confusion under King Solomon's rule, and when he died, many in Israel turned to idols."

"Sounds like King Ahab," said Seth.

Michael stopped and turned, looking hard at Seth. "Yes. You saw the way King Ahab abandoned God and allowed Jezebel to encourage idolatry and Baal worship. You saw the damage and disarray it caused the Israelites. You saw the people slain in the valley today because they worshiped Baal."

Seth tilted his head, remembering the dead priests of Baal, heaped on the carts at Mount Carmel.

Michael's eyes still bored into him. "You saw today that there are grave consequences for those who ignore God and his ways. King Solomon lost his passion for Almighty God and even allowed his wives to bring their gods into Judah. So he also, like Ahab, experienced a judgment of God sent from heaven. A prophet announced that Almighty God would split the nation in two because of Solomon's decisions. After King Solomon died, all of us in the heavenly host stood in silence and watched the prophecy come true. Rebellion and war broke out in Israel after King Solomon's son, Rehoboam, claimed the throne."

Michael stopped and motioned for Seth to sit under a cypress tree. He stooped to his knee, smoothed the ground again and wrote more names in the dirt. "Let me show you how the families divided themselves," he said.

Solomon—(Son of David)

JUDAH (Two tribes)   ISRAEL (Ten tribes)
REHOBOAM (1ˢᵗ king - new Judah) JEROBOAM 1 (1ˢᵗ king - new Israel)
Abijam   Nadab
Asa   Baasha, Elah, Zimri, Tibni, Omri
Jehoshaphat   *Ahab*

Michael drew a line under the first two names, *Rehoboam* and *Jeroboam*. "It all began when ten of the family tribes chose Jeroboam as their new spokesperson and leader. These ten tribes rallied around Jeroboam, hoping he would present their grievances to Solomon's son, King Rehoboam."

"I'm confused," said Seth. "I thought Israel grew and prospered under Solomon's rule. What were they complaining about?"

"Well," Michael hesitated. "Solomon started his reign like a cool summer morning and ended it as a muggy, gray afternoon. In the early days of his reign, he pleased the Lord with his choices, and God granted him great wisdom and wealth. He wrote and taught a thousand wise things, but he failed to live by his own wisdom. It didn't take long for him to overtax his people and draft his citizens to build his magnificent palaces, the temple, and the spectacular city of Jerusalem. It took thirteen years just to build his personal palace! He acquired fourteen hundred chariots and twelve thousand horsemen and built four thousand stalls for his stables. Yes, he gave Israel prominence and splendor, but at great cost to his people and their families. He chose to impoverish the Israelites for the prestige of his crown. The Israelites wanted relief from the harsh labor, but mostly, they resented the favor he showed to the people in his own tribe, Judah. It didn't take long to see the nation pull apart and become two. Rehoboam, his son, was a foolish young man and would not listen to the wise men who had advised his father. Instead, Rehoboam rejected the advice of the elders and turned to his friends. They told him that he was king now and advised him to ignore the people and increase their hardships."

Michael slammed his fist into the palm of his hand. "The downfall was quick, just as God had said it would be. The ten tribes who followed Jeroboam rebelled, and the nation divided. Only two tribes remained together under King Rehoboam: Benjamin and Judah. They took *Judah* as their country name and called themselves the House of David after David's family line. The other ten tribes who followed Jeroboam continued to call themselves Israel."

"But our family split up too," Seth argued. "It seemed like the right thing to do. Cain and Father didn't agree about hardly anything, and after Abel was killed, things got worse. When Cain didn't regret killing Abel, God cursed him and drove him away from us. His descendants live near us, but Mother says they're unbearable. I don't get it. Why can't families forgive and forget their problems with each other, and just go on? Why do we keep making things so difficult for each other?"

"There is no promise that life will be easy and everyone will get along," Michael said. "People sin and must bear the consequences of their choices. But that doesn't have to be the end, like it was for Cain. If you confess your wrongdoings, God will forgive you and help your heart to change. Even though they no longer live in the garden, your father and mother accepted God's forgiveness and want to follow him. Seth, people make choices everyday to agree with God's ways or not."

Michael paused. "God is good, and he will help those who follow him. Throughout the ages this will be true, because God does not lie. He even promised Jeroboam, the new leader of Israel's ten tribes, that if he would trust God and obey him, he would bless the new nation of Israel. He promised to bless Jeroboam's family just as he had blessed David's."

"And did he do it? Did Jeroboam listen to God?" Seth asked.

"Sadly, Jeroboam took matters into his own hands and trusted himself rather than God. He quickly abandoned the ways and promises of God and led his people into idol worship, just as King Ahab would do later. So, to answer your question—no. Jeroboam and Israel lost the blessing. The kings who ruled Israel after Jeroboam, including King Ahab, never gave their full allegiance to Almighty God. The people and the nation suffered under their own rebellion."

Seth furrowed his brow. "But what about those two tribes who stayed with King Rehoboam? Were they afraid when so many left to go with Jeroboam? Did they recognize God and remain faithful to his ways?"

"Yes, they tried. But they trusted their new king, Rehoboam, more. It made us sad that he continued to take advice from inexperienced young men who encouraged him to believe his choices were better than God's. Rehoboam struggled to be a wise king for Judah, but like King Jeroboam, he thought he knew better than God. But God Almighty's plan will not be stopped. The people of Judah, the House of David, always had a strong group of people who remembered the promise God had given to Abraham, Isaac, and Jacob. As a nation, Judah grew in power and strength and had many kings who followed David's example and led the people with wisdom."

They walked quietly until they reached the top of a small hill. A broad smile spread across Seth's face. He recognized the rich green valley sprinkled with palm and olive trees. Saffron plants mingled with caster beans, and grapevines were full with fruit.

"Michael, I'm almost home!" Seth shouted.

Acknowledging the joy he saw in Seth's face, Michael nodded

and smiled. "Today, Almighty God has shown you what will take place in the future. Treasure the memories and the truths he has revealed. Make your choices wisely. They will determine the destiny of your children—and all of their descendants."

Then, as quickly as he had arrived, Michael disappeared. Seth stood alone, but questions filled his head. *What choices would he have to make for his future? Would he ask God for direction and trust him even if things were difficult? Would his own children choose to trust God Almighty? And what about the future kings of Israel and Judah? Would they follow the ways of God like King David, or would they follow the inclinations of their own will? How would their choices shape the destinies of their kingdoms?*

Seth rubbed the knuckles of his rough hands. He thought of the revelation he had received—that Abraham, and all the people of Israel, were *his* descendants. Then he turned his palms up and formed his fingers to hold an imagined bowl, which he held out in front of his chest like an offering to God. "One thing I know for sure: God knows me, and he has a plan for my life."

BOOK TWO

The Brotherhood

———◆———

CHAPTER 8
A Boastful Breed

Seth's stomach growled as he pulled another apricot from the heavily fruited tree. He fingered the velvety fruit before he popped it into his mouth, pit and all. His cheeks bulged as he chewed the seed loose from the pulp and spit the pit to the ground. He swiped his fingers over his chin, wiping away the juicy fruit droplets, and turned toward the river.

At first it was only a soft whimper. Seth stepped quietly toward the sound. In front of him lay an empty basket, discarded near the willow tree. Recognizing the basket, he froze in place. Jutting his neck forward and squinting, he focused on the crumpled form below the swaying branches. A choking sob rippled through the air.

Seth took a short breath and ran to the tree. "Rizpah, is that you?" He pushed the branches aside and fell to one knee beside the weeping girl. He lifted her chin with one hand and rubbed her back with the other. "Sister, what happened? Are you hurt? Why are you hiding here?"

Rizpah looked into his face, inhaled with staggered breaths, and buried her head on Seth's shoulder. He wrapped his arms around her shaking body. "Tell me what's wrong."

Rizpah caught her breath and sobbed. Seth rocked his sister back and forth. "Shhh, shhh, shhhh. It's going to be all right. I'm here. I'm here."

Finally, Rizpah choked out, "I was gathering fruit for Mother when the brothers of Nod found me. They mocked me because I'm your sister. They said you're brainless and I am a skinny crow.

They made hawking sounds and threw their arms around like birds. One of them said our family is weak and poor because we don't bow down to their storm god."

Rizpah buried her face in her hands. Tears rolled down her cheeks when she looked back at Seth. She wiped her eyes and nose. "They put the food I had gathered for Mother in their bags and pushed me around until I screamed for help. I was so afraid! One of them shoved me to the ground and put his foot on my back and laughed. When I struggled, he laughed again, and before they left, he threw my basket at the willow."

Her shaking stopped, and Rizpah pulled away from Seth. "I was hiding under the branches of the tree when I heard your footsteps. I thought they had come back."

Seth leaned in and brushed the tears from her cheek. "They are bullies, Rizpah. They look for someone to tease so they can feel powerful. They may be bigger than you, but don't be afraid of their words. Don't let their teasing shake you like this. They're rebellious and angry. They don't look to Almighty God for direction, so they think they have to act rowdy to impress everyone."

"That's easy for you to say," Rizpah said. "I was alone. I can't help being scared."

Seth gritted his teeth. "I should have been here to help you. But you weren't alone. God was with you even though you didn't see him. You resisted them, Rizpah, and they left. Stand firm and fear only God."

Seth sighed, and images of his time with Michael filled his mind. How well he remembered Elijah, seemingly alone, and yet guarded by legions of angels. "Be still now, Rizpah, and know that he is *your* God. He will support you and give you courage to face your enemies."

Rizpah looked up at Seth and whimpered, "I did ask him for help."

"Good. And, Rizpah, even though you may not realize it, he

heard your prayer and protected you." Seth reached over and touched her hand. "Don't be afraid. You can be strong and even courageous, because God is always with you—and he *did* protect you today, with his strong right hand." Seth smiled. "I know this is true, Rizpah. He's done it for me too."

Rizpah nodded and leaned against Seth as they sat together under the cover of the willow branches. Finally, Rizpah straightened her body and took several deep breaths. Seth rose and offered his hand to help her stand. "Now, let's go home."

Back on her feet, Rizpah smoothed her hair and straightened her skirt. Then, stooping for her basket, she grinned. "First, help me pick some fruit. I don't want to go home empty-handed."

A warm breeze tickled their faces, and the afternoon sun streamed brilliant rays of light through the silver clouds, washing them in its luster. Seth raced to the apricot tree ahead of Rizpah and gathered an armful of ripe, juicy fruit. She laughed. "Where were you when I needed you today? And what is this newfound courage you seem to have in your heart?"

"Sure, sure," said Seth with a smile. "Fill your basket, and I will tell you a story about our God on the way home."

CHAPTER 9

Besieged

A curl of smoke hovered above the ashes of the fire pit, and the cold night air filled the house. Waking with a start, Seth bolted upright and sprang to his knees. A troubling dream about King Ahab crowded his mind until he remembered the comforting voice: *Do not fear, Seth. My strength will be with you.*

Sweat beaded on his forehead as he reached for his cloak and tossed the blankets to the floor, searching for his hunting knife. Spotting it near his sandals, he grabbed both the knife and sandals and bundled them together with the cloak. Quietly, he stepped away from the family sleeping corner into the gathering room and went outside. Still panting from the dream, Seth surveyed his surroundings and let out a deep sigh. The sheep were sleeping, huddled near their gate; the cow didn't make a sound. Only Storm, the old sheepdog, raised his head to acknowledge Seth's presence.

Seth scanned the wispy clouds that thinly veiled the crescent moon. Walking to the stone bench, he sat down and sorted his bundled clothing. He slipped on his sandals and cloak and tucked the hunting knife into his ankle strap.

Old Storm stretched his skinny body, shook himself awake, and ambled over to the bench. The shaggy dog plopped his head on Seth's knee. Instinctively, Seth began to massage the dog's head and ears. "Nothing bothers you, does it, boy, except maybe that mountain lion that prowls around and gets hungry for our sheep." *I can't shake the feeling that something is going to happen. Why else would I dream about trouble for King Ahab? Is something going to happen with the brothers of Nod? God, are you trying to show me something?*

Seth watched the dawn creep into the morning sky. He rested his hand on Storm's head and prayed, "O Lord God, the brothers of Nod are a danger to my family. I'm afraid they'll do more than just taunt Rizpah. She is a quiet and gentle girl. They know my father is a peaceful man who works hard to feed his family. He doesn't want to fight with his neighbors. But they're a bad-tempered clan who disgrace your name and even curse their own brothers. How long will it be before they begin to steal our animals and harm our family? How long until they turn as violent as Cain?"

There was no answer from the heavenly realms, but Seth rested assured that God could hear him. Even so, he felt troubled. If only he were more confident—more able to face these dangers. Seth patted the old dog's head. "Elijah would have stood up to the brothers and challenged them to return to you, O God. If only I had his courage and boldness. He even challenged King Ahab over the choices he made when he ignored you and your ways. But Elijah trusted you, Lord, to judge the king's decisions."

Seth looked into the big brown eyes of their faithful dog. "Will I ever be able to stand up for my family or defend their honor? Even you bark and growl when the brothers of Nod come near." Seth shook his head. "Ha! I would probably run and hide from them. I don't want to face their sneers and threats any more than Rizpah does. It's easier to just avoid them altogether. Maybe I am a pushover."

An air of calm settled around Seth. Before he felt the strong hand on his shoulder, he heard the deep, familiar voice saying, "Do not fear them or be upset by their sneers. They are a rebellious household."

Seth leaned into the protective presence behind him, then turned to see the familiar angel and smiled. "Michael, you're here. I prayed you would come. I had a bad dream about King Ahab. He was leading his armies into battle, and thousands of enemy soldiers surrounded him. Did this really happen? Is he all right?"

A broad smile spread across Michael's face when Seth reached around to touch the brawny hand of the archangel. "The Almighty God has sent me. Come with me, Seth. You are to witness another battle for the soul of King Ahab. He is to be given another chance to follow the true and living God. The Lord's eyes are on those who seek him and place their hope in him alone. Perhaps this time, King Ahab will realize it is not the size of his army that will save him, but his faith in the unfailing arm of the Lord, whose strength is invincible."

Once again, the air began to tingle around them. The bells grew louder and louder until a sound like rushing waters surrounded them, and sparkling crystals danced overhead. Purples, greens, yellows, blues, and reds rapidly changed positions in beautiful snowflake patterns before their eyes. Melodic harmonies replaced the roaring waters, and Seth watched the clouds part as they began their journey through the heavens.

They came to rest on a large, fortified rooftop that surrounded a spacious open area below. Seth scanned the beautiful patios. Men in regal clothing were gathered, and soldiers stood guard at each door of the palatial courtyard. Several children played with wooden toys near the trunk of a large tree, while women picked ripe olives from its heavy branches. Under the awning at the far side of the inner yard, attendants were preparing platters of food for a group of men gathered near the stone benches at the sidewall. Seth noticed their long sleeves and striped tunics swirling around their ankles as they moved, suddenly self-conscious of his own meager dress and cloak that barely covered his knees. A veiled woman walked from the sizable pool in the middle of the courtyard and approached the men with a large jug. She filled the pitchers on a side table with water from the cistern.

The husky voices under the awning stopped when one of the men reached into the girdled fabric wrapped around his waist and pulled out a rolled parchment. He motioned for the others to join him at a nearby table, where he spread the map in front of them. They hovered over the war plans, whispering back and forth. One pointed out the location of the approaching armies.

"Watch them carefully, Seth," Michael said. "They are King Ahab's advisers. God Almighty has brought you here to witness a great war that is brewing for the king, and these men may have news for him." Seth recalled his dream and sat down at Michael's feet. *Will this be the same battle I remember from my nightmare?* He positioned himself on one of the square roof stones and crossed his legs. Michael stood at his back, blocking the strong sunshine and scanning the palace courtyard for trouble.

"I've thought a lot about the choices the king made with Elijah on Mount Carmel," Seth said. "I thought that after he experienced God's incredible power, he would change his mind and remove the idols of Baal from his country. He and Queen Jezebel could have turned Israel around after all the prophets of Baal were killed. It was the king's opportunity to see God's power return to Israel. If he needs a second chance to follow God, then he must not have learned anything that day on the mountain!"

Michael took a deep breath. "You know that King Ahab declared Elijah his enemy. And you are right! The king has not yet changed his mind about Elijah or about Almighty God. He continues to rebel, and so far he refuses to change his course."

Seth threw up his hands. "How can he be so foolish? How can he turn his back to the God who created his world and sends rain and sun for the fields of his kingdom?"

Bending one knee, Michael crouched beside Seth. "The Almighty wants everyone to turn to him, the only true God. He has certainly given the king many chances to repent of his stubborn nature, just as he does for everyone. But there comes a time when God knows that a person's rebellion has hardened his heart and that he will not respond to God's truths."

⟫— ⟫— ⟫—

A door burst open under the columned roof inside the palace, surprising the busy group in the courtyard. King Ahab strode into the expansive area, followed by his royal attendants. The people stopped their activities and bowed when the king approached. The mothers hustled their children back to their quarters, and the servants attended to their work.

King Ahab marched toward his advisers and flicked his hand to halt his attendants, who quickly dropped back from his side. "Where is Ben-Hadad now?" shouted the king. "What have you heard from the scouts?"

A small, lean man in a military uniform stepped forward and bowed before his king. "Syria is moving horses and chariots throughout Israel. Ben-Hadad is heavily armed and has endless supply wagons following thousands of soldiers. He has mustered his entire army and placed his siege forces at many of our major cities. They are locked up tight, and our people will soon run out of food and water."

Grim-faced, the man looked directly into the king's eyes. "But not only that, my lord: thirty-two powerful kings from east of the Tigris River have now joined the king of Syria, along with all their armies. They have set up camps surrounding the great walls of Samaria. They can't get to us, but their siege is well positioned, and there are only a few paths out of the city that might allow our scouts to move. It will be very difficult to get supplies to our people from other parts of Israel. The enemy hordes of foot soldiers, charioteers, and cavalry will cripple our precious capital."

Noticing the map, Ahab stepped toward the table to join his advisers. "I've just returned from a meeting with the provincial commanders. They have prepared for war, but their hearts are not ready to face this massive army. How long can we withstand their threat?"

Omar, the king's chief adviser, smoothed the parchment and planted his finger on the kingdom of Syria. He tapped on the map twice. "Syria has been a threat to us and a stone in our sandal for twenty years. Now, with these tribal chiefs joining them, they are a powerful force. They are strong enough to do us grave harm. They are determined to extend their control south into Israel while Assyria is expanding in the northeast. Ben-Hadad wants to secure the south to withstand a two-front war from the aggressive Assyrian forces."

Omar looked up from the map, directly into King Ahab's eyes. "We are caught in the middle of these two powerful nations. King Ben-Hadad knows that if he controls Israel and Judah, he may deter Assyrian violence against his kingdom."

The king of Israel paced back and forth, looking nearly as anxious as he had when the priests of Baal failed to call down fire from heaven. "My father knew the powerful position of our great fortress city, Samaria. We sit high on this majestic hill and command perfect views of the plain. Our double limestone walls are formidable, and the rugged terrain makes it difficult to use ramming rods against us. But still, we may have no choice but to bend our knee to Syria's massive armies. Perhaps Ben-Hadad will only want tribute."

Ahab stopped and looked at Omar. "Until we are sure he can defeat us, we will not surrender."

Michael was the first to rise from their vantage point on the roof. His muscles flexed, and his powerful body bounded up when he spread his mighty wings above his head.

Seth jumped to his feet when he heard the soft whirling wind and felt its gentle breath on his cheeks. He remembered this sensation from the last angelic gathering above Mount Carmel. He turned to see Michael, the vigilant archangel, standing strong and alert. Without a word, they watched the sparkling crystal clouds float closer and closer. The sky began to glow with iridescent shades of blue, yellow, pink, and white. The glimmering lights radiated and transformed before their eyes. Joining Michael were hosts of angelic beings. In every direction Seth turned, and as far as he could see, the sky was filled with breathtaking angels: angels in golden gowns with flowing sashes, angels with trumpets and cymbals, and angels draped with breastplates and prepared for war. Each one was vibrant and glowing with colors of fire and light.

Before Seth could utter a sound, Michael raised his finger to his pursed lips. "Shhh! We must be quiet, Seth. Later we can talk. For now, we have been instructed to watch the activities of earth. We are not to participate. Like you, the angels are here to observe the actions of men. This is King Ahab's opportunity to remember God and honor only him. God has resolved to reward every man who shows that his heart is with the Almighty. We will see what the king chooses to do this time."

"But in my dream, he is surrounded and in trouble. Can't you warn him this time?" Seth whispered.

"Shhh! This is not the time for talking! Watch."

Two winded messengers jumped from their horses. One collected the reins, and the other followed the soldiers into the palace. King Ahab straightened his jeweled crown and sat erect, regal in his purple robe. His hands gripped the carved wooden arms of his throne. Omar, his chief adviser and personal administrator, stood in the aisle before the throne and waited for the message from the king of Syria, Ben-Hadad.

Bowing, the messenger held the scrolled letter in both hands. His voice was weak. "Ben-Hadad has this to say to the king of

Israel." He hesitated, then cleared his throat. "I have surrounded your cities with my armies. We have cut off your food and water supplies. Our siege will kill your people, and our fires will destroy their homes and land for years." The messenger hesitated again for a brief moment. "And now look at the armies of thirty-two kings who sit at your gates. What choice do you have but to surrender your treasures and the cities I surround? Your gold and silver are mine, and your best wives and your children are mine."

The messenger handed the scroll to Omar, who took it to the king. The servants, soldiers, and advisers stood like statues while they waited for the king's response.

King Ahab opened the scroll to read the words the messenger had just recited to the court. Rolling the parchment into its cover, the king groaned and handed the letter to Omar. "I have no choice. Tell Ben-Hadad it shall be just as my lord says. Everything I have is his."

The messenger bowed his head. "Of course, my lord, but that is not all. At this time tomorrow, King Ben-Hadad will send his officials to search your palace and the homes of your officials. They are to seize everything you value and take it back to him." Again, the messenger bowed, then he turned to leave the room. Four palace guards, two in front and two in back, escorted him to the outer court.

King Ahab bolted from his throne and paced the floor. He rubbed his mouth, curled his lower lip against his teeth, and glanced at his advisers. The advisers huddled together, frowning and whispering softly. The king pressed his fist to his mouth and mumbled under his breath, "Ben-Hadad is not just subjecting me to his rule, he is humiliating me in Samaria. What will I do? How do I retain *any* power over the people of Israel if they think he has crushed my crown?"

He jerked around and stared at his advisers. His voice boomed, "This man is looking for trouble! When he asked for my wives and children and gold and silver, did I refuse him? No!" The king dropped his shoulders and glared at Omar. His eyes pleaded for help. "But now, what am I to do about his threat to search the kingdom and confiscate my treasures? This is too much!"

Omar motioned for the palace elders to join him at the throne. "O king, this is a deplorable situation. If we don't obey his demands, he has the strength with all these armies to choke us off and starve our people with his blockade. On the other hand, he is not just subjecting you to his strong rule, but to his selfish exploitation of your kingdom. He wants to make you a mere puppet king before the other nations, and on top of that, belittle your authority with your own people. We will lose more than territorial power if we submit to his search and seizure. Perhaps you should be prepared to fight against his full demands."

The elders nodded and began to whisper in agreement. Omar's words were strong. "Don't listen to him or compromise our position; stand strong on this point. Tell the people that for their safety, you were willing to surrender all your possessions, even your wives and children. But now Ben-Hadad wants to search their homes and take their valuables as well. Tell them you cannot allow this to happen. You must defend the people of the kingdom. They will admire your courage and join in support of an attack against the Syrians. Give them the chance to fight for Israel and defend their homes. We are a strong people and should not bow to such a humiliating demand without a fight…perhaps even to death. Besides, if he has the power, he will have his way, no matter."

The king slouched into his chair and rested his chin on his hand. He stood and looked over his elders, advisers, and commanders. He raised his voice. "Tell the couriers to return to Ben-Hadad with this message: 'My lord, your servant will do all you've demanded. My wives and children are yours. My gold and silver is yours. For the peace of my people, I submit to your strong hand. But this last demand I will *not* allow. You will *not* search my capital nor the homes of my people.'"

The royal scribe copied Ahab's words on a royal parchment. After he rolled and tied the official document, he handed it to the guard for the Syrian messenger. The messenger turned and marched toward his companion. They mounted their horses and returned to the army of their king.

Watchful and quiet, Michael, Seth, and crowds of angelic beings kept their eyes on the scene below. Seth remembered the fear he had seen in Rizpah's face and the dread he had felt when she had told him about the confrontation with the brothers of Nod. *I wonder what I would have done if I had been there with Rizpah?*

A different memory popped into his head as he remembered the story of how Cain had announced that he was moving away from the family. He had laughed and shouted, "God may drive me from this land and hide his presence from me, but I will survive on my own. By my own hand I will build a city for my own kind. I am Cain, and I will do it!"

Seth trembled as he thought about his brother's boastful proclamation and how he had secretly wished Cain's bravado could be his own when he faced the brothers of Nod. *But I don't want to be like Cain. He is arrogant and belligerent!* The daring stand King Ahab had just shown with his advisers seemed all too familiar to Seth. *So, King Ahab…is it courage or is it pride that drives you to defy Ben-Hadad? I pray you are confident in God's strength today.*

Riders on horseback rushed toward Ben-Hadad's royal tent. The horses' nostrils flared, and their sides heaved from their rapid and treacherous journey down the rocky hillside of Samaria, the watch-post city of King Ahab. The messengers dismounted, and one of them approached the king's guards. The guard held out his hand, "The kings are having dinner. Give me the message. I will deliver it to the royal adviser. Wait here!"

Before long, the courier mounted his steed and galloped back up the rugged hillside toward the Samaritan gate with Ben-Hadad's reply to King Ahab.

"Let him pass! Let him pass!" ordered the soldiers guarding the palace. Once again, the courier delivered the message to the chief official of King Ahab's court. He approached the throne and held out the document to the king.

"Read it to me," Ahab scowled.

Omar loosened the ribbon and read Ben-Hadad's command aloud: "Watch my armies, one handful of soil at a time, build a dirt ramp higher than the walls you trust. May the gods treat me even more severely than I am going to treat you, if I don't turn Samaria into a bowl of dust as my men's reward for destroying you and your people!"

Throwing his crimson robe from his shoulders, King Ahab marched tall toward Omar. The king stared into his dark eyes, nose to nose. "Oh, he's pompous to presume we have no strength to withstand him. Tell Ben-Hadad this: 'One who puts on armor for battle should not relax like one who has finished his war.'"

Seth furrowed his brow and turned to Michael. "I don't understand. What is he saying? What does the message mean?"

Michael smiled at Seth. "It sounds as if he is telling Ben-Hadad not to count his victories before they are won. King Ahab is going to stand up to this invader."

The courier once again hurried back to the tent palace of King Ben-Hadad. He stopped abruptly at the raised hand of the guard. Boisterous laughter and raucous shouting flowed from the men gathered inside. "The kings are celebrating their coming victory against Samaria," said the guard. "They're waiting for King Ahab's surrender. You are to come with me and give the message to the royal adviser."

The guard escorted the young Syrian scout through the door and stood at alert.

The royal adviser unrolled the message, read it, and approached the king. Ben-Hadad was leaning on the banquet table with one arm and drinking wine from his goblet with the other. The intoxicating drink splashed onto his face and ran down his beard. He motioned his adviser to read the response and confirm that Israel had surrendered to his demands.

When he heard King Ahab's arrogant response, Ben-Hadad pushed himself back from the table and staggered to his feet. He slammed his drinking goblet on the table. "Prepare the troops for siege. Station them in camps around the city, garrison by garrison. Ahab is a fool!"

Glancing over Seth to the horizon, Michael saw the faint gray cloud appear. He gripped the handle of his great sword and nodded the alert to his angelic commanders. He searched the skies and earth below for signs of further demonic interference. His angelic commanders were standing alert and ready to call their warriors to battle if necessary.

The stocky figure marched toward King Ahab, wearing a cloak that covered his head and fell loosely over his shoulders. He stopped before the throne and planted his walking staff firmly on the mosaic medallion under his feet. The man stroked his bearded chin and waited for the king to acknowledge him.

King Ahab glared at the man standing before him. He brushed his attendant aside, grabbed the arms of his throne, and sat forward. "Ha!" laughed the king. Then he slumped back into his seat and glared at the old prophet from the plains of Jezreel, obviously an associate of Elijah. "Now what? What good could you possibly bring me?"

The prophet of God approached the throne. He raised both arms to the king and his adviser. "This is what the Lord has to tell you: 'You see this vast array of armies surrounding your city? Today, I will give tens of thousands of your enemy's soldiers into your hands so that you will know that I am the Lord, the Almighty God, from everlasting to everlasting.'"

The king jumped to his feet and drew in a surprised breath. His eyes danced, and a smile changed his stern face. He stepped down from his throne. "How will this victory happen? Who will accomplish it? What am I to do?"

The prophet raised his chin, "The victory will belong to God Almighty. It will happen by the hand of the young men of the provinces, not your seasoned soldiers. These young men will go to battle at your command."

"But they are unskilled for war, and there are not many of them. How can this help us?" Ahab frowned. "Should I strike before Ben-Hadad attacks?"

"Yes!" The prophet pointed his finger directly at the king's face and stared into his inquiring eyes. "You must attack first, with the

young men of your provinces. Attack first and take no prisoners."
He turned and marched from the palace, leaving King Ahab to
wonder and stare at the back of the prophet's shabby brown tunic
and robe.

CHAPTER 10

Bedlam in the Barracks

King Ahab stepped away from the powerful stallions harnessed to his royal chariot. "How many young officers have come from the provinces? Has each district sent its leader?"

"We have found only two hundred and thirty-two men altogether to serve as officers, my lord," Omar said, bowing. "They are courageous and will lead the charge at noon, as you have commanded. There are seven thousand of your armed soldiers within the walls of the fortress city of Samaria. They are assembled and waiting for your signal."

"Then what are we waiting for? Send the message to move the young soldiers down the hill! Let the march begin." King Ahab returned to his chariot and took the reins from the commander. Loosening one and tugging on the harness strap with the other, he turned his horses for the downhill journey.

With a steady pace, they pulled the king's chariot down the hillside road to the observation point, where he reined the horses to a halt. The ground was relatively flat, and wide enough for half a dozen charioteers to gather. The king's engineers had fortified the area with a massive stone retaining wall to hold the hillside and offer protection if needed. From this vantage point, he could study the siege armies below and observe the ensuing battle. He handed the reins to his commander and stepped from the chariot to see the enemy scouts disappear into Ben-Hadad's royal camp.

Following their instructions, the young provincial officers of

King Ahab made their way down the hillside to confront Ben-Hadad, who laughed when he heard about the size of their envoy. The Syrian ruler took another serving of roast lamb from the huge platter before him and tipped his goblet for a refill. His commanders mingled with the vassal kings and joined in their raucous festivities.

Ben-Hadad smiled and mumbled to his chief aide, "There is no need to disrupt the camps for this confrontation. Find out what their intentions are. Perhaps they come to surrender."

He smiled, smug and satisfied. "Tell the troops to take the small band of Israelites alive, whether they have come for battle or truce."

Michael unsheathed the hardy sword from his belt and rested the blade in his left hand. Again, he scanned the skies for any approaching danger to the Israelite troops. His angelic commanders readied themselves for trouble.

Seth hardly noticed the cautious act. Mesmerized by the battle scene below, he watched a second set of young officers move like antelope around the craggy hillside and fight their way through pockets of Syrian soldiers, downing them before they could retreat to their camp. An Israelite scout sent a message through the troops that strengthened their fervor to push forward: "The kings are still celebrating, and their soldiers are at rest. Only those on guard are wearing battle gear." Soldier after soldier repeated the message until all the Israelite soldiers had heard.

Seth noticed the voices and laughter that trickled through the Syrian camp. The enemy army was clearly not prepared for what was coming its way. Tents sheltered snoring soldiers. Shouts rang out from the happy winners of dice and coin-toss games. And not far beyond the camp, where only a few paltry guards moved about, Israel was about to attack.

Seth watched the young Israelites advance and easily overtake their idle enemy. In moments, the entire camp of the Syrians collapsed. Panic and disarray spread like wildfire. Syrian soldiers scattered in all directions, searching for their weapons. Taking advantage of the chaos, Ahab signaled his waiting army to join the battle. Thousands of soldiers charged from the city gates and fought their way into the enemy encampments surrounding their fortress city, Samaria. Taken by surprise, the allied armies of Ben-Hadad abandoned their armor and weapons in their rush to retreat. They fled for their lives, along with their kings and commanders.

In quick pursuit, the Israelites chased them down and overpowered the fleeing soldiers, even those on horseback and in chariots. Ben-Hadad shed his royal robe and grabbed the reins of an abandoned horse. Jumping on its back, he galloped through his deserting armies toward Damascus, leaving behind a thousand empty campsites strewn with weapons, armor, and treasures for Israel.

Seth could hardly believe his eyes. A big smile spread across his face as he watched King Ahab standing with his mouth open and his eyes wide with amazement. "Michael," Seth whispered, "*now* the king will trust God, won't he? He has seen the Almighty deliver Israel from this enormous army! God has saved them from the ravaging hoards of Ben-Hadad."

Michael shook his head. "Perhaps. But this isn't over yet, Seth. Ahab will surely face this battle again. Ben-Hadad is very ambitious and will not accept defeat. Already, his officers are gathering around him with new plans against Israel. God gave King Ahab victory this time, but it will not put an end to the Syrian king's determination to conquer Israel."

Michael sheathed his sword and signaled the angels to stand down. They would not need to defend God's children today. He put his powerful hand on Seth's shoulder.

"Remember, Seth…" He hesitated. "Despite their faithlessness,

Almighty God loves King Ahab and the rebellious Israelites. He is patient with all men and does not want anyone to perish. However, men have choices, and choices have consequences for good or for ill. Even though God does not want to give up on the king, there will come a time when he will judge his heart and his life. Then the Almighty will give Ahab what he deserves, either in life or in death."

King Ahab drove his horses and chariot back to the palace. Micaiah, the familiar prophet who had foretold the victory, stood waiting at the palace door.

"Prepare yourself for another attack," the man of God said. "The king of Syria will be back to fight you again. Gather the spoils of your victory. There are hundreds of chariots and horses to round up. Almighty God has made you wealthy with the gold and silver the kings have left behind. So prepare, and remember the Lord's instructions when you are victorious next time: 'Do not leave the enemy alive to threaten you again.' The Syrians think the Lord Almighty is only a god of the hills and not a god of the valleys. They will draw you into battle in the valley against their vast army. Ben-Hadad will replace his mighty armies and replenish his chariot brigades. But do not fear his masses. This is what the Lord says: 'I will deliver you a second time, and you will know that I alone am the Lord, the God of Israel. Follow me.'"

Michael reached down and took Seth's hand. The sky began to swirl overhead, and dazzling lights rained down around them. Again, the tingling sound of moving crystals sang in their ears, and a soft wind lifted them from their vantage point above the palace.

Everything changed around them. Light and darkness flashed before their eyes for what seemed to Seth to be only a moment—yet he sensed that time was passing in front of him. Eventually the dark flashes gave way to soft white, yellow, and pink hues. As the sky changed around them, their feet settled on the firmness of a colossal cumulus cloud.

Seth caught his breath. *Where am I? Is this a different day, or maybe even a different year?* Even without answers, he could feel that things were different here. Michael stood beside him, unshaken. Behind them stood the hosts of heavenly angels, again waiting for battle. Looking down, Seth surveyed the gathering armies on earth. He gasped.

Thousands and thousands of soldiers were marching toward the smaller Israelite forces. Only this time, the king's city of Samaria was nowhere in sight. Stretched in front of the Israelites were the plains of Aphek, the spacious valley east of Samaria. Seth shook his head. "The prophet was right. King Ahab did have to muster his army to face Ben-Hadad again. But look at them, Michael...they look like two little flocks of sheep compared to this vast army of Syrian soldiers! How can they survive without God's help?"

Michael raised his wings but didn't move. "You are right, the Israelites will fall quickly if God Almighty does not intervene. Prepare yourself to see the strong right arm of the Lord. This battle is his, and it will be won in his time and by his strength."

Seth watched the contentious armies camped across from each other. He could not begin to count the Syrian soldiers, dressed and ready for combat this time. Seth considered Ben-Hadad's advantage. *Not only has he fully replaced his soldiers; it looks as if he has more horses and chariots than he did for the battle last year! I can't see a way for Israel to live through a war against this vast, innumerable army.* Seth felt his heart race and his stomach churn. His brain could not process the number of soldiers his eyes tried to scan in the valley below. *They are like sheep facing slaughter unless God Almighty saves them.*

Michael crossed his arms and waited for Almighty God to call the angelic army to battle. The kings would see, one more time, the awesome power of God.

CHAPTER 11
Ahab's Betrayal

A soft light began to push away the gray-black tones of night. "Another day! Seven days, seven days! Nothing happens!" King Ahab grumbled as he strapped the heavy breastplate onto his body and stomped past his attendant to the door of his tent. Porters scurried nearby to pour juice and cut stale bread.

Omar stood and stretched his shoulders back. He took the goblet of fresh orange juice from the porter's tray and handed it to the king.

"When will they attack? What are they waiting for? They taunt us, knowing we won't start this battle." Ahab snatched the cup and reached for the bread. He gnawed on the hard, crusty piece.

Israelite scouts had moved throughout their camp, continually advising the king and his commanders of enemy movements. Soldiers on both sides had faced each other for six straight days. All remained in full uniform, dressed for battle. The front lines rotated small sections of troops for meals, rest, and sleep. No matter their other activities, both militaries were armed and ready for the coming battle cry.

"Don't let them worry you, my lord," cautioned Omar. "The prophet told you the God of Israel would deliver this vast army into your hands."

"Yes." Ahab rubbed his lip with his thumb. "He said I would know that *his* God was Lord." Ahab walked back into his royal tent and paced back and forth. "My grandmother told me a story about a battle for the citadel of Jericho—something about seven days. Yes, Joshua conquered the Canaanites on the seventh day."

On the cloud high above, Michael laughed. "Yes, the king is correct, but he has forgotten how Almighty God gave his servant Joshua the victory! The Lord told Joshua that the mighty warriors waiting within the walls of Jericho were already defeated. Joshua knew an important truth about winning his battle against this strong enemy. Yes, he had heard that the warriors of Jericho were strong and mighty men, but more importantly, he trusted God, and he believed what God told him was true: *they were already defeated!*"

Seth pointed at the Syrians. "Those armies don't look defeated."

"Neither did the men of Jericho," Michael said. "They were surrounded by impenetrable walls. Joshua did not know *how* they were defeated, but he knew that God had secured his victory because God had said so. Even when the others were afraid, Joshua was courageous because he trusted God for success and believed he would keep his word."

"I wish Ahab would trust like that. He seems so worried."

"Joshua was a man of integrity," Michael answered. "He followed God's ways and made decisions based on what he knew about God. He remembered how the Almighty had helped them in the past, and he made up his mind to follow the Lord no matter how bad things looked. He even told his people, his friends, that they could make their own choice about God, but he and his household would follow the Lord. His mind was made up for God, and he would not let his circumstances or anyone else's opinion change his mind."

Nodding, Seth remembered Rizpah's encounter with the brothers of Nod. His chest tightened, pressing the fear he carried in his heart. *Where is my courage? Do I really believe God will protect us if their threats turn into hateful acts against my family or me? What will I do? Will I choose to trust God, like Joshua? I know God can provide for us. But still, do I really believe he will do what he says?* Seth tipped his head to the side. "Did the Israelites trust Joshua and follow his leadership? After all, God didn't speak to them, just to Joshua. And did they really believe they could win the battle against the warriors of Jericho?"

Michael leaned in and smiled. "Oh yes! The Israelites followed Joshua because they could see that Joshua trusted God and his power for victory. They saw Joshua's faith and courage and chose to believe God's words for themselves. When they believed God was with them, all the Israelite army had to do was follow God's instructions. They were to walk around the city once a day for six days and on the seventh day blow the trumpets. Seven priests were to follow the army, just ahead of the ark of God."

Seth raised his eyebrows. "How could that work? And what was the ark of God?"

"There is always victory when someone agrees with Almighty God," Michael said, chuckling. "And the ark is a glorious gold trunk that holds several items from days of old, reminders of God's law and his miracles. When the people think about it, they remember how God saved them in the past."

Michael spread his feet and clasped his arms behind his back. He scanned the skies for a moment, nodding in confident satisfaction at the ready state of his armies. "Remember, Joshua had already determined in his heart that he and his household would follow the Lord, no matter what God asked of him. Jericho wasn't hard for him. But the Israelites had to learn the rewards of following Almighty God. The Israelite army and the priests all agreed to listen to Joshua and follow the instructions. So they marched around the city walls for six days. On the seventh day, the priests did as God had instructed. They blew the ram's horns, and the people of Israel gave a loud shout."

A wide grin spread across Michael's face. "Ha! If only you could have seen what happened then." Michael threw his arms above his head and swooshed them down in one continuous movement. "The walls of the mighty city of Jericho fell to the ground! Joshua and his soldiers rushed in and overpowered the surprised army of Jericho. The soldiers of Israel fought with courage and valor and captured the city for Israel. The angelic army was ready to do battle with them, but we were hardly needed that day. Today may be a different story. We will see if the courage of Israel is based on what God tells them or on their own physical strength."

Omar leaned over to whisper in King Ahab's ear. "Perhaps we should surprise them with an attack today. The Syrian armies are unsettling our troops by delaying the fight. The longer we wait for them to attack, the more uncertain our men become. They recognize the force of our enemy. It's impossible for them to see a victory ahead. But no matter, they will follow you, even to their deaths."

Ahab frowned, but Omar's words seemed to please him. "Hmm, you may be right. The prophet did say that I would see this vast army delivered into my hands. If it is true, we will have success from Israel's God. You're right about a surprise attack. Let's move out in battle and trust the prophet's God. We are too small to overcome them in our own strength. But if God is for us, we have nothing to lose and everything to gain."

Michael signaled the angelic army to ready themselves for battle. Seth watched many of them divide into small groups and position themselves throughout the Israelite camp. High above, countless angels with trumpets, harps, and flutes remained in the heavens. Their flowing robes and majestic sashes seemed to surround the airspace and command attention. Seth took in their beauty and power, then settled himself near Michael for the coming events.

The deep blast of ram's horns sounded, signaling that battle was to begin. He watched the Israelite soldiers move into quick formation. They positioned themselves side by side and began their forward march against the foe. Simultaneously, the angelic orchestra broke into energetic, rhythmic melodies that exploded through the heavens. The powerful music shot through Seth's soul, and he joined the multitude of voices singing, "Thanks and praise to the Almighty God of heaven and earth, forever and ever! His hands hold salvation and glorious victory, forever and ever. Amen!"

Seth listened to the chorus of angels continue their concert of praise. "What is happening, Michael? The battle is about to begin, and I don't feel the same dread as I did when you fought for Elijah. I don't even have the concerns for King Ahab that I had in his last battle. And yet, the Syrian army is so vast and powerful!"

Michael unsheathed his great, shining sword and turned to Seth. "You are safe and in the strong right hand of the Almighty God. The battle today is not the same as you have seen. This battle will be won with a courage that comes only from praise. Watch! For the victory belongs to God, and he has called his holy chorus to lead the fight for Israel."

Michael raised his wings and joined the angelic warriors on the ground. As Seth watched in wonder, the great archangel joined the Israelite soldiers in fierce hand-to-hand combat. But something else was different—this was not like it had been when Michael's warriors fought the demons before.

Seth's eyes widened. "They're visible!" he gasped.

The Syrian soldiers froze in fear when they saw the angels of God positioned throughout Israel's army. The Israelites, who could not see the avenging angels, fought their way into the enemy camp, leaving a trail of enemy blood as they moved forward. Hundreds of men on each side were injured. But one by one, with the help of God's angelic army, the Israelites defeated the thousands of Syrian invaders. More and more fell with mortal wounds.

Michael told Seth the figures later: A hundred thousand enemy foot soldiers died on the first day of battle, along with many on horseback. Empty chariots littered the bloody grounds. The remainder of the enemy soldiers fled to the fortified city of Aphek, hoping to escape the slaughter. But the wall of the city collapsed on top of them. It killed twenty-seven thousand more of their soldiers, except for Ben-Hadad, who hid in the cellar of a house there. His advisers found him crouching behind a cabinet, dripping with sweat.

Horses stamped and snorted as the commanders left their chariots to approach the command post. King Ahab pounded his fist on the rugged camp table. "Where is Ben-Hadad? Is he still alive? How could he escape our assault? We have destroyed his army and taken victory from his hand. If he is alive, we must find him!"

One of the commanders of Israel's army turned to Omar and whispered in his ear. Omar walked straight to the king. "There are three Syrian officers from outside the camp who are wearing sackcloth and have looped themselves with rope. They come with a request from Ben-Hadad. Do you want to hear them?"

"Ha! He is alive!" The king laughed out loud. "Bring them to me."

Soldiers pushed the men into the middle of the gathering. King Ahab stood tall, lifted his chin, and shouted, "Speak!"

"Sir," one officer replied, looking at the ground, "we have heard that the kings of Israel are not savage but merciful and gracious. Ben-Hadad is now your servant and begs you to let him live. Be merciful, and he will forever be your servant."

Without hesitation, King Ahab fired back, "He is still alive?"

Michael whispered in Seth's ear, "The prophet said Ben-Hadad should not live to fight again. But Ahab wants him alive to make peace with his people and put Syria under his foot."

Ahab looked the enemy officer in the eyes and smiled. "Then he is my brother."

The Syrian soldiers gasped at his words and nodded their heads. "Yes, he is your brother and pleads for your hand of mercy, as a brother."

"Go, and bring him to me." The king waved his arm at the officer and watched him march away, followed by his companions.

Then King Ahab rested a hand on the top ridge of his chariot. He leaned against the sturdy frame and waited. Finally, Ben-Hadad approached, bowing several times before he knelt in front of his conqueror, rigid and surly. Wearing no protective armor, his uniform was torn and stained with blood. Only his decorative boots revealed his royal status.

A slight smile softened King Ahab's face when he reached down to touch the shoulder of his defeated foe. Ben-Hadad looked up and accepted his rival's outstretched hand.

"Come," said King Ahab, "step into my chariot, brother. I will not harm you, don't worry."

Puzzled, the captive warrior joined King Ahab in the royal chariot. Ben-Hadad stuttered, "I will remember your kindness my whole life. Of course, I will return all the cities my father took from Omri, your father. You may come back to Damascus as your forefathers did. Set up markets and trading posts again. We can live together in peace."

"Yes, we have had a peace treaty in the past. A treaty that *you* broke." Ahab stared at Ben-Hadad for what seemed like a full minute. Then he smiled. "But I am a generous man, and I will let you live. We will make an oath: your life for my cities and trade routes. Agreed?"

A chill went through Seth's body when he heard the king promise to let Ben-Hadad live—in direct disobedience to God's command through Micaiah that the invaders should die. He watched the Syrian king leave the camp with his soldiers. Michael shook his head and slumped down on one knee. The air became heavy around them, and the angels wept.

"Why?" Seth whispered.

After a while, Michael rose and looked toward Seth. "The king has rejected the Almighty God again. Even this miraculous victory has not changed his heart. He continues to choose the treasures of earth and his own selfish wisdom over the good and perfect ways of the Almighty. Sadly, he will reap what he has sown. If only he had learned from his grandmother's story about Joshua. The king cannot serve two masters, himself and God."

Seth nodded. Tears were pricking at his eyes. "But why is it so hard for Ahab to remember God and choose his ways? How did Joshua do it?"

"Joshua was always loyal to God first," Michael said. "He did not waver because he had decided to keep his heart for God and follow his ways. Decisions were easy for Joshua. He just asked himself, 'What would God want me to do about this?' If he did not know the answer, he would pray, like Elijah. God is faithful and will show us his way." Michael looked directly at Seth. "And...God was good to Joshua and gave him great successes in his life and with his family."

Seth and Michael heard a commotion on the road below. They recognized the prophet who had brought the good news to Ahab about God's victory over the armies of Ben-Hadad. He wore a bandage over his eye and was draped in the bloodstained clothing of a wounded soldier. He sat on the side of the road, watching the soldiers pass by.

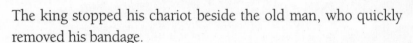

The king stopped his chariot beside the old man, who quickly removed his bandage.

"Micaiah!" the king gasped. "Well, you were right to say we would defeat Ben-Hadad again." He smiled and threw up his arm. "We return to Samaria, victorious!"

The prophet was not moved by the king's proclamation. Micaiah stood next to the chariot and pointed his knobby finger at the king. "This is what the Lord says," he declared. "'You chose to free the man I told you must die. Now, *you* will die in his place. It is your life in place of his life, and your people will perish instead of his people.'"

King Ahab pursed his lips and frowned. "You are a fool! Go away!"

The old prophet shook his head, turned, and walked down the road. Furious, the king struck his horses with the whip and drove them past the prophet of God.

CHAPTER 12
A United Banner

dreadful silence fell around them. Seth felt nauseated. He stared in shock at the king's chariot, fading into the colored plains of Aphek. Speechless, he looked at Michael.

"Again the king realizes the Lord is the God of Israel, but he will not follow him!" Michael's voice was cold, angry. For the first time, Seth felt uneasy with his guide.

Seth caught his breath when Michael faced him and then pulled the mighty sword from its sheath. Michael touched the tip of the shining blade to Seth's shoulder and waited for their eyes to meet.

"The Almighty will always be on your side, Seth, even as he was for the king during the battle today. But Ahab ignores God's instructions and continues to go his own way. The Almighty has no choice but to let him suffer the consequences of his decisions. King Ahab continues to dismiss the safety God offers to those who believe his invincible words of truth. But Ahab hopes to receive his blessings anyway."

Michael pulled the sword away from Seth and rested it in both hands. "Seth, you will see that God will not be mocked. The king has called this judgment on himself."

Michael looked up into the heavens and nodded his head. He slipped the sword back into its sheath and took Seth's hand. "Come with me. The Almighty has instructed me to take you back to Samaria. But prepare yourself, for time has passed, and things are grave for Ahab. Ben-Hadad, his Syrian 'brother,' has again become his enemy."

Seth recognized the delicate sounds of chimes in the distance and took a deep breath when darkness covered them like a blanket. He felt Michael's firm grip on his hand and relaxed. Wide-eyed, he turned to watch the changing kaleidoscope of colors: this time purples, blues, greens, and magenta. The moisture and cold that had enveloped his body changed to warm, dry vapors and a gentle wind. Sweet smells of orange blossoms filled his nostrils, encouraging him to breath in their fragrance. Again, the colors faded, and the earth came into view below their feet. Michael released Seth's hand, and they came to rest on the now-familiar roof of the palace of King Ahab.

Smoke rose from the fire pit, delivering the delicious aroma of roasted lamb and beef throughout the palace grounds. Seth felt his stomach growl. Looking around, he watched attendants struggle to remove the succulent roasts from the scalding spit for the evening banquet.

"The meal must be perfect for the king of Judah," instructed Omar. "It is imperative that we repair our relationship with our southern brothers. King Jehoshaphat is a fit ally for Israel, and we need his help."

He leaned over to get a better look at the roasted meat. "Take it to the chef for slicing. Be sure to save the juices for moisture."

"Yes, my lord, we will not disappoint you or our visitors." The chief kitchen aide patted his forehead with a towel.

Omar smiled. "I trust you will outdo yourselves tonight. The king expects nothing but your finest foods." He watched them lay the heavy roast on the large wooden platter, then turned and hurried into the palace to join the amiable kings.

Inside the palace, Ahab raised his silver goblet to toast the young King Jehoshaphat.

"I've had word that your son is a good husband for my daughter. Now I wait to hear that there is laughter of little children coming from their windows." Ahab's smile turned serious. "Jehoshaphat, you have been ruler in Judah for several years now. You've proven to be a wise man and an able soldier. Your people honor you, and Jerusalem has prospered. Under your strong leadership, Judah has taken back territories from Syria, Edom in the east, and even Moab in the south."

Jehoshaphat tipped his goblet toward Ahab, and they both took a drink.

Ahab continued. "It's time to put the strife between your father and me to rest. I have invited you here to consider joining in alliance with me, to take back our beloved city of refuge in Gad. Ramoth-Gilead, you know, belongs to Israel, and neither of us have done a thing to rescue it from Ben-Hadad. This walled city has been in Syria's hands for too long. Our people there are his vassals and pay him tribute. It's time to bring them back into the family. Don't you agree?"

King Jehoshaphat smiled. From all appearances, he was enjoying himself thoroughly. "Perhaps. What are you thinking?"

Ahab stroked his beard and leaned close to Jehoshaphat. He spoke softly. "Ben-Hadad is at peace with us for the moment. He is busy fending off Assyria on his northeastern border. He won't be prepared to fight against us as well. Besides, our combined armies will overwhelm him before he can muster more troops to the city. Will you join me and send your army with mine?"

Jehoshaphat inclined his head and smiled. "We are brothers. Abraham is our father. We should stop this family fighting and reclaim our city. My people and my horses are at your command. But first," he said, looking directly at King Ahab and becoming suddenly stern, "we must seek the Lord, to be sure this is what he would have us do. I will not enter into an alliance before I have his word on it."

"Of course." King Ahab clapped his hands. "Omar, send word to as many prophets as you can locate. Tell them to join us here tomorrow to tell us what the Lord says." He motioned for his aide to refill their goblets. Then the kings toasted in agreement.

Seth squinted at the rising sun on the eastern plains and put down the flat bread he had found in his pocket. He tugged on Michael's sleeve for attention. Men in long tunics and brightly colored head-pieces were heading toward Samaria. Some had already made their way up the hill and were gathering at the gate of King Ahab's fortress and capital city, Samaria. Soldiers moved about the streets in chariots and on foot, changing positions with weary night guards. Merchants set up tables and booths to sell their wares, and women gathered around the city cisterns with their water jugs.

"Yes," frowned Michael. "The prophets are arriving, but I don't see a prophet of Almighty God among them. So far it looks like only prophets who worship Baal and the prophets of their sacred cow are here. Seth, watch King Jehoshaphat. He is a man with a different character than King Ahab. He has chosen to follow the ways of Almighty God and has had great successes in Judah. Every day he tries to do something good for God. He is highly honored by the neighboring kings. They send him gifts to remain in his favor. Yet, he is here, today, discussing an alliance with King Ahab, who tolerates the worship of Baal. It is dangerous for him to listen to Ahab, who has shown himself to be stubborn toward God Almighty. Jehoshaphat is stepping onto a slippery rock in a moving river and thinks he can avoid getting wet if he falls."

Michael and Seth watched the prophets in their festive robes greet each other with nods and smiles. Seth sat down on his knees, and Michael stood beside him with crossed arms. "Unlike King Ahab, Jehoshaphat smashed all the statues of Baal and the statues of Asherah in Judah. He even sent teachers into the land to teach the people about the ways of God. Judah has become prosperous and safe under his wise decisions."

"I remember you told me that King David loved God and wanted to follow him with his whole heart. Is Jehoshaphat like David was?" Seth asked with wide eyes.

"Few will ever be like David. But Jehoshaphat does seek God and asks for his guidance to help him lead the people of Judah. These prophets of Israel are double-minded. They try to worship the God of Israel *and* the gods of Baal. They will not help Jehoshaphat make this important decision for Judah. If he decides to join Ahab in this battle, he will experience the consequences that come when you yoke yourself to someone who does not follow Almighty God."

⋘ ⋘ ⋘

The two regal kings sat on their royal thrones. The threshing floor at the main gate of Samaria was their stage. King Ahab, in his purple robe and jeweled crown, rose and looked over the hundreds of prophets gathered in front of them. The participants quieted. The king motioned for Jehoshaphat to stand beside him on the platform. In a commanding voice he asked, "Are we to go to war against Ben-Hadad in Ramoth-Gilead, or not?"

Many began to answer at once. "Yes, go! You will overtake him like you did before. The gods have already given you the victory." Then hundreds of voices cried, "Attack, attack! You cannot lose. Victory is yours."

One of the prophets, who wore iron horns on his headpiece, danced around. He shouted, "Like the bull, you will gore the Syrians until they are annihilated!"

King Jehoshaphat turned his head away from the crowd and strained to speak to King Ahab over the clamor of the voices. From

Seth's post, his voice could be clearly heard. "Isn't there a prophet of Almighty God here we can ask? I want to hear from him."

King Ahab frowned. "Yes. There is one—but he doesn't like me and never has anything good to say."

"Is he Elijah?" questioned Jehoshaphat. "I have heard he speaks truth from God."

"No, and it's a good thing he's not Elijah! The last time I heard from *him*, he accused me of murdering a Jezreelite for his vineyard. It took me a long time to recover my peace after his harsh words." Ahab raised one hand to those gathered and motioned to his adviser. "Omar, send for Micaiah, the prophet, the son of Imlah. Bring him at once."

Under his breath Ahab muttered to himself, "He will be happy enough to prophesy bad things for me."

Omar left the staging area and approached a nearby guard. "You heard the king. Go and bring Micaiah to us quickly. Tell him all the other prophets are predicting success for the king, and so should he. Tell him to agree with them and favor the attack on Ramoth-Gilead. The king doesn't want to hear bad news."

Omar glanced back at the staging area where the kings had returned to their seats with a magician entertaining them. Omar studied the scene, then smirked, shook his head, and made his way back to stand near his king.

The guard returned with Micaiah. The prophet was dressed in a pale gray tunic and brown cloak. The two men approached Omar. "Sir, I told him to reply favorably as you commanded."

Micaiah straightened his stance and squared his shoulders before Omar. "As surely as the Almighty God lives, I will say nothing except what he tells me to say."

Omar grimaced. "Then you bring on your own fate, you simpleton. Go, give the kings your prophecy!"

Seeing the prophet of God approach, Jehoshaphat stood, followed by King Ahab, who took a deep breath and addressed Micaiah. "So, shall we go to war to free our city from the hand of Ben-Hadad, or shall we let our brothers die there as his vassals?"

Micaiah tipped his head to the side and shrugged his shoulders. "Go ahead. Attack, and take your great victory. Haven't all of these men told you to go?"

King Ahab bolted a step toward the prophet as though he would physically attack him. "Don't taunt me! How many times have I told you to say only what the Lord has shown you? Tell me the truth, in the name of the Lord!"

Micaiah stepped forward and answered, "Very well. Before me, I see all Israel running like sheep scattered on the mountain when their shepherd is slain. And the Lord says, 'The people have no king. He is dead. Send them home in peace.'"

King Ahab threw his arms in the air. "See! I told you he would have nothing good to say about me. He always has bad news." Ahab turned back to his throne, but Micaiah continued to prophesy.

"I saw the Lord Almighty sitting on his mighty throne with the angelic armies all around him. And the Lord said, 'Who will go for me to entice Ahab to attack his enemy and meet his death at Ramoth-Gilead?'"

Pausing, Micaiah lowered his voice and stared at Ahab's rigid frame. "Several suggestions were presented, until finally an angelic spirit stepped up to God and said, 'I will go. I will entice him to go into battle and meet his judgment.'"

Micaiah turned and pointed to the crowd of men before him. "Don't you hear the lying spirit in the mouths of these prophets you have gathered to encourage your war? You hear what you want to hear, but the Lord God has declared your defeat. Disaster is coming to you!"

The prophet who wore the iron horns stepped up to Micaiah and slapped him in the face. "So, when did the Spirit of the Lord leave me to go and speak to you?" he demanded. "Your words are not true. Didn't Elijah say that dogs would lick the king's blood in Jezreel at Naboth's vineyard? One of you is wrong. Elijah is the greater prophet and the first to be believed. You are only trying to upset the king's plans."

Micaiah shook his finger at the man. "God will judge between you and me. He will give you the answer to your questions when you find yourself alone and shivering in your room."

The veins on King Ahab's neck bulged, and his eyes narrowed. He glared at the prophet of God. "Take this man away immediately! Put him in prison and give him only bread and water until I safely return with victory in my hand."

Micaiah cried out in a loud voice, "Mark my words, man! If you return with your life, then the Almighty God did not speak through me today. Remember what I have said!"

Jehoshaphat stood motionless and watched the guards drag Micaiah from the assembly area. The crowd broke into shouts and jeers. Several men near Micaiah threw stones and jabbed him with their walking sticks. "You are wrong; the king will have victory!" they shouted.

Micaiah was not alone. Two angels appeared and walked next to him as the guards dragged him to jail. Several angelic warriors stood on the stage of the threshing floor near King Jehoshaphat. Others began to gather around Seth and Michael.

Seth turned to see Michael greet the heavenly army. He waited for him to instruct his commanders, and then Seth asked, "Where have they been? How did the angels know to come now?"

"Remember, Seth, the eyes of the Lord roam throughout the earth to strengthen those whose hearts are fully committed to him. Micaiah is a bold and courageous man. His respect for Almighty God is greater than the fear he has for man. The Lord will give him inner strength to endure his coming hardships. The angels will stand by his side to encourage and help him."

"Jehoshaphat looks shaken," Seth said as he stretched his neck forward. "I don't think he should go along with King Ahab. He shouldn't go to war, should he? The prophet said they would meet disaster if they war with Syria."

"Well, Jehoshaphat is a militant king, just like King Ahab. He has had his own battles to fight for the safety of Judah. As a wise soldier, he would not come into Israel without his army. After all, Israel and Judah have warred against each other for generations, even though they call themselves brothers and make treaties. Jehoshaphat is always ready and prepared to defend and protect his country. Perhaps he was not convinced by the testimony of Micaiah. And he did not see anything happen to Zedekiah, the prophet of the sacred cow, after he slapped Micaiah. Perhaps Jehoshaphat and Judah will join Israel and follow King Ahab's lead. Perhaps he will fight alongside Ahab to reclaim Ramoth-Gilead for the brotherhood. We will soon see."

CHAPTER 13
The Last Bastion

a richly striped blanket of blue, red, and gold draped the stallion. Threads sparkled throughout the embroidered design, highlighting the royal emblems of the house of Omri. The horse's neck was protected with wide bands of tooled leather, painted in bright blue and yellow and laced together with ribbons. The two-wheeled chariot was fitted with straps to hold an extra sickle sword. Hardened leather encased its sides.

Dressed in battle clothing, Jehoshaphat stood by the side of Ahab's colorful chariot and signaled his armor bearer to bring the breastplate and ornamental helmet. A soldier held the reins and stroked the mane of the restless animal while they waited for the battle cry.

"You've made the right decision," Ahab said, slapping Jehoshaphat's back. "Together we can claim victory in Ramoth-Gilead. Not only will we take back control of this strategic city, we'll also regain the timber of these lush green hills. You know, as a frontier city, Ramoth-Gilead separates our kingdoms from assault by the Assyrians. We must control it. These brutal invaders will not stop at Damascus. Ben-Hadad will eventually lose his capital, and they will push their forces southwest into Israel. We must be ready if they advance against us. Ramoth-Gilead is an important victory for both of our nations."

Jehoshaphat breathed in the cool morning air. "Yes, yes, I have agreed to join you and take back our land, the land acquired by King David. But if this is a wise decision, why do I have this knot in the pit of my stomach?"

"Ha!" laughed Ahab. "You ate too much mutton for breakfast, that's why! There's nothing to worry about. Just follow my plan."

Jehoshaphat walked back and forth. "It does seem to be a good diversionary tactic. The Syrian soldiers will have orders to kill you first before they turn their full force on your men. But by disguising yourself as a charioteer, you can blend in with the Israelite soldiers." Jehoshaphat slipped the heavy armor over his head, buckled the straps, and secured his belt and sword. "Hopefully, when the Syrians spot the royal robes and headgear, they will think it is you and chase after me. We will draw them into our ambush and make quick work of their attack. If the trick works, your commanders will break through the enemy ranks, storm the city, and capture the guard station. It should be easy for our men to kill the soldiers left inside the walls."

King Ahab nodded in agreement and straightened his own armor.

"I like your plan," voiced Jehoshaphat. "What I don't like is the wall of chariots I see waiting for us in front of the city. I'm told they have thirty-two chariot units and thousands of seasoned warriors waiting for us. This strategy must work." Jehoshaphat raised his brows and tipped his head to Ahab. Then he stepped into his chariot and shouted out, "May God be with us and fill us with the joy of his presence!"

Seth chewed on his fingernails and scurried back and forth from atop his vantage point. He glanced from Michael, who was pacing in semicircles and shouting orders to his angelic commanders, to the fierce earthly battle between the able forces of Syria and the armies of Israel and Judah. The sounds of clashing swords and crushing metals mixed with the howls and cries of the brutal warfare on the rough terrain below. Bloody Syrian chariot soldiers pushed through the Israelite front lines in search of the king.

A voice shouted from the fray. "There he is! There's the man we want, the king of Israel!" The Syrians wheeled their chariots around when they spotted the royal robes and regal steed of the king. Jehoshaphat led them toward the waiting ambush in the eastern range. Seth held his breath and watched the Syrian infantry force their way through the protective defenses around Jehoshaphat. The cries grew louder, and blood-soaked Judean soldiers fell to their death while defending their king from the enemy onslaught.

Jehoshaphat saw the Syrians come closer and closer, attacking his men with slashing swords and spears. He turned his chariot into the fierce attack and cried, "O Lord, in you I take refuge! Come to my rescue!" Pulling hard on the horse's reins, he stopped the chariot and stood tall. He threw off his helmet and raised his sword. Screaming out to the approaching warriors, he cried, "I am Jehoshaphat, of Judah! I am not King Ahab!"

Wild screams spread through the ranks. Syrian commanders barked orders. "Stop! Retreat! Retreat immediately and find King Ahab!"

Seth watched in frozen silence as spears flew through the air and violent hand-to-hand combat left thousands of soldiers wounded and stumbling to their deaths. Countless angels appeared in the milieu, whipping heavy swords from their belts. Many surrounded Jehoshaphat and shielded him from the aggressive enemy assault. Others lifted fallen Judean and Israelite soldiers to their feet and defended the overrun charioteers and breathless horses. Bolts of lightning lit the sky, and thunder roared through the heavens while angels held and soothed the dying warriors.

Seth searched the manic crowd, peering through the smoke

and rising dust to locate King Ahab. *Lord, God Almighty,* he prayed. *Where is he? Protect him.* A frenzy of arrows shot through the air, blanketing the eastern battleground. Seth felt the strong presence of the archangel beside him, but he couldn't shake the nagging fear that plagued his mind.

Sword in hand, Michael pointed toward a flurry of activity at the far edge of the field. He noticed the stress Seth wore like a tunic and took the young man's chin in his free hand. The archangel's face was deathly serious.

"The face of God Almighty is set against those who do evil, Seth. God has handed the king's life over to his enemy. Because Ahab chose to spare the life of the Syrian king, Israel continues to suffer. Ahab has thrown his victory and his life to the wind by choosing to defy God. Now, he will die as the prophet said, and Israel must reap the destructive whirlwind."

A ray of sunshine broke through the gray sky, targeting Ahab in his chariot. Seth watched Ahab's commanders fight valiantly alongside the royal guard to protect their leader and king. Soldiers fell under the barrage of arrows targeting their position. Without warning, the king slumped over and grabbed his chariot for support. Blood ran down his armor. His driver wheeled the chariot out of the battle zone.

Seth furrowed his brow and stared at the king. "Michael, what has happened? Why is he leaving the battle? Look at him. There's something sticking out of his side between the joints of his armor." Seth raised his hand to his forehead to shadow his eyes from the glare of flashing swords. "He's been hit! King Ahab is wounded!"

"My lord," begged the driver, "we must get you to the physicians. You are badly hurt. I fear the arrow has hit your lung."

"No!" groaned King Ahab. "It is impossible to withdraw now."

He grabbed his side and struggled to stand against the back of the chariot. "Set me up here in the chariot so my army will fight with Jehoshaphat and Judah. Otherwise they will despair and desert me."

The driver helped the king sit comfortably. He took the decorative cords off the neck of the horse and wrapped them around the king's chest, bracing Ahab against the back of the chariot. Blood continued to run down his side and pool on the floor of the chariot.

"Ahhh," exhaled the king, "take me back into battle with my soldiers and face my chariot toward the Syrians. Be sure they can see my face for as long as it takes to turn the enemy back to Syria."

The fighting raged all day between the armies of Judah and Israel and the armies of Syria. One pushed forward, and the other counterattacked. Infantry column after infantry column came against Israel and Judah. Arrows continued to cross in the sky as the bodies mounded upon each other and blood stained the ground. Throughout the day, Jehoshaphat's voice was heard shouting to his troops, "Be strong, take heart, and trust in the God of Israel!"

When evening approached, dark, formless creatures darted over the soldiers and swarmed in and out of the battle. Seth dropped to his knees and put his hands over his ears, trying to muffle the vile cursing, cries, and sneering laughter. The Israelites took their eyes off the enemy and stopped their fight to chase the voices. Shielded Syrians moved forward and cut them to the ground with sickle swords and hand daggers. The Israelites battled against the Syrian infantry to hold their line of defense. Screams and groans echoed through the land as the warriors endured the horrific hand-to-hand combat.

The angelic army watched the ghostly figures flit around the Israelite and Judean armies. They waited for Michael to receive his instructions from the heavenly throne. Suddenly, he dashed into the sky and drew out his golden sword. Stretching his powerful wings above his head, he signaled his heavenly warriors to follow him into the fierce counterattack. Legions of angels thundered from the sky with furious swords, thrashing the demonic spirits until they pushed them back into the darkness of the horizon. Reenergized, the Israelites went on the offensive again, finally overpowering the enemy. The Syrian infantry welcomed the call to retreat and stumbled back to the safety of their camp.

"It is almost over now," breathed Michael when he again appeared beside Seth.

"The king is dead! The king is dead!" the scout cried throughout the ranks of Israel. "Return to your lands, return to your homes. Gather the weapons. The king is dead. Return to your lands!"

Michael stood in front of the angelic army, watching the soldiers place King Ahab's body on the cart for transport to Samaria. There was no celebration.

Michael released his commanders to their legions and turned to Seth. "We knew this day would not turn out well for Ahab. He tried to outmaneuver the decree of Almighty God. The four hundred prophets told him what he wanted to hear: 'Go to war.' But he ignored the lone voice of God's prophet."

Seth nodded as tears blurred his eyes. "And King Jehoshaphat was almost killed in the gruesome battle too." *Is this how Father and Mother felt in the garden after they agreed with God's enemy...thinking they could become like God themselves? They must have been overwhelmed when the power of God's truth stripped away the enticing appeal of Satan's lies. Oh, the consequences of their selfish rebellion! Jehoshaphat has barely escaped death today. I hope he realizes that ignoring God's warnings encouraged Ahab to start this war. And now Ahab is dead just like the prophet said he would be if he didn't heed God's advice.*

They watched the soldiers of Israel gather armloads of weapons from the slain warriors and throw them into the supply wagons. Other carts came by to collect the wounded and fallen Israelites. Michael shook his head, grief evident in his features. "Weeping will be great in the land for the thousands of lives lost here today. Ahab's disguise was clever, but it almost cost the life of another king and put two kingdoms in jeopardy."

"So Micaiah was right when he said the Lord showed him that Ahab would die on this mountain. But what about the prophecy from Elijah that said the dogs would drink his blood?" Seth lifted his palms. "What did that mean?"

Michael pointed to the bloody chariot the king had died in. "They are going to take his chariot back to Jezreel, to clean it and preserve it for his memory. What they do not yet realize is that they will wash the chariot in Naboth's field, next to the king's palace in Jezreel, and the dogs will lick the bloody water that runs out. Jezebel gave that field to Ahab after instigating a riot to kill the owner, Naboth. He was a good and noble man, but the king and queen confiscated his vineyard, property that did not belong to them. Think about this, Seth. Both prophets spoke God's judgment for Ahab, and both judgments will come to pass."

Seth tipped his head and considered Michael's statement. "Hmm." He bit his lip. "It looks like Ahab could ignore God's word and even try to defy it. But in the end, what God says will happen *is going to happen.*"

A weary smile spread across Michael's face. "You have seen that the word of God Almighty is always the last word. Because you believe God accomplishes what he says he will accomplish, Seth, you can face your own future with courage."

CHAPTER 14
The Buttress for Courage

S"eth, there is King Jehoshaphat, standing in his chariot."
Michael pointed at the king of Judah. His strong, commanding presence gave way to resignation and sadness.
"He is waiting for his commanders to regroup their units for the trip back to Judah. Thousands are buried here now and will never see Jerusalem again. He is their king and wants to lead the survivors home."

Seth watched weary soldiers move in all directions and fall into loose formations, leaving the battlefields behind. They looked like hordes of ants deserting their hill. Slowly, they merged into long lines and followed their king.

Jehoshaphat handed the reins back to his driver and stepped onto the wet palace grounds at his home in Jerusalem. He smiled at Moza, his friend and chief administrator, and accepted a warm cup of broth. "Ah, you think of everything; thank you. Now, prepare a bath and gather my children in the throne room. Tell the kitchen staff to bring in apricot juice and the sweets they love."

"Jehu the prophet has been waiting at the palace door all day. He will not leave until he speaks to you. Shall I have him wait inside while you refresh yourself?"

"No, I'll talk to him now. Perhaps he has an encouraging word for me." Jehoshaphat motioned for Moza to lead. He walked toward the door to the palace, where a man was waiting.

"There he is." Jehoshaphat stepped forward. "Jehu! Welcome."

"You will not welcome the Lord's rebuke. Why have you helped the wicked and loved those who hate Almighty God? Because you have aligned yourself and all of Judah with Ahab, a man who does evil in God's presence, the wrath of Almighty God is upon you. You even took Ahab's daughter as a wife for your son. You have joined Baal to Judah and allowed its evil root to grow and corrupt the kingdom. Everything is uncovered and laid bare before Almighty God. Did you think he could not see your heart?"

As though he had been struck, Jehoshaphat sank to his knees and covered his eyes with his hands. "Your words are true. I have foolishly denied the standards of the Lord and gone my own way. I tried to hold the hand of Almighty God and the hand of his enemy at the same time, and in doing so I have lost both. I accept the justice of the Lord." Tears began to run down his face.

Moza rushed to his side. "No, my lord! You are a valiant warrior, and you thought the alliance would protect Judah. Success would have made our country richer and stronger. Perhaps it would have even strengthened Israel and Judah as brothers."

Jehoshaphat put his hand out to stop Moza. "Yes, I thought our alliance would strengthen our position against Syria. I even agreed with Ahab that it would present a strong defense against the forces of Assyria. But already, my mind was made up. Even before the prophet of God spoke, I knew I would join Ahab and fight for Israel."

Jehoshaphat rubbed his sleeve across his forehead and confessed, "The truth is that Ahab's prophets impressed me with their rich ceremonial robes and encouraging words of victory. Even so, I sensed their cheers were full of empty promises. Why didn't I listen to the tug at my heart and the strong warning from the prophet of Almighty God?" Jehoshaphat shook his head and looked at Moza. "Now Ahab is dead, and I live."

Jehoshaphat stood slowly, and he met Jehu's piercing eyes. "May God have mercy on me. And may God have mercy on Judah."

Jehu the prophet stepped toward Jehoshaphat and extended both palms. "Look at yourself! You live because the Lord protected you. He is not finished with you. Only God knows the intentions of your heart and sees how you act when no one else is watching. Your actions seem good to others, but the Almighty knows your secret thoughts."

Jehoshaphat lowered his head. "Then God knew it didn't matter to me *what* the prophet would say. He knew the decision had been made in my mind long before the prophet arrived."

Jehu pulled the hood of his robe off his head and said, "He knows all of our selfish intentions, and he knows when our hearts want to please him. But there is some good in you," he encouraged the king, "because you have gotten rid of the carved images of the goddess Asherah in Judah. It is not as easy for the people to worship Baal on the mountains as it was before. Your people know you have chosen to seek after God and follow the way of David and your father Asa. So now, commit yourself to the word of Almighty God and follow his ways. If you choose to listen to a voice other than his, you choose to be deceived. Determine to trust the word of God and act as he directs you."

Jehoshaphat stood up and nodded. "Yes, may God search me, show me the offensive ways of my heart, and lead me with his strong right hand." He turned away from Jehu and Moza, combed his hands through his hair, and prayed, "Help me to listen and follow you, O Lord."

"Michael, you're right." Seth looked up at his mentor. "King Jehoshaphat is a different kind of man than King Ahab. But do you think he will remember God's words first before he makes future decisions?"

Michael focused his eyes on Seth and said, "Jehoshaphat is a man who loves Almighty God. But he, like so many in powerful positions, fell into Satan's trap by thinking he had a better way than God. Then, when he heard what he should do, he was unwilling to admit his mistake and choose God's way."

"Well," Seth continued, "he sure didn't pay attention to the words of the prophet. But it looks like he knows he failed, and now he wants another chance."

A recent event came to Seth's memory, and he bit his lip. *Father has given me plenty of chances to change, especially after I let my temper go and lit into my little brothers. I hurt more than their feelings in that last fight. Joshah ended up with a broken arm when he tried to stop us, and he fell into the river. But they teased me too many times about being afraid of the brothers of Nod. I just wanted them to stop. I guess I let their taunting feed my anger, and I reacted to stop them instead of being rational and brushing off their fun. Father told me I used my anger as a weapon to hurt them, instead of as a tool to help me see my own problem: I was letting my fear defeat me.*

Michael picked up on Seth's comments about Jehoshaphat's confession. "Fortunately, God is always looking for those who recognize their failures, whether in their behavior or in the thoughts of their hearts. He waits with open arms to forgive them and show them a better way. Jehoshaphat seems determined to listen to God first now and do what he says to do. What do you think, Seth? Do you think he has really changed?"

"Well, Ahab didn't, even after acknowledging that God gave him the victories. He still continued to disregard God and choose his own way. I hope Jehoshaphat is different, like you said."

"His future choices will show us the answer. He will make more changes in Judah," Michael answered. "I was there when he went a second time into his country to tell his people about the God of their fathers who promised to make them a mighty nation and bless them. Jehoshaphat went into all the cities of Judah and appointed judges over the people and instructed the judges to listen carefully to the complaints of the people, just as God would do."

Michael grinned, enjoying the memories. "Yes, he is different from Ahab. I remember when he reminded the judges that they were not judging for the king but for the Lord, who was always with them when they gave a decision. They were to judge carefully, because there is no partiality or injustice or bribery with Almighty God."

Michael shrugged his shoulders. "You saw how Ahab and Jezebel judged. They decided what was best for them and then decreed it to be so. Because they had no regard for God, his justice was severe toward them, and the nation suffered. But Jehoshaphat is different."

"Do you think Almighty God would let me see King Jehoshaphat again?"

"Ask him, Seth." Michael saw the doubt in Seth's eyes, and he continued, "Your prayers are always heard. When you believe that God hears your prayers, his divine order sets his answer in motion, and heaven's full attention is focused on your need. Almighty God will answer your prayer in a way that is best for you, and his answer is not always 'yes.' Sometimes it is 'wait.' So, never hesitate to talk to him and present your requests."

"I do believe he hears my prayers." Before Michael could respond, Seth closed his eyes and whispered, "O God, I see that you are over all my comings and goings. You know me, inside and out. You care about how I live and will live my life. So, if it would be all right with you, I would really like to see what happens to King Jehoshaphat before I return home. I would like to know if he remains a good man and a good king before you. I think you want me to remember his life and learn from his example, good and not so good. Thank you for listening."

Seth opened his eyes and gasped. He looked from Michael to the sky and back to Michael again. Clouds began to move overhead, and the sky became bright orange and iridescent yellow. A large golden door opened in the heavens, and before their eyes stood an angel clothed in translucent hues that sparkled like crystal. Michael approached the heavenly being, crossed his sword over his chest to his shoulder, and greeted the angel with a bow. "Gabriel."

Seth's jaw dropped, and his eyes moved from Gabriel's head to his toes. *I haven't seen another like this angel!* His face was shining and reflecting off the gold threads embedded in the fabric of his gown and robe. His shoulders and chest were covered with golden emblems. Even his hair was like golden silk. *He looks so different from Michael and the others,* Seth thought.

The angel pulled a scroll from his belt. "Greetings, Michael, to you and to Seth. I have come from the throne of the Almighty God of heaven and earth to bring you good news."

Gabriel looked directly at Seth. "God has heard your prayer and wants you to see why he established the kingdom of Judah under King Jehoshaphat. The people of Judah are happy with Jehoshaphat and honor his wise rule with gifts and treasures from their own wealth. They have added great amounts of gold and silver to his treasury. But even so, the king has not been swayed by their flattery and offerings. His heart has been devoted to the ways of God, and he has tried to do what is right in the eyes of the Lord."

Gabriel spread his wings and raised his voice. "Now go, and behold the ways of Almighty God!"

Michael reached over and placed his hand on Seth's shoulder as sparkling colors swirled around their feet and legs, cocooning their bodies in twinkling rainbows of light. Seth recognized the harmony of melodic chords as the music of stringed instruments entered his ears. The light began to fade into darkness, and soft, whispering voices replaced the pleasant instrumentation of the harp.

When Michael released his grip on Seth's shoulder, Seth focused his eyes on the figures surrounding him. As far as he could see in all directions were glowing angelic beings. He squinted and blinked his eyes and tried to focus on the faces appearing in the crowd. Brilliant bursts of light shot from one to the other like blazing fires. It was difficult to define their figures. He recognized the shining armor and the large bronze shields of the warrior angels. Throughout the thousands and thousands of angels shot flames of fire like lightning.

Michael watched Seth turn around and around, gazing toward the distant horizon. Everywhere they looked, they saw images of glimmering angels, who in the distance looked like burning coals and flaming lamps.

Seth could only breathe out words of awe: "Amazing! Glorious—spectacular!" He heard the familiar bells, followed with cymbals and singing. Melodious instruments mingled with sounds of trumpets and horns throughout the throngs of angels. Seth felt the strong, familiar grip of Michael's hand on his shoulder, but he couldn't take his eyes off the scene. He felt weightless and began to float. Leaning into Michael's arm, he was lifted into wispy clouds that softened the blazing picture below. As they rose together above the multitude of heavenly beings, he mumbled, "O God, am I dreaming? This is indescribable splendor. What can this mean? What is happening?"

Michael relaxed his mighty wings, and they glided onto a small raised platform above the bursts of flashing lights. A big smile spread across Michael's face, and he inhaled deeply. He raised his arms over his head and nodded repeatedly as if agreeing with an unheard voice.

Then Michael turned toward Seth. "Almighty God has enabled you to see the angels he has called to carry out the details of your heart's prayer. There is much for you to witness, but first we must see what will happen back in Israel. King Ahab is dead, and his son, Ahaziah, is now king. He is following the ways of his father and mother and worships worthless idols. God has seen his heart and judged his rebellion. Ahaziah has set another contest in motion between the gods of Baal and the Almighty God of heaven and earth. Take my hand. We are going back to Mount Carmel."

CHAPTER 15

A King's Folly

Seth opened his eyes and took a deep breath to clear his mind. Traveling through time continued to overwhelm and excite him, even though his fears were diminishing. Michael was always near. *How can I worry with this awesome archangel by my side? He has the strength of an ox and the agility of a lion. He comes against his boldest enemy with the force of a tornado. Yet he stands here beside me as a gentle dove. O God, you have created a masterful creature in Michael.*

Embers shot through the air when the juicy meat of an evening meal spit and sizzled above the fire. Seth fastened his eyes on the nearby figure sprinkling water on the fire and calming its blazing heat. Seth's eyes sparkled when he recognized the familiar man of God. *Elijah! O God, you heard my prayer!* After fussing over the fire, Elijah reached out to turn the spit of roasting quail.

A soft wind tickled the back of his neck before Seth heard the voice of the angel who appeared behind Elijah. Once again, this angel was not like the others Seth had seen. He seemed more like a man—and yet, there was something strange and indescribably holy about his presence.

"Stop what you are doing, Elijah," directed the angel of God. "Ahaziah is the new king of Israel now that his father Ahab is dead. Go and meet his messengers, who are going to Ekron to consult the prophets of Baal. King Ahaziah has fallen from the roof of his bedroom and is injured. He wants to know if he will live or die. When you meet them on the road, ask them these questions: 'Are you running to Baal for an answer about the king's health because there is no God in Israel? Or are you trying to avoid the words of Almighty God?' Then tell them to take this message back to the new king: 'God's answer to his question about whether he will live or die is final. He will not get out of the bed he lies in. He is dying already.' Get up and go, Elijah. They are coming now." The angel looked up at the sky and was gone.

Elijah dumped water on his fire and walked quickly to the road to deliver the message. He stood in the middle of the path and waved his arms at the approaching horsemen, who stopped their panting steeds and listened to Elijah's words for their king. As soon as he delivered the message, he strode away.

"What should we do?" the courier gasped. "If this is the word of God concerning our king, we must return immediately to the palace with the prophecy. If we go on to Ekron, the king could die before we deliver the message."

"Yes, we must return to the palace." His companion pulled at the reins and turned his horse around. "We have an answer to the king's question, and for the sake of Israel, he must know."

Michael and Seth stood in the corner of the king's bedroom and watched the attendants come and go with food and drinks. Candles were burning on the tables, and a pot of healing herbs was simmering over the fire. The smells of mint and cinnamon wafted through the air. Several of the king's administrators stood at the foot of his bed, discussing kingdom business with their ruler, when the messengers appeared at the door.

The king lifted his head and tried to sit up but moaned and fell back on his pillows. "Why have you come back so soon? You couldn't have possibly reached Ekron in this short time."

The messengers hurried to his side, bowing. "We met a prophet on the road who told us to turn around and give our king a message from Almighty God."

The king glared at the speaker. "Well, tell me then. What did he say?"

The messengers exchanged glances, then one of the men stepped closer to the bed and leaned toward the king. "The prophet said, 'God's answer is clear. He wants to know why you are running off to Baal for an answer about your health: do you think that God is not in Israel? Because you have done this, you will never leave your bed. You will surely die.'"

The messenger straightened, stepped back, and waited for the king's command.

The king closed his eyes and furrowed his eyebrows. After a moment or two he let out a steady sigh and looked at the messengers. "Tell me about this man. Who was it? What did he look like?"

"He didn't stay long enough to give us his name. But he was a big man. His hair was long and shaggy, and he wore a brown scruffy garment with a leather belt."

The second man added, "His manner was abrupt, and he was not afraid of us."

"I knew it!" the king exclaimed. "It must have been Elijah." He turned his attention to his advisers, his voice bitter. "He was a pest to my father Ahab, and now he is questioning my authority and the power of Baal to heal me. Send a captain with fifty men and arrest him immediately. We'll see how brave he is in the dungeon."

"Oh Michael," Seth groaned. "I thought Elijah would be safe now that King Ahab and Jezebel are dead. Elijah did what God told him to do, and now he'll even suffer under the hand of this new king."

Michael stood erect with his hands on his hips. His powerful wings rested behind him in peaceful tranquility. "When God commands Elijah to speak, the prophet does not let danger stop his tongue. He is an effective tool in the hand of Almighty God. In fact, many Israelites have put their trust in God alone because of the courage they see in Elijah." Michael looked at Seth, who was leaning against the wall of the king's chamber. "Don't worry about Elijah, Seth. The word of truth and the power of God is his armor of righteousness against any foe. God will empower those who seek him and strengthen their weak hearts with faith."

For a moment, Michael's face looked sad. "But Elijah will not serve in Israel much longer. His days are numbered by the Lord. Even so, his influence will last long after he is gone."

Seth felt his body relax as he followed Michael from the room. When they reached Mount Carmel, the site where Elijah was camped, they found the prophet kneeling at the top of the hill, praying. Michael and Seth settled down on a boulder and waited for the approaching soldiers.

Elijah lifted his face and said, "A fool confesses in his heart that there is no God. And before you, O God, there are none that do right." He raised his hands and called, "Look down from heaven and see how we turn away and do not call on you in our distress!"

Seth heard the thud of horses' hooves and the clatter of armor, but he kept his eyes on Elijah, who ignored the intrusion and continued his prayer.

"You know that even I, your servant, can shake with dread," Elijah continued. "But you are my help, my strength, and my vindication. Why do I worry? Cleanse my thoughts, and have mercy on me because of your faithful love. When the voice of my enemy rings in my head and suffering stalks me like a shadow, I will trust in you, O God. I will not be afraid."

The captain and his soldiers made their way through the trees and halted their horses within view of Elijah. The captain steadied his horse, his face grim. "I will take that loudmouth preacher to the king, alive or dead," he muttered. He dismounted and called up the hill to Elijah. "Prophet of God, come down! The king of Israel has need of you."

Elijah stood and looked calmly down at the soldiers. "You call me a prophet of God, and yet you come with all these men to take me to your king. Well, if I am a prophet of God, then I call on him, my king, to strike you with fire from heaven—you and your men!"

Michael jumped to his feet and shielded Seth with his outstretched wings. The sky burst open before their eyes, and bolts of fiery lightning shot to the ground and devoured the captain and all his men. Nothing was left but smoke and ashes. Peals of thunder rumbled in the distance.

The blast knocked Seth to the ground. Michael reached out to help him up and brushed the twigs off Seth's cloak.

Elijah weaved and staggered at the top of the hill. He balanced himself with his staff and stood tall, with his feet apart. His hair blew in the gentle breeze. Breathless, he stared at the smoking ground.

Seth leaned over and put his hands on his knees to regain his own stability. He panted, "What happened?"

"It is an awesome event to fall under the judgment of the Almighty. These men brought the king's challenge to the very door of heaven. Remember, Seth, God will not be mocked. No one can defy the word of God and prosper. But this is not over. The king is Ahab's son and has learned to defy the God of heaven. Elijah knows that this challenge has just begun."

King Ahaziah handed the silver cup to his nurse and rested on his pillows. "Call my advisers in." He groaned, "Where is that scout I sent to find my captain and his men? They should have found Elijah by now. He is only one old man! How could he evade their strength?"

Two men entered the room. One was dressed in fine linen with blue and gold trim, and the other wore a military uniform. The officials approached the king and bowed. The king scowled. "Well, what have you heard from the scout?"

The adviser took a deep breath. "O king, the scout has just returned with a dire report from Mount Carmel. The captain and all his men have been killed by fire. Nothing was left but a runaway horse and ashes at the foot of the hill. Elijah was not harmed and is still residing on the mountain." The adviser swallowed hard. "It seems his God has protected him."

The king closed his eyes and grimaced. "Then send another captain and his fifty troops to capture Elijah. He will face his prison cell, whether I live or die."

Orders were given, and the soldiers left at once to bring back Elijah, the lone prophet.

As this second group approached the mountain, the captain instructed his soldiers to stay behind him. They were mounted with swords drawn, ready for a fight. The captain spoke to his men. "I'm going to speak to Elijah alone. I will try to convince him to come to us. Listen and be ready to take him by force if necessary."

Elijah heard their voices and started down the hill to meet them. He heard the captain shout, "Holy prophet of God, the king of Israel says, 'Come down. Come down now!' Listen to the king, and come back to Samaria with us!"

Elijah looked at the soldiers, shook his head, and shouted, "If I am a holy prophet of the living God, then expect fire from heaven to destroy you and your men!" Elijah stepped back and shielded his face when the bolt of lightning shot from heaven like a fiery arrow. The captain and his fifty men were consumed, along with all the horses and weapons.

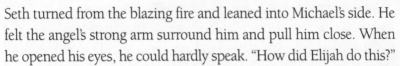

Seth turned from the blazing fire and leaned into Michael's side. He felt the angel's strong arm surround him and pull him close. When he opened his eyes, he could hardly speak. "How did Elijah do this?"

"Elijah did not do this, Seth," Michael countered. "A judgment came from the hand of God. Elijah is only mortal, but he knows that God is on his side. He trusts that whatever happens, God is in control and will not be maneuvered by the decisions of man—king or pauper. But man is controlled by the decisions he makes about God. The consequences of a man's decision will bring either blessings or curses."

Seth glanced at Elijah and looked into the clear blue sky. "I don't understand. Where are the other angels? They haven't been here for Elijah."

"There are countless angels in God's service, and they work in many ways. The angel you saw speaking with Elijah just after we arrived was God's most special angel. He is called the *Angel of the Lord*, and he is the holy representative of God himself! He appears to God's people in human form, to give an important revelation about what God has planned. Elijah was chosen to hear this prophecy and judgment concerning King Ahaziah. The Angel of the Lord is God's agent of righteousness, and he announced God's judgment, not his mercy, on the king."

"So that's how Elijah knew these soldiers would be struck down with fire and die," Seth replied.

Michael nodded. "Almighty God can do whatever he chooses, and it is right. We, his holy angels, wait for his commands without question." Michael looked directly at Seth. "I do know this: Elijah wears his faith in Almighty God as a garment of protection and stands on the truth of *God's* words, not the mumbling kings of this world."

Seth watched the royal scouts discover the second massacre and scurry back to the palace. *Will this news stop the king? Certainly he will give up this vengeful quest for Elijah!*

When Seth noticed the shadows changing around him, he looked toward the sky. The clouds thickened and moved in rapid chase through the heavens. He felt the warm presence of Michael at his side and waited for events to change. Brilliant sunlight and starry nights twirled around them until at last the dark night ushered in the dawn of a new day.

Seth couldn't believe his eyes. "Michael, here comes another captain and fifty more soldiers! Is the king crazy? Why would he send more troops when it is so obvious that God stands with Elijah? This has been disastrous for the king, a powerful rejection. Is he really that stubborn?"

"Just watch, Seth," instructed Michael. "This is the day the Lord has planned for Elijah, the new captain, and the king of Israel. And you may be quite surprised. Wait for the Lord; be strong of heart."

The third captain gestured for his men to wait at the bottom of the hill, below the scarred and ashy area where one hundred men had died just days before. Trembling, he approached Elijah and fell on his knees. "O holy man of God, please consider my life and the lives of my men. I know that your God has sent fire from heaven two times and devoured two captains and their soldiers. Nothing is left of them. But I ask you to respect our lives and be merciful to us." He bowed his head to the ground, waiting for Elijah to respond.

Suddenly, a different angel, dressed in a golden robe, stood before Elijah. Flaming embers shot from his body like lightning. The supernatural being spoke to Elijah and said, "It's all right, Elijah. Go back with him to Ahaziah, and do not be afraid. I will not leave your side."

"Stand up." Elijah looked at the captain and raised his palm. "Nothing is going to happen to you today. Take me to the king."

The captain wobbled to his knees and led Elijah to a waiting horse.

Michael and Seth followed the soldiers and Elijah to the palace. The captain was announced to the king and ushered into his bed-chamber with Elijah at his side.

King Ahaziah was propped on his pillows. He glared at Elijah and spoke with a weak voice. "Why have you said that I will die?"

Elijah approached the king's bedside and stared back at the king. "God's word to you is this: 'You acted as if there were no God in Israel to consult for your healing. Instead, you asked the prophets of Baal in Ekron for a word about your life. Because you disregarded Almighty God and have chosen another, you will certainly die in your bed.'"

The king turned his face from Elijah. "Go away," he scowled.

Elijah shook his head and left the room. No one tried to stop him.

Seth stared at the stricken king. He was speechless.

"Come with me," said Michael as he took Seth's hand for another journey.

CHAPTER 16

The Testing

ou are here to witness the awesome power of the Almighty." Michael gestured toward the temple in Jerusalem, the center of worship for the Israelites in Judah. Its massive walls rose above them. Marble pillars, gold overlay, and sparkling metals and jewels made the temple shine. *I couldn't even imagine a place like this!* Seth thought.

Michael took in the scene around them and said, "When the evil grip of Satan seems impossible to break, God gathers his special angelic forces. They are reserved for those who know the Almighty and call out to him for help and rescue. You will see what happens when God answers the prayers of the faithful. This time we visit Jerusalem and King Jehoshaphat in his own capital city. He will need the help of God's specialized angelic army."

Seth stepped closer to Michael, overwhelmed by the beauty and grandeur of the temple. Surely God was in this place!

Michael nudged Seth and directed his attention to the men who stood nearby. They were huddled near an ornately carved door that led to a spacious hallway. The men were very serious, and their deep voices forced Seth to step closer to understand their words.

"A massive army is on its way to attack Jerusalem," whispered one man to a small group of temple officials.

"I've heard they are already on this side of the Dead Sea and camped to the south, at the oasis of En Gedi. They are only days away," another said quietly.

"It's Syria again!" a bearded man said. "After years of silence, they have joined with other kings to declare war on Judah and on King Jehoshaphat. They want Jerusalem, and this time their force is bigger than ever. What is the king going to do?"

The man turned to a shrouded figure. "Moza, you are the king's chief adviser. Can you tell us what you know?"

Moza looked over the expansive courtyard. Appearing comfortable that no one outside the small group of men could hear his voice, he answered, "It's true. The king is badly shaken by the news, but he is determined as always to pray to the Lord for help. He knows there is no time to waste, so he has ordered all the people of Judah to fast. He has asked them to stop eating for a while and use the time and energy to persistently seek God's help. He knows the vast armies of our enemies will devour us if God does not come to our side."

"Yes, yes," chimed in the man next to Moza. "He has told us time and time again that the Lord hears and answers all prayers. But God is especially aware of the prayers offered by those who admit their failures and accept his forgiveness. We must certainly seek his favor."

"The king says the Lord gives him inner strength and peace when he prays. He knows God hears him and will answer his cry for help." The bearded man rubbed his hands together. "We must have God's advice and help now. We cannot win this battle without him."

Moza nodded toward the temple gate where crowds were clustering together, many wearing torn clothes and sackcloth. "Look! Already people are beginning to gather in the temple grounds. They must be here to pray for God's help and deliverance as the king requested." The shadows of evening were falling across the ground. "Soon the singers will come for the evening sacrifice and service. I must go and tell the king. Gather your own families and come back." Moza left the men and made his way into the passageway that led from the temple to the royal palace.

Heavy clouds moved across the sky over the city of Jerusalem. Spring rains threatened the evening's events. Priests were busy at work throughout the temple grounds. They carried wood to the bronze altar in the inner courtyard to feed the fire for the evening sacrifice. Some poured water into the large bronze basin the priests used to wash themselves before performing their temple duties. Around the sides of the temple walls, men tended the animals needed for the offering. Pens held sheep, cattle, and cages filled with doves. The aroma of sweet, burning incense in the holy place escaped through the tall lattice windows. A cool breeze mingled the fragrance of candles with the smell of musty animal fur, straw, and burning wood. More and more people made their way through the gates into the temple. People who could not find space inside the temple area gathered outside the walls.

King Jehoshaphat locked the door to his bedroom. He removed his crown and placed it on his dressing table. Flinging his outer robe onto the bed, he walked to the window and watched the activity in the courtyard. Then he pulled the drape cords, closing himself inside the shadows of his room, away from the distractions of the world outside. He ran his hands through his hair and began to pace back and forth. Finally, he crumbled to his knees and wept.

Seth stood very still in the corner of the king's bedroom with Michael, mesmerized by the sight. He had not been this close to the earthly activities before. Seth looked around the shadowed room—when a freezing chill shot from the top of his head straight to his feet. He saw a large, ominous presence slither close to the king, dominating the space between himself and the king. Michael stood behind Seth, put his comforting hands on Seth's shoulders, and pulled him to his side. Seth stepped behind Michael and peered out from under the angel's left arm. Michael pressed him close.

Unsheathing his sword, Michael flashed its tip toward the dark, foreboding spirit, who instantly thrust his own mighty sword into the air and lunged at Michael, barely missing his throat. Seth fell to the ground and scurried away. Sparks flew from the clashing blades as the enemies rushed to be rid of one another. Seth's eyes filled with the horror of glowing green eyes dancing around the contestants. The demon spirits circled the room cackling and shouting, "Slay the foolish warrior of heaven! Splatter his blood throughout the palace! Our Prince is supreme!"

"Enough!" shouted the Prince of Darkness. He fell back to regain his balance. Michael stood firm, planted to the floor, waiting. The great angel and the dark spirit glared at one another, swords held ready, each anticipating the other's attack. Seth felt his heart pound at his chest like a crazed animal trying to escape the appetite of the approaching beast. Frozen with terror, he held his breath. Michael moved his way and motioned for him to follow close behind.

The ominous, evil presence hissed and swayed around the room. *This demon is not the same as the ones I saw before! I don't even want to look at his shadow. Has Michael met his match?*

Michael stopped and stood tall before his archenemy. His left arm was tucked behind him, enclosing Seth. Eerie squeals bounced off the walls and ceiling as more dark shadows filled the room, surrounding them with heavy, moist breathing and uttering profanities against God and Jehoshaphat.

The booming voice of the mighty archangel broke their frenzied cursing: "I am a soldier of the Almighty God. There is none like him! The glorious power of his right hand can swallow the earth in its grip. There is no one who can stop him as he rides through the heavens to help his children on earth. Your envious passions and jealous resentments have guaranteed your heavenly defeat and your eternal destruction to come."

Michael made short circles with the tip of his sword as he took a step toward the shadowy figure. "You, Satan, are the ancient enemy of God Almighty, and he has decreed the day of your destruction. You know that your time to rule the earth is limited."

At the revelation of this creature's name, a chill ran through Seth, and he clutched Michael's robe. This was the Great Deceiver himself, the Prince of Darkness. *Satan!* This was the one who had spoken to Seth's mother in the garden and brought about all the devastation and pain he had witnessed since. His throat tightened. This was the liar who had convinced his family that life would be better if they rejected the truths of God. Now they faced each anxious day working till their hands bled, to provide food and shelter that had once been at their fingertips. He knew they still mourned the death of Abel and feared the violence of Cain and his descendants in Nod. Seth felt his muscles freeze as he thought about the havoc Satan had caused his family. At the same time, a new thought went through his mind. *I don't need to be afraid. If God has brought me here to see Satan at work, he will keep me safe through the event.* His own confidence startled him. *Where did that idea come from? This is Satan we're talking about!*

And yet—somehow he was not afraid.

Michael stared into the hollow, yellow eyes of his enemy. "You know that Almighty God has granted you a short time to speak to Jehoshaphat. Have you come to deceive him with your lies and remind him of his failures?"

"Jehoshaphat is already sinking in his own misery," the Prince of Darkness hissed in reply. "He needs only a few suggestions from me to seal his fate. His eyes have filled with enemy armies. Already he has swallowed his miserable circumstances and is drowning in self-pity!"

"You are the father of lies. You are here to accuse Jehoshaphat. I know your tricks. You never change your tactics."

Satan curled his mouth and bellowed a horrific, guttural laugh. "These stupid people fall for my ways every time. Why would I change my strategies? It's so easy to convince them that they can't trust God. Why should they call for his help? Their fear always puts them in my hands."

"Try as you may, but you will not find it so easy with King Jehoshaphat. His heart reaches hard after Almighty God!" Michael eyed his old enemy with courage and continued, "And Almighty God is Lord of all!"

Michael swung his mighty sword over his head. Satan mimicked his action and flicked his sword back and forth, taunting the archangel to action.

Michael steeled himself and warned, "Take care, Satan, what you do here. The Lord keeps his distance from the wicked, but men like Jehoshaphat have his constant attention."

"Why would your god care about this dreadful little king and the puny city he makes his capital?"

"You know that Jerusalem is the city of God and the only city on earth he has chosen for his Name to rest upon. He gave the city to King David, and Jehoshaphat is David's heir. Almighty God hears his prayers and the prayers that rise from within the walls of the holy city. The people of Jerusalem look to the God of their fathers for counsel, and they trust his ways for salvation. Jehoshaphat knows in his heart that God's answer to his prayer will be good for Israel and good for him."

Michael narrowed his eyes. "I would drive you out now if I could, but God has allowed you to be here. Remember, you only have a short time to try your crafty wiles on Jehoshaphat."

Michael lowered his sword and swept it toward Jehoshaphat.

Seth watched the huge figure slowly turn away from Michael, but his piercing eyes lingered. Seth choked in panic and held his breath when the terrifying stare bore into his own. He felt himself wilt within, helpless, and drowning in feelings of hopeless despair. *God save us!*

After what seemed an eternity, the Prince of Darkness moved

toward Jehoshaphat with a rush of putrid air. His large, bony hand, sparkling with jeweled rings, reached out of the black cloak to rest on Jehoshaphat's shoulder. Seth recoiled. He couldn't believe his ears as the commanding voice cursed and shouted vile obscenities into the room.

"Quiet! You've gone too far!" Michael screamed. "You darken your lying council with vulgar slander? Speak your piece quickly, and return to your lair!"

The belligerent figure flashed his grisly eyes toward Michael and rolled them back into their sockets, leaving bulging red orbs for all to see. Seth winced and quickly turned his head toward the floor. This was a scene he wanted to forget!

Satan turned back to his prey. A chorus of shrill, screaming demons invaded the room, and chilling winds circled like cyclones around them. The Dark Prince growled like a pouncing lion upon his prey. He leaned in close to the king and whispered, "You wretched, sniveling bag of bones. You *should* feel lost right now. Your country faces annihilation, and you cannot stop it from happening. Blood will fill your streets, and your children will be mutilated in front of your face! Your precious city will be plundered, and your palace will burn with the bodies of your women."

Satan paused as terror took root in the king. Then with a soft, kind voice, the Master of Evil continued. "Look at yourself. You are exhausted from meetings with your advisers, hour after hour, and you have not slept for days. Of course you have a right to feel sorry for yourself. After all, you are all alone, and no one can understand the pressures you face as Judah's king. This is an impossible situation for anyone."

The king let out a sob.

The depraved spirit waved off his demon spirits and circled around the king. "It is time to surrender your people and save yourself from this perilous loss! Give them over to the invaders, and save yourself…and your family. Wouldn't you like to breathe freely and be rid of these burdensome responsibilities? You think too much about the welfare of all these people!"

Jehoshaphat shook his head, but Satan was unrelenting. "Maybe you should just get on your horse and ride away. God will choose a new king, and perhaps he will save Jerusalem—you can't help them now. You certainly have no strategy against this vast army that is coming to kill you! You have failed your people and your country."

The Tempter swept his arms open and moaned, "And look how you have failed your God! You are no good to anyone now. Even your children fear that you cannot protect them. Maybe you should just fall on your own dagger and be done with this impossible situation."

The tempestuous shadow towered above Jehoshaphat before he backed away. Again, shocks of cold air shot through Seth. He shivered as he watched the eerie figure throw back his head and shoulders and puff out his chest. Seth couldn't see his face, but when the shadowed being turned toward Michael, a deep, foreboding, laugh rumbled from his belly and joined the cackling giggles of his minions surrounding the king. Instantly, Satan disappeared, but his hellish demons remained and flurried around the room.

Seth breathed in a small breath of air, exhaled, and fell against the wall for support. *What will happen now?*

The king struggled to stand. He reached for the bedpost and steadied himself before walking to the bench near his dressing table. His elbows rested on his knees, and he buried his face in his hands.

Out loud, Jehoshaphat spoke in a somber voice: "I can't think this way. I must face what is really true, not just what I am feeling. No, I have not always made the choices God would want me to make, but when I have asked him, he has corrected my course and set me straight again. He has always forgiven me and helped me to remember his wisdom and goodness. Who is like him? There is no one! He is my God, the Creator of heaven and earth, and he will not fail me now!"

Around him, the demons began to flutter, their whispers growing in urgency. But the king's voice drowned them out. "Whether I live or whether I die, I will trust him, and I will do the job he has called me to do. I will lead the people of Judah in his way and listen for his voice to direct me. I know that nothing is too hard for him."

A slight smile broke on the king's face, and he closed his eyes. "So in you, O God, I place my strength. You are my help and deliverer."

There was a rush of wind against Seth's face. The shadowed demons flew wildly around the room, and one darted close to the king's ear. "No, no! Stop saying those things. God will not help you this time. You are lost, and your kingdom is going to be given to another ruler!"

Seth waited to hear more of the king's prayer, but instead the king remained still and silent. While Seth kept his eye on Jehoshaphat, his mind returned to the horrible battle scene at Ramoth-Gilead. *What are you thinking about, Jehoshaphat? Your defeat was devastating, and you barely escaped with your life. Both you and Ahab paid a high price for ignoring the warning God gave you through his prophet. You are older now, and years have gone by since that battle. Maybe you are fighting thoughts of failure, like Satan said? I know I would be. I would still blame myself for joining forces with someone who didn't honor God…I would probably be shaking with fear if I were in your sandals. Ha! I can't even face the brothers of Nod with their threats and criticism. I don't even know what to say to them when they threaten me. I just want them to leave my family and me alone. And I have allowed my fear to push me into sin too—I've been violent and angry with my own little brothers.*

Seth scowled and bit his lip. *How could I ever face what you must be facing today?*

Seth heard a soft knock at the door of the bedroom. He turned and shook his head to clear the depressing thoughts.

Jehoshaphat ignored the knock and the other sounds around him and rose to his feet. He raised his head and hands. He stood tall, looked toward the ceiling, and prayed, "Almighty God, please hear me! You have shown me the path of life, and more than ever, I don't want to stray from it. In the past you have guided me and given me accurate directions. Even at night on my bed, you have heard my anxious thoughts and filled my heart with your truth and counsel. You are my God, my rock, and my savior. In you and you alone I trust. Please hear my prayer. Show me again if my heart is not right before you. Is there any wrong deed I have committed against you or my neighbor? Does anything stand between me and your blessing?"

A louder knock at the door surprised the king. He jumped. "What is it? Come in."

Moza approached the king. "Sir, I am sorry to disturb you, but the people have heard your order to put aside food for prayer. They have come from all over Judah and are filling the temple grounds to pray. Perhaps you will want to address them before the evening sacrifice."

Jehoshaphat's face showed his conflicting emotions. "I'm not sure I am ready to face our people yet. I know I can trust God to help me, but I still can't shake the blame I feel for Ahab's death at Ramoth-Gilead. Now, all his children and Jezebel are dead too. His brother is on the throne, and Israel is very weak under his rule. Our brothers will fall under the strong hand of the Syrians if the Lord doesn't intervene. I know God has forgiven me for ignoring the warning, but I can't seem to forgive myself and move on. God help me!"

Jehoshaphat looked at Moza and breathed out a loud sigh. "But

Judah is my concern today, and my worst fear has become a reality. Everyone knows that the Syrian mob is marching with their southern allies to annihilate us. Their armies appear to be invincible. They threaten to swallow our people and destroy our precious city of Jerusalem."

Moza stepped forward and embraced his friend and king. "Oh Jehoshaphat, I have known you all your life, and you are no longer the man who doubts Almighty God. You have experienced his discipline like a son who has wronged his father. You have also experienced his goodness, and you know the joy of his forgiveness. Do you not trust him now?"

Jehoshaphat nodded. "Yes, I do—but do I deserve his mercy?"

"Of course not!" laughed Moza as he released his hold on the king. "No one ever will. But he is for us anyway, even when we are against ourselves. You know he will strengthen our hearts when we ask for his forgiveness. So don't even open a small window in your heart with doubts. God's eternal enemy will see the crack and push his way in to do battle with your thoughts. If you listen to his accusations and taunts, he will magnify your fears, and you will forget the promises of God Almighty. Remember what you have heard and believed about God. It will shield you from the fiery darts of the enemy when he showers you with doubts and worries. Hold up your convictions and remember that what you know is really true. How can you trust God when you only think about yourself? Instead, concentrate on him and his abilities and goodness, and the enemy will run from you."

"You're right again." Jehoshaphat lifted his chin. "That's why I listen to you! My father would tell us that man is made to carry the burdens of only one day at a time—no more. If we try to carry the burdens of yesterday and tomorrow, we will crumble to the ground."

"Yes, and God said he forgives our sins and remembers them no more, so why should you? Do you think he lies to you about this?" Moza smiled and held out his hand. "Come now. Let's go to the temple and remember together the amazing things God has done for our people. You are a man of integrity and courage. Make up your mind today to trust God, and don't let your fears smother your faith."

Moza slapped the king on the back and smiled. "God will help us and give us the strength we need to face this great army."

CHAPTER 17

The Petition

ichael led Seth through the palace to join the gathering crowds in the temple. Unseen, they made their way to the top of the eastern gate, the main entrance to the temple. Below, they could see the stream of visitors coming up numerous steps and passing through the immense double-doored gate into the temple grounds.

Seth sat on the massive stones above the gate. "Michael, this sure is a beautiful palace, even more beautiful than the palace of King Ahab."

"This is not a palace, Seth." Michael tussled Seth's hair. "This is the house of God, the temple for God Almighty on earth. He designed it himself, as his special place, to meet with his people. Remember King Solomon? He was David's son, and he built the temple when he came to the throne. The people come to the temple to worship God with songs, prayers, and sacrifices."

Michael pointed to the large altar in the center of the inner patio court. "That is the altar for the people's sacrifices. Sin comes with a cost. Just as your father taught you to offer God an animal for your wrongdoings, these people offer their animals as payment for their bad thoughts and actions. Their sins separate them from Almighty God. When the priest kills the animal, it reminds them that God will forgive them and always be with them."

Seth wiggled. "I don't understand how a lamb can pay for my sins. I offer them as Father tells me to do, but I don't really know why."

"God uses something innocent, like the lamb, as a picture to show you how serious your rebellious ways are to him. He does-n't ask for *your* life because he loves you so much. But Almighty God is also just and cannot let your sins go unpunished. The animal takes the judgment instead of you. When you realize that God has made a way to forgive you, it is possible to accept his forgiveness and face a new day with him. Your mistakes and sins are gone, and he forgets about them forever."

Seth mulled over Michael's words. *What would happen if Cain recognized his sins and offered an animal sacrifice? God would forgive him, too, and things might change in Nod. He doesn't have to be like King Ahab, who kept rejecting God.* He thought, too, of his own wrong actions and attitudes. It seemed like even when he wanted to do well, he ended up making mistakes and sometimes sinning.

"I guess that's why we need to keep offering sacrifices. Because we go right back to our sinful ways, every time." Seth shook his head, thinking now of Ahab and his son, Ahaziah. Even Jehoshaphat had failed to follow God fully.

"Yes," said Michael, his eyes glittering. "But these animal sacrifices are only temporary. Someday God himself will make a sacrifice for your sins that will last forever. The lamb he has chosen will be the last sacrifice, the last lamb that ever needs to die for you. The Lamb of God will take away the sins of everyone on earth. Those who accept his sacrifice as theirs will live with God forever."

Seth collected his thoughts, wrestling with the sense of wonder that jumped up in him at Michael's words. He thought of all the animal sacrifices his family had offered—the cries of the lambs and the smell of blood. And he thought of his many sins and failings that needed to be paid for. "That *is* good news!"

Excited voices drew their attention to the noisy crowd gathering in the inner court. They watched as people moved aside for Moza, who escorted King Jehoshaphat and his attendants. The king and his entourage made their way up another set of steps into the new courtyard in front of the temple.

The king took his position in front of the people of Judah. He stood in somber silence. Then he raised his hands and ordered, "Humble yourselves with me before the God of our fathers."

The crowds in the temple courtyards stopped talking. As people began to pray, a quiet hush swept through the crowds, both inside and outside of the temple walls, until even the children were quiet.

King Jehoshaphat continued, "You, O God, are the God of the heavens above and the ruler of all the kingdoms below. No one can stand against your power and might! We remember how you drove out the people who lived here when you brought our ancestors back into this land, the land you promised to Abraham forever."

People throughout the assembly responded, "Yes, you are our God!"

"We stand here today," the king said, motioning around him, "in the temple your people built for you. And we believe you will hear our cry for mercy and help us. You have always heard our ancestors during their times of calamity, distress, famine, and disease. Hear us now and rescue us, O God our Father."

"Yes, yes. We will not survive without your help!" cried men throughout the crowds.

Jehoshaphat shouted, "You can see that the invading armies are coming to take the land you gave us, God! We can't stop them this time. We are helpless against this mighty army and don't know what to do without your help. Hear us, and save us from this brutal assault! We have no hope but you. Rescue us, O Lord!"

Without a word from Michael, angelic beings began to move toward the temple. Seth watched them float onto rooftops and line the walls all around the area. Angels were everywhere he looked, too many to count. Most of them wore armor for battle, but those who stood among the crowd were different. He had not seen this kind of angel before. They wore flowing robes in lustrous whites, with hues of violet and pale yellow. Across their chests were ribbons of blue and yellow. Their hair was glowing and iridescent. Seth studied their beautiful faces, which were smiling and peaceful. Each seemed to reflect a reverent calmness. He glanced at Michael, who also stood relaxed, smiling, and radiant. Seth saw more angels in the crowd than people. They filled the rooftops and overflowed into the masses outside the temple walls. *What are they doing here? They don't look like warrior angels. Are they here to support the king, or are they here for you, Michael?*

Seth crouched on his knee and leaned forward, resting his weight on his hand. Scanning the temple grounds, he saw men with their wives and children standing almost motionless, eyes closed, praying. Many raised their arms and looked into the skies. Others fell to their knees and bowed their heads. Countless angels joined them. Seth breathed deeply, filling his lungs. His tension disappeared, and he whispered his own request. "I don't know what is going to happen to these people, God. But it looks like even the angels are joining their prayers and expecting your help. The people are counting on you, O God. Will you help them?"

Seth felt a ripple under his feet like a vibration deep in the ground. Michael and the angels raised their heads and looked at the surrounding skies. Seth narrowed his eyes to focus on dark clouds of successive smoke that seemed to billow from the outer limits of the horizon. He felt dizzy as things began to wobble and rock up and down. He reached for Michael's hand and steadied himself against the angel's immovable frame. Everyone around Seth, except the angels, remained quiet and unaffected by the strange events. The people continued praying as if nothing had happened.

"The Almighty has heard them, Seth." Michael didn't take his eyes off the dark clouds. "He knows they are overwhelmed and almost paralyzed with fear. They are facing imminent death for themselves and their families and the destruction of all they cherish. But they have called out to God Almighty, and he has heard their cries."

Michael pointed to the horizon, "Look at the billowing clouds in the heavens. Already the smoke is turning into a blazing fire."

"Are the demon warriors coming back?" Seth gripped Michael's sleeve.

"Perhaps, but we are ready to fight if they come. *This* fire is stoked by the immeasurable powers of God, and it shows us the amazing energy and zeal he has for these people and the promises he has made to them. He can part the stratospheres of heaven and ride his great and mighty angels on the wings of the wind to answer the prayers of his people. He has heard their honest cries for help, and he will drown their fears like cool water on flaming coals. He will give them the courage they need to face the vast, destructive army that moves toward Jerusalem, the city he calls holy."

Seth felt his fingers tingle from the strong grip Michael had on his hand, but he didn't move from the angel's side. Seth heard his heart pounding in his head as the moving earth relaxed its waving motion, and his feet felt solid footing beneath him again.

When Seth's body stopped swaying, Michael waved an arm toward the crowds. "Listen to their prayers, Seth. They are powerful and have moved the Almighty to respond. Listen to what they say."

Seth concentrated to hear their words. "I hear them saying that God is good and merciful and reigns justly over everyone." He strained to hear more. "It sounds like they are thanking him for things he has done for them in the past: saving them and their ancestors from their enemies, giving them the land they live on and the water they drink."

"The true words they speak are like swords that slice away at their fears and doubts. But not only that," Michael said, "they have admitted to themselves and to God that they have no hope in their own plans or their own strength." A broad smile spread across Michael's face. "This is when the Almighty can really move heaven and earth for them: when they realize they are helpless without him."

Seth nodded. He took another deep breath and released Michael's hand. "Yes, I guess that's why they asked for so much. They asked for miracles, didn't they? They asked for protection and victory over their enemies. It would be impossible, unless God stepped in and rescued them. One little girl even asked God to keep her chickens and goat safe if the bad people hurt their family."

"Ha!" laughed Michael. "God loves to answer the prayers of children. They come to him in faith, knowing that he hears and understands their needs. They believe what God says, and they act on it. Just as children expect their earthly fathers to take care of them, they also expect God to love and care for them, because he has said he would. They know they are safe coming to Almighty God and can leave their concerns with him. They do not hold on to their worry as tightly as adults do. They can let it go, because they trust God to make it happen."

"Hmm." Seth brushed the hair from his eyes and responded, "It sounds like they put their faith in God, not in their feelings— like Moza told Jehoshaphat to do. Wish I could learn to do that." *Then maybe I could live in peace with the brothers of Nod—and follow God as faithfully as I would like to.*

CHAPTER 18

The Power of Courage

Seth tingled from the sudden sensation that ran through his body and filled his head with anticipation. Michael raised a finger to his lips and held his other palm up, signaling Seth's attention. Seth took a deep breath and exhaled as a peaceful stillness enveloped them, heavy with the sense of—something holy and powerful.

This seems familiar to me...the same as it was on Mount Carmel when the angels saw the heavens open and the Lord reach out to protect Elijah. Michael is waiting for something to happen. Seth gazed into the blue, spring sky, scattered with white frothy clouds. *It is so quiet! I don't see anything unusual.*

"Wait," Michael whispered. "The unseen Spirit of Almighty God is moving through the assembly. He is searching the hearts of the people to find someone who will be courageous to speak God's words to the people."

Michael stood in silent attention with all the angels. Again their faces were showered with light, reflecting a calming stillness. Seth leaned in to search the crowds as he waited with Michael and the angels for someone to speak.

One of the priests held up his hands and raised his voice: "Listen, everyone—people of Judah and Jerusalem, and especially you, O King Jehoshaphat! This is what God says: 'Believe in the Lord your God. Do not be afraid of these invading hordes from the other side of the great sea. The battle that is coming is not yours, but God's! Tomorrow, go out to attack the armies of Edom and the armies of the Ammonites, Moabites, and Menuites. In God's hands, they are as the Syrians hordes who do not know the Almighty and march boldly to their destruction. When you see them heading for the slopes of Jerusalem, move out to meet them. You will find them in the mountain pass of Ziz, at the end of the gorge. But do not lift your swords to fight! Just take your positions and stand firm. Then, watch as the Almighty God rescues you from their hand. Do not be afraid tomorrow, but march out with courage.' God is with us!"

Jehoshaphat fell on his knees and leaned forward with his face to the ground. Everyone followed his example. They praised God, shouting, "He is our help against the enemy! His love is better than life. His right hand protects his children, and all the earth will fear him." The people filled the air with their strong, clear cries of worship. They hugged each other, danced, and sang, "God is with us! We are saved from our enemies!"

Smiles broke across faces in the crowds. Men slapped each other on the back, and women hugged each other and laughed with the children. Then, one by one, the people of Jerusalem made their way through the narrow streets to their homes. The visiting pilgrims built fires and camped nearby, resting through the night.

Early the next morning, Jehoshaphat stood before his commanders in full battle attire. He scanned his soldiers in the thousand military units scattered before him.

"Men of Judah," he shouted. "How do we face our fears today? We will saddle our horses, put on our armor, and trust God. Do you believe you will return home again? Soldiers of Judah and Jerusalem, listen to me. Believe in your God, the God of Abraham and the God of David, and you will live! Believe what the prophet has spoken, and we will have success. Wear these truths like an unbreakable belt around your waist. Carry your faith with you like an invincible shield to fight your fears. Everything will turn out well for us. Trust God today!"

King Jehoshaphat stepped into his chariot and waved his bronze helmet over his head. He shouted, "We have sought the Lord, and he has heard our cry. Now, wrap yourselves in God's promise! Let his promise protect your heart like armor around your chest. Nothing can take away what the Almighty God has already done for us, or from what he promises to do for us today. We can be victorious against this great enemy because we are his children; he has called us 'his people.' We cannot trust in our own skill or our horses and chariots, but we can trust in Almighty God who will fight our battle today. He has promised us victory. Believe he is for us today, and see his victory come. Encourage each other with the truths of Almighty God."

Turning his attention to the commanders of his army and the leaders of the people, Jehoshaphat secured his helmet and instructed, "Now go to your men and communities and remind them of the prophet's words to us this morning. The prophet said we are to take our positions for warfare and wait for God to act for us."

For a moment, the king's face creased in deep thought. "Surely there is *something* we can do to show we trust him while we wait. Tell the troops to pray while they wait for the work of the Lord. They can pray for themselves, their families, their country, and their fellow soldiers."

"But sir, shouldn't they remain alert in case of attack?" one of the commanders asked.

"They can be alert to the enemy and still pray," Jehoshaphat answered. "I believe it will prepare them for battle and help relieve their fears. When they concentrate on the power and strength of Almighty God, they won't concentrate on themselves or the troubles in front of them. Prayer will be like a helmet for their thoughts. It will help them make up their minds to believe that God will save us one way or another. Tell them to pray, believing their prayers will touch the nerve that moves the mighty hand of God for us today. God's victory is coming, and he will do even more than we can ask or imagine. It will be done by his power, and he will not disappoint us."

One of the commanders slapped his arm across his chest. "You are right! I agree; prayer will convince the army to expect God's victory."

"It will keep them calm while they wait. And who knows? Perhaps this is how God will give them courage," echoed another.

Several more nodded in agreement.

"There is one thing more we must do." Jehoshaphat looked each commander in the face, acknowledging them one by one. "I've called the men's choirs together to lead our march into the valley. They are wearing their special ceremonial robes and will sing songs of thanksgiving to the Lord. Please make a path for them to pass to the front of the troops."

The commanders gasped, and one of them stepped forward. "Sir, to the front of the lines? They will face the first attack. They should *follow* behind the troops at a safe distance."

Jehoshaphat shook his head. "Where is your faith? Do you believe this battle is the Lord's, as he said? If so, everyone will return home safe, even those without weapons. Let's put flesh on our faith, and show everyone we believe this battle is going to be won by the Lord and not by our own strength."

The commanders nodded in agreement and returned to their units. Throughout the armies of Judah, the message was proclaimed: "Make way! Clear the path! Let the temple choir pass to the front of the line! They will lead us to God's victory!"

The choirs made their way through the soldiers while the commanders instructed their men to be alert for battle, even as they waited and prayed. Jehoshaphat expected details from his scouts on the proximity and strength of the enemy forces. His scouts had crossed the rugged mountains facing the Hebron Valley to gather information about the eastern invaders. Even now, they made their way up the hill to Jerusalem to give their report to the king.

Moza greeted the scouts. "The king is waiting for your strategic analysis of the enemy. Come with me, quickly."

The scouts followed Moza through the gate and approached the king. Before speaking a word, they bowed and dropped to one knee. Jehoshaphat sat on his regal stallion outside the East Gate of Jerusalem. "Brothers, please rise and tell me all you learned about our enemy."

Still panting from their hard ride to Jerusalem, they rose to attention. The lead scout stepped forward, eager to relay the news they had gleaned. "O king, we watched the dust from their advance move steadily westward across the Judean wilderness three days ago. They broke camp this morning and marched northward, from the southeast, and are now nearing the desert of Tekoa, only twelve miles away. We saw no end to their armies of horses and chariots. And their foot soldiers are innumerable! Their armies are greater than those we faced against the Syrian invasion into King Ahab's Israel. They have at least two hundred thousand men with large swords and spears, and the same number with small shields and bows. They are advancing like a flood to surround Jerusalem."

Jehoshaphat exhaled and placed his hand on his scout's shoulder. "Well done! Have faith in God Almighty. He will deliver the invaders into our hands. Go now. Refresh yourselves and join your units. See what the mighty hand of God will do for us."

The king turned to Moza. "Alert the commanders and tell the priests to sound the trumpets. We are ready to move forward. To God be the glory for what he is going to do for his people!"

At the sound of the trumpets, the choirs led the march through the hills that separated Jerusalem from the approaching enemy. The choirs marched ahead of the soldiers and sang again and again with hearty, harmonious voices, "Give thanks to our God; his love will last forever." Their choruses echoed through the air, with the king himself joining in their boisterous praise.

Seth watched the heavy layer of storm clouds approach from the eastern sky, blurring the rising sun. He looked around for Michael and spotted him nearby with his angelic warriors. His wings were fully extended, and his sword was in his hand. All the angels stood at attention and listened.

"Expect to fight with all your strength against the forces of darkness," Michael commanded. "Stay on your guard and be ready for battle. But remember, Almighty God will bring the victory. Satan will send his strongest and most able warriors to foil God's plan and defeat God's people. You are stronger than his demon warriors, and you are ready. Go, and honor God with your service!"

The angelic army crossed their chests with their swords and vanished. Seth stood up and waited for his instructions.

Michael flew to Seth's side and folded his wings. "Watch the skies carefully, Seth. The Lord God Almighty is here. He has sent warrior angels to wait for the Ammonites and their partners, who anticipate victory against Judah today."

Without warning, streams of intense light shone through the clouds. Streaks of fire and hailstones hurled through the heavens. Great shouts like thunder roared, while bolts of lightning tore through the stampeding clouds.

"Watch, Seth!" shouted Michael as he wrapped his strong arms around Seth's waist and stood his ground against the torrential winds.

Seth dropped his jaw and gaped when he saw what looked like a massive hand reaching through the raging clouds and bursts of lightning. The open hand pointed into the valley where Jehoshaphat and his choirs were singing and his armies were praying.

Michael swept Seth up in his arms and carried him to a nearby mountaintop that separated Judah from the invading hordes. They heard the sounds of music and singing drifting their way. Over their heads, God's angelic warriors battled with demonic creatures. The sounds of clashing swords and shields grew louder in the heavens. But Seth still heard the music of the men's voices cutting through the thunderous conflict. Angry bolts of lightning scorched portions of ground throughout the battlefields. Jehoshaphat's choirs kept up their singing while demonic warriors appeared out of nowhere, swooping in to join the fight. They droned and growled throughout the fearsome onslaught against the angels of God.

Group after group of angels gathered and circled the heavenly battlefield. Most joined the warring spectacle, but many more praised God with loud, strong voices, singing and shouting, "Glory to our God and King! Your word will last forever and forever. Glorious power and greatness are yours! Stretch out your hand and swallow the enemy by the truth of your word!"

The sky turned to utter darkness. Pandemonium broke out in the valley opposite the mountain where Jehoshaphat and his people stood. God's blinding lights ricocheted from one enemy soldier to another. Horses reared up and bolted off in all directions. Shouts and screams mixed with clashes of thunder. Sporadic fires sent smells of sulfur and burning ash into the air, and smoke wandered through the valley of death. Intermittent blasts of deadly lightning made it difficult for Seth to see the battle, but as he focused, he couldn't believe his eyes. *The enemy armies have stopped their advance and…are they turning around? No, they have raised their swords and are fighting…each other!*

Seth and Michael watched the confused Ammonite and Moabite soldiers turn against their allies. Their commanders shouted orders to their units. "Attack!" Slashing swords and battle cries spread throughout the enemy armies.

"Michael," Seth shouted. "What's happening?"

"The heavenly armies have overcome Satan's warriors, and now Almighty God will show his victory for Judah! He released his tremendous, invincible power as the choirs lifted their songs of praise." Michael pointed into the fray. "Look, the enemies of Judah are stunned by the hand of God and don't recognize their enemy! They hear the battle cries and see the one next to them as the avenger."

The angel set his jaw, his face grim. "The invading armies and their allies will fight each other…until the last man is dead."

The choirs of Judah saw the approaching storm clouds but were not moved from their course. They continued to sing and bravely lead the Judean soldiers to face the vast armies that had come to destroy them. One by one, they began to stutter and gasp when they reached the mouth of the gorge, near the pass of Ziz. Before them lay massive numbers of dead bodies, crumpled in the weeds and dirt.

"Call the commanders! Get the king!" shouted several of the singers. "The Lord our God has delivered us from the hand of our enemies! As far as our eyes can see are dead soldiers. They are everywhere. Not one warrior from the attacking hordes has escaped the sword. God be praised!" The message continued through the singers and the soldiers until it reached the king.

King Jehoshaphat had joined his commanders on the hilltop to survey the miracle. He trembled and shook. "Our God has avenged us! He is indeed our only fortress and strength. How could we ever doubt his hand of deliverance? The Lord is the only great God."

Jehoshaphat looked again at the bodies of the invading armies tangled together on the valley floor and shouted, "God Almighty is King of Kings! There is no other! Pass the word to the soldiers of Judah and the people of Jerusalem. Spread the joy and revel in the salvation of our God!"

"Sir." Moza appeared at Jehoshaphat's side. "It will take at least three days just to gather the plunder from the corpses and bury the bodies. The armor and weapons will fill storehouses in Jerusalem, and who knows what else God has given us from their supply tents?"

"Of course." Jehoshaphat gripped Moza's arm. His eyes were dancing with joy and tears at their incredible deliverance. "Call the troops together. Let's get busy so we can celebrate with everyone at the temple of God. Send word to the priests to prepare the orchestras and singers for our triumphant return. How can we ever forget this miraculous day and the power of Almighty God? Our God is able. He can do more than we ever ask or even imagine. And look how he works in our hearts to help us trust him!"

Seth turned his attention to the changing skies. The darkness seemed to lessen, and sunbeams pushed their rays through the breaking clouds. Angelic choirs stirred around Michael and Seth. They watched the warrior angels move into loose formations. A powerful trumpet blast sounded in the distance. Again, blood drained from Seth's face. His knees trembled, and he staggered to catch himself.

Michael and the entire company of angels dropped to the ground in a wave of motion. They shouted, "All thanks to you, Almighty God, who has always been and always will be! You are the only true and living God! You have used your great power to save your people from their enemy. You are the everlasting Father, the Prince of Peace. You do not change; you do not grow weary!" Seth sank to his knees and listened while the angels continued to praise and honor God.

Just as suddenly as the skies had darkened, the dark faded away. The vast company of angels on earth and in the sky looked up. They opened their wings in unison and lifted into the heavens.

As he watched them go, Seth felt the warm sunshine on his back, and he stood to join Michael. They were again alone on the mountain. From the valley below, they heard the shouts of voices as soldiers worked to clear the killing fields of plunder and bury the bodies. Seth sat on a large, smooth stone near Michael and exclaimed, "Wow! Who would ever think that such a victory could be won! The soldiers of Judah never even lifted their swords. God did it all! All they did was pray and sing songs of praise and thanksgiving."

"Yes, but they heard God's promise of victory and decided to believe him." Michael rested his strong hand on Seth's shoulder. "They pushed their fear away with their faith. Now they will be stronger for the next attack. Courage comes with faith and knowing the true character of Almighty God. But the Israelites had to *use* the courage God was working into their hearts and stand before their enemy, believing God's promise. They will never forget his mercy and power. They will always remember the miraculous victory he gave to them today."

"That must mean they're going to have to face this kind of assault again." Seth put his hands on his hips. *Courage comes with believing God is who he says he is and will do what he says he will do! I will need to remember this, no matter what I must face. I know the Almighty will hear my prayer for help.*

Michael sat on a boulder next to Seth, "Well, I have good news for you, my young friend. The word is going to spread to the surrounding towns and kingdoms about God's victory and his favor for Judah and for Jehoshaphat. Those kingdoms will hear how the Almighty descended on Judah's enemies today. They will be afraid of Judah's great God and humble themselves before the kingdom of Judah. Jehoshaphat will reign over Judah for many more years, and his strong faith will help him to choose God's directions and ways."

Michael tapped the handle of his sword. "We will not need to fight again for Jehoshaphat like we did today, because as long as Jehoshaphat reigns in Judah, peace will reign in the kingdom."

Seth jumped up and pointed his finger at Michael. "You've already been in his future, haven't you? You know he will choose wisely from now on. I'll bet his people will even listen to him and try to follow God's ways."

"With God, time is different." Michael looked at Seth. "Mankind doesn't experience time the same way he does. With God, there is no beginning or end. Yes, he set the earth in motion with start times and a stop time. But he reigns above it all: men and animals made with flesh and blood, rulers and powers and authorities in this dark world, spiritual forces of evil that roam in the heavenly realms with his own angels, everyone and everything. He can see from the beginning to the end of time, Seth, and he has given you this amazing privilege and allowed you to learn from the times and lives of others. You have seen that the choices made in life come with blessings or consequences."

"I'm not sure I understand why God has allowed me to do this," Seth said.

Michael smiled, but his expression was still sober. "The results of your choices will not affect only you. Your small decisions today will set up larger decisions in your future, and together they will influence the future of your descendants—even Jehoshaphat." A large smile stretched across Michael's face. "Now, *you* must work out what Almighty God has worked into you during your travels. Take up the courage he is planting inside you."

Seth ran his hand through his hair and looked at the ground. *If God reigns above everyone and everything, then he also reigns above the brothers of Nod. I wonder if they're listening to the lies of Satan's demons. Hmm. I wonder if I'm listening to the lies of demons when I fall into fear because of the brothers? But their threats are so real!*

A muscle tightened in Seth's jaw as he thought back to a night not long ago, after one of Cain's grandsons had taunted him and threatened to burn Seth's home down in the night and kill his whole family. Adam had tried to talk to the young man, to tell him that if he did what was right, what God expected from him, God would help him overcome their hard circumstances and have a better life. But Cain and all his descendants were angry and blamed God for their troubles. They said they could live without God's blessings. *Hmm!* Seth thought. *That's what Ahab thought too, and look at how his life ended up and all the people he hurt!*

Seth had lain awake in bed the night after Cain's grandson had made his threats. He had let his thoughts go wild, and he'd even devised a plan to stop their hostility once and for all. He would poison their well!

Seth shook his head and grimaced at the thought. He realized he had been thinking just like Cain. *What would Father think if he knew my angry thoughts about Cain and his family? Sometimes it is so hard not to hate them! But Father forgives them and prays they will return to God's ways.*

Seth bowed his head, and tears filled his eyes. He wanted so much to follow God faithfully, like Jehoshaphat, and believe and trust in his promises. But it seemed like his own heart was full of anger too, just like Cain's.

Help me, God, to think about what is right and good and true. Help me to guard my heart and mind and remember what I know about you and your promises for me. Help me to trust you and your ways more than my feelings. Seth blinked when he felt Michael staring at him.

"Seth, God has a plan and purpose for your life, just as he does for all of his children. Everyone will have choices to make, just as these kings and prophets have had to make choices. We talked about this before. Your family and others you know will be affected by your choices, not just yourself. One way or another, even the lives of your future descendants will be impacted by the choices you make every day."

"I'm just one person," Seth said. "Do I really matter so much?"

"Think about it, Seth," Michael answered. "You can't throw a rock into the pond and not expect it to make ripples in the water all the way to the edge of the shore. In the same way, your life will affect those around you and even many you will never meet, and often those choices reach far into eternity."

Seth sat back down. He lowered his head and closed his eyes. "I don't always do what I should. Sometimes it's just easier to do what everyone else is doing and be quiet about it."

Michael chuckled. "King Solomon once said, 'The wise man will see danger coming his way and seek safety, but a fool keeps going and suffers. His bad choice can kill him and his complacency can destroy him.' You are correct: It is not always easy to make a wise choice. Sometimes it is easier to go along with others. I have seen many men get lazy in their hearts and fall into trouble because they would not choose to take the right path."

Michael gazed into the sky, then looked back at Seth and continued, "When you decide to choose God's ways, the light of his wisdom shows you which way to go, and your conscience is free from guilt and accusations."

"Is that why I always feel better after I tell someone what I've done?"

"Of course. But it is more than just recognizing your bad behavior and thoughts. When you tell them to yourself and to God, he can forgive you and heal you. Just like a spider bite can make you sick, keeping your offenses and sins inside will poison your whole life and eat away at your happiness."

Michael reached out and gripped Seth's shoulders. "After all, Seth, it is yourself you hurt the most when you turn away from God. He is the best friend and counselor you will ever have. Don't run from him. Be courageous, and ask Almighty God to forgive you when you know you have made mistakes. His miraculous power will rescue your life from shame, just as he rescued Judah from destruction and death today."

CHAPTER 19
Battle of the Mind

As Michael and Seth finished talking, clouds began to swirl and scatter around them. The stars moved closer and sparkled like icy crystals. "We must leave now, Seth. The Almighty is sending us back in time, to the northern kingdom of Israel. You have seen God give his people victory in impossible situations: battles were fought to protect the Israelites of Judah and the northern kingdom from their enemies. These victories showed them God's power and strengthened their belief in God's love for them. Now we are going to see one of the most difficult battles of all, and it is *not* fought on earthly soil, but in the mind of man. It happens to every man, in every generation. It will happen to you."

Michael wrapped his strong arm around Seth's shoulders and spread his wings for flight. His swift and nimble movement through time and space shattered approaching beams of light and scattered prisms of color into the atmosphere around them.

Seth's heart jumped when he saw the familiar terrain around Mount Carmel in the distance. Before he could blink, they came to a standstill in a rocky desert. When Michael released his grip and stepped away, Seth looked around and saw nothing but sagebrush and dusty whirlwinds. Out of the corner of his eye, he noticed a figure sitting under a broom tree, mumbling. They walked closer until Michael motioned him to stop.

"Just take my life, Lord. I can't take any more from this woman, Jezebel!" cried the shaggy man in a ragged cloak, tied with a long leather belt. "She has soldiers searching for me to kill me. I am no better than a frightened bird or wounded rodent running for my

life! Her threats overwhelm me. I have nothing to live for now."
The man laid his head on the ground, drew his knees to his chest,
and closed his eyes.

Seth looked closely at the figure and gasped, "That looks like
Elijah! What has happened? Is he dying, Michael?"

"No, but he has lost his love for life and thinks that perhaps
God has forgotten him. His fear of Jezebel is greater than his faith
in Almighty God. Look at him. He is giving up on himself."

Michael and Seth walked toward Elijah. "I have been here with
Elijah before, Seth. This is a crucial time for him. A powerful battle is raging in Elijah's mind. He must decide one more time
whether to believe that God is who he says he is or to let his feelings and circumstances shade the truth about God. He will either
accept that what God says is true and live on with courage, or he
will believe the lies swirling around his head. If he gives up and
believes the lies, he will become just another notch on Jezebel's
scepter."

Elijah opened his eyes and struggled to sit. He pushed one
hand into the dirt and rested against the tree trunk.

Michael grabbed the hilt of his sword, but he did not pull it
from its sheath. He moved away from Seth and Elijah and stared
at the muddled gray cloud moving toward the bedraggled prophet.
Gaudy, gnarled hands, like talons, stretched and withdrew from
the haunting blur of the creeping fog. Distorted figures with hollow, protruding eyes jutted through the misty cloud and hovered
overhead.

Seth threw his hands to his head and plugged his ears, trying
to quiet the squeals from the cloud. The screeching sounds grew
louder, and he ducked when the eerie shapes flew overhead and
surrounded Elijah. Seth watched some of the demons attach themselves to Elijah's head and beard. Others landed on his clothing.

"Michael, help him!" Seth shouted.

Michael stood by, shaking his head. "Almighty God has not

released us to defend Elijah at this time. He must face his fears and stand against these demons with the truths he has stored in his heart. When God commands the battle, we will rush to save Elijah from these nagging demons. Satan has sent his lying spirits to confuse his thoughts and to convince him to give up on the strong right hand of the Almighty. Elijah has been one of the Lord's strongest voices in Israel. He has told the people how they have betrayed their God and honored the idols of Baal. Satan wants to devour Elijah and stop him from speaking to the people forever."

Elijah shivered, rested his tangled, hairy head on one hand, and swatted the air around his face with the other. "What good came from the miracle on Mount Carmel?" he cried out. "It didn't take long for those scandalous Israelites to reject you and return to the idols of Jezebel. She has killed all the prophets, and I am probably the only one left." He moaned, putting his face in his hands. "Now she's going to kill me too."

Elijah rolled over and clutched the soil at the base of the tree. He filled his hands with the rocky dirt and threw handfuls of dust in the air. Before long, his face and eyelids were coated in dust. "Agh!"

Exhausted, he fell to one elbow and went to sleep. The demon spirits withdrew and hovered in a pack a short distance away, yet kept their eyes on Elijah.

Seth reached for Michael when an angelic figure appeared beside Elijah. The angel's curly auburn hair rolled off his shoulders when he stooped to touch the old prophet. "Wake up and eat this warm bread, and drink the water in the jar here beside you. You are exhausted from the spiritual battle on Mount Carmel, and even though Almighty God gave you the victory, Satan has convinced you that Jezebel will see you dead."

Elijah sat up, speechless, and stared at the angel. The angel looked directly at Elijah and continued, "Who are you listening to? You say this woman wants you dead. But what has God said?

Only what *he* declares is true. You know the voice of Almighty God. Did he tell you that Jezebel would kill you?"

The angel lifted Elijah's face in his hands as the prophet remained speechless. "No! You are listening to your own fear and the lies of demons. Truth about God never changes, just as God never changes. Now, eat, drink, and sleep. When you are rested, be on your way. The Lord has much for you to do. Start walking south. In forty days and nights you will come to Horeb, the mountain of God, at Sinai. Wait there for the Lord."

As quickly as the angel appeared, he was gone, leaving food and water for Elijah's recovery.

A quick smile flashed on Michael's face, and his eyes sparkled. "God will never leave his children, and he is not finished with Elijah. Even though Elijah does not feel good about his life now, he will take hold of what is true about God and be strengthened. He will work out the faith God has worked in him. For the time being, Elijah has given false power to Jezebel and feels intimidated by what she has threatened. He has agreed with the enemy of God! Now he is worried and afraid of the harm she may cause him. There is a mighty battle going on for Elijah's heart and mind, and for now, he has handed a temporary victory to Satan because he fears Jezebel more than he trusts God. But he will gain strength and courage when he remembers that Almighty God truly reigns over the universe and over Jezebel. Elijah must fight his fear and determine to believe that God is on his side. Then he will have courage to stand against Jezebel's decrees."

Seth wrinkled his forehead. "I don't understand. How could Elijah doubt the power of God to protect him from Jezebel? Surely he can't forget how God kept him safe from King Ahab all these years!"

"It is never easy to stand up for God when you think you are alone. And it is true, Seth, you will not win every battle in life. People fall and stumble when they make quick and careless choices, just as you have done at times. And you have had greater temptations and sins, haven't you?"

Michael's eyes seemed to look into Seth's heart. He averted his own gaze, thinking of the night when he had wished to poison his enemy. Yes, he had done much worse than be irresponsible or foolish. He had hated another human being and allowed himself to think the unthinkable.

Michael continued, "In the heat of action, it is hard to remember that God will fight to do something great *in you,* not something easy that you can do yourself. But remember, you can always start over with God. Just recognize your mistakes and decide to walk with him again. His goodness is new every morning."

Seth scuffed his foot in the dry dirt. "But it's hard. Especially when I'm with someone who doesn't care about God. Some people seem so comfortable with their lives, and they appear stronger than I am and maybe even smarter. My younger brother Joshah tries to follow the ways of God, but he makes it sound okay to sometimes ignore God too. I know I shouldn't listen to his reasoning, but I do anyway. He makes it so easy to go along with him and do what he says. And besides, I don't like being alone. I want others to like me and to think I'm smart and strong like them. Sometimes, I just want to be a hero for my own brothers. Is that so bad?"

Seth's mind flooded with memories of the day he and one of his little brothers were chasing a runaway goat. His father had told him to leash the goat and take it to his cousin, Gera, who lived near Nod. He had wanted to go around the meadow so he wouldn't run into the boys from Nod, who often stripped the fruit from the trees there. But instead, he had listened to his brother's complaints about how long it would take to walk around the meadow. Besides, his brother had wanted to stop for pomegranates in the meadow. *He looked up to me and thought I was invincible. How could I disappoint him?*

As the memories flooded over him, Seth felt the chilling fear of that day return and rush through his body like a cold plunge into his favorite pond. *I couldn't hold the crazy goat back when the snake hissed and lunged at us. The animal kicked and ran ahead until he tore away from my leash. I ran after him, but when I tripped on the root, I couldn't catch up. What was I supposed to do, follow it all the way to Nod? And besides, what would have happened to my brother? If I'd kept running after the goat, he wouldn't have been able keep up with me.*

Seth stared into the desert and scratched his forehead. *But the truth is, I was afraid. I didn't want to run into the ruffians from Nod. And I was right to think that, too.* Some of the brothers of Nod were gathering firewood in the meadow and caught the runaway goat. One of them picked it up and dared Seth to come and take it from him. The others called Seth a sneaky, little lizard. He tried to convince them to give him the animal, but they just laughed and told him that the goat was their property now. His little brother ran back to get help from their father.

Seth shook his head at the memory. *I must have felt like Elijah does today. I was alone and afraid they would hurt me if I tried to take it back. It was easier to just let them have the goat. Why didn't I listen to the little voice that nudged me to go around that meadow in the first place? I felt like such a coward. I was even afraid to face my father when I got home.*

Adam had been angry at first, but he reminded Seth that God had been there and would have helped him. Why hadn't he asked for help? Seth's father had even tried to show him how to stand tall when facing a foe and trust God to help him. He had told him to have courage and speak with authority. *Ha! A lot of good that talk did. They are too strong, and I'm not very brave. Ah, but God is strong and brave, and I've seen that he is always ready to help me. I pray I'll remember that when I have to face the brothers next time.*

Seth glanced back at the lonely prophet. *Maybe Elijah will decide to trust in God's strength again. He certainly can't face Jezebel's soldiers on his own.*

Looking at Michael, Seth tugged on his sleeve. "What will happen to Elijah? Will he get his courage back and go to the mountain as the angel told him?"

"Yes," replied Michael. "Sometimes God's followers can feel alone, but they never are, Seth. Elijah is going to feel alone when he goes to the top of Mount Horeb, but Almighty God will be with him. He won't make his appearance in a big windy storm or a powerful earthquake. No, he will speak to Elijah in a gentle whisper to remind him of his truths. As long as Elijah chooses to walk with God, he will never be alone."

Michael tipped his head toward Elijah. "Almighty God continued to speak through Elijah to King Ahab and Jezebel, the two people Elijah feared the most. The old prophet may look like he has lost the battle, but soon he will remember what is true and right and honorable, and he will be strengthened for the days ahead. He will learn to ignore the insults and bullying of others. It is important to remember that what God says about you is true, not what others say about you. I have seen men forget this many times and lose hope. The enemy will use his lies as a weapon against you if you let him. But take heart, God has overcome the enemy and will always be there to remind you of his truth and give you strength. Just be sure to listen and respond."

Michael turned to walk away from Elijah. "Come on, Seth. Elijah will win the battle today and continue to speak the truths of God, no matter what bitter circumstances come his way. But for now, we are going to watch the events at the end of the war for Elijah's life. Come, God wants you to see Elijah's most exciting day, even more exciting than the day of God's powerful miracle of fire on Mount Carmel!"

Seth stepped toward Michael and took his hand, and in a blink of his eye, the scene changed.

CHAPTER 20
A Prophet's Reward

"Yes, Lord, I hear you," whispered Elijah. "I am ready to leave the young man, Elisha, to do your work when I am gone. He is full of energy and wants nothing more than to be your voice to the people. After announcing a new king to replace Ahab's evil son, as you told me to do after you came to me on Mount Horeb, I called Elisha to follow me as your prophet. He has always been eager to take on the job."

Elijah chuckled. "He thinks he's my son and follows me everywhere. I can hardly be alone. I'm glad I'm finally coming home to you, Lord. Elisha is ready to carry on."

"Everything is arranged for our departure, Elijah," interrupted the younger prophet, Elisha. "The animals are packed with food from the women of the city." He laughed. "Can't you smell it? But we should go quickly—the young prophets in Bethel are waiting for you to come to their school. They expect more of your stories about Almighty God, and they want to be with you as long as possible."

Elijah rose from his knees and looked at the animals. He walked over to the mule and rubbed its mane, lifted the animal's head with his hands and stared into its eyes. Then he turned toward Elisha. "You are not coming with me this time. I'm not yet too old to go from Bethel to Jericho. I will do this alone."

"Oh, no, my lord! It is a dangerous journey into Jericho," Elisha exclaimed, reaching for Elijah. "As I stand before God today, I will not let you go by yourself." He whispered into Elijah's ear. "Besides, like you, I and the other prophets have heard that God is going to take you from us today. I won't leave you alone. Please let me stay with you until the Almighty takes you to himself."

Smiling and shaking his head, Elijah threw up his arms. "Yes, yes, you may come along for a while." He cocked an eyebrow at the heavens as if to say, *You see?*

Elijah and Elisha walked without a word through the city of Bethel and on toward Jericho. Elijah kept his eyes on the road in front of him, not looking to the right or to the left. The city had been an important site for the people of Israel and Judah for centuries. For a time, the ark of God had been kept there. But now, the prophets saw it only as a center for idolatry and a house of wickedness.

Several of the younger prophets, who had studied the Scriptures with Elijah in Bethel, saw the two men of God pass by. "We must spread the word quickly. Elijah is on his way to Jericho and will not stop at the school." Before long, a small group of young prophets gathered. One of them said, "We should not disturb them with our questions. Let's stay quiet and follow at a distance behind them. Perhaps he will invite us to join them later."

As they continued the journey, other prophets joined the group. By the time their caravan reached the Jordan River, there were fifty young prophets of God traveling behind Elijah and Elisha.

"The river is too deep for us to cross." Elijah turned to Elisha and said, "Wait here. Please!" Elijah took off his cloak and rolled it on the ground into a long rope of leather. He gathered one end in his hand and swung it over his head before sharply striking the water of the Jordan with the other end.

Elisha's eyes opened wide. "Look! The river has stopped moving!" As they watched, openmouthed, the water of the Jordan began to divide, just as it had done for Moses when he led the people out of Egypt. The water from upstream stood very still, ending right in front of them as if an invisible hand were holding it back. Even the ground under the river was dry.

"It's a miracle of God, Elijah!" Elisha exclaimed. Elijah smiled, nodded, and stepped into the riverbed, crossing ahead of Elisha, who pulled the mule up the rocky bank to the other side. Once they reached level ground and caught their breaths, Elijah and Elisha turned to see the water pound and splash down between the riverbanks. It rolled over and over, forcing its way downstream. On the other side, the young prophets stopped abruptly to watch in amazement as the river settled into its banks.

After Elijah and Elisha had gone a few more steps from the riverbank, Elijah reached down and picked up a smooth stone. He rubbed it clean with his cloak, then headed toward a nearby mound of rocks and placed the stone on the pile. He held up his staff and closed his eyes. "Thank you, Lord. Thank you for everything."

He turned to see Elisha place his own stone of remembrance on the crude monument.

"I'll never forget this," Elisha said as he stepped back.

Elijah smiled and put his hand on Elisha's shoulder. "You know the Lord is going to take me away soon." Elijah paused. "What can I do for you before I am gone?"

Elisha blurted, "Please give me two portions of your prophetic power." He blushed at his own boldness, but kept going. "You have stayed on the course the Almighty laid out for you. You kept on going, proclaiming his truths, and endured hardships and even persecution. It is as if you could see God before you, and you followed him without swaying from your goal. We both know God called me to come behind you, and I will face this rebellious people in your place. I, too, want to walk behind the Lord and not flinch when troubles block my path and come at me from all directions. How can I follow in your footsteps without your abilities?"

Elisha dropped to his knees and stared up at the senior prophet. "Please, give me a double portion of your God-given power."

A broad smile spread across Elijah's face. "Well, that's a difficult request for me to give. Of course, it will all be up to Almighty God, the Giver of all good things. But don't worry, if he has called you for his tasks, then he will provide all you need to do the work. He will accomplish his purpose in his time and through his strength and his power. But he will not take you farther than you are willing to go. If you refuse to listen and follow him, he will call another."

He paused, chuckling down at the sight of the younger man on his knees. "It is a good thing you are willing to go so far." Elijah squinted into the sun. "If you see me when the Lord takes me to himself, your request will be granted. Otherwise, it won't. It is the Lord's will, not ours. Let's walk together. Come by my side."

Seth and Michael walked behind the two men, listening to the older prophet advising the younger. "Let your love be sincere and honest. Devote yourself to God, and he will direct your life and strengthen you by his own Spirit and power."

Seth couldn't take his eyes off Elijah, who had stopped and again put his hand on Elisha's shoulder. Seth strained to hear Elijah's counsel.

"I know I've told you many times to hold on to what is good and despise what is evil. If you resist evil and trust God, evil will run from you." Elijah hesitated. "Also, never think too highly of yourself. Let others measure your accomplishments. What will last is what you do through the power of the Almighty, not your own strength."

Elisha nodded slowly and quietly repeated the wise words of his mentor. "Will I remember these things when you are gone?"

"Oh yes," laughed Elijah. "It's obvious you love the Lord with all your heart and soul and strength. Stay true to your decisions for him, and he will show you his ways and make your path straight before you."

Seth heard the words of Elijah as though they were speaking

straight to him. *Stay true to your decisions for him, and he will make your path straight before you*...even if that path led to confrontation with the brothers of Nod.

Michael nudged Seth and pointed to the scarlet horizon. Seth looked, puzzled. They stood peering into the sky, when suddenly a huge, whirling fireball swooped down from the heavens. Inside the fiery swirl of smoke was a blazing chariot surrounded by fire and drawn by two flaming horses.

Seth could just barely make out the details of the spellbinding sight. Golden wheels whirred with shooting flames that danced behind the speeding chariot. Blinding lights reflected off the glassy skin of the horses as their fiery hooves stoked the jumping flames beneath them.

Seth couldn't believe what his eyes saw next. The chariot and horses swooped down between the two prophets and pulled Elijah into the center of the whirlwind. The old prophet was whisked out of sight and into the heavens.

Nothing moved, except the fading smoke trail in the sky.

Elisha saw it all, and he shouted after Elijah, "My father! My father! Chariot of God!" He crumbled to his knees and ripped his gown open from his neck to his waist. Seeing Elijah's cloak, he scooped it up and clutched it to his chest. "My father," he cried.

Seth stood speechless.

The afternoon sun hid the brilliance of its face behind the distant cypress trees as Seth and Michael walked into the pale pink horizon. "You are quiet, Seth. Has this last view into the future disturbed you?"

Seth shook his head slowly. "I keep thinking about the awesome picture of the chariot of fire and the blazing horses, and how Elijah was snatched up into the heavens. Will he come back? Will anyone ever see him again? Why didn't he die like others do, and why did God let me see all of this?"

"You may never have answers to all your questions, but you will remember that true power belongs to God Almighty. His word created the heavens and the earth, and with his hands he fashioned your father and formed your mother. All authority is his in heaven and on earth. There is nothing he cannot do when he wants to reward his servants. Elijah was his faithful prophet. You have seen how he followed the Lord. God Almighty could depend on him, so he strengthened him with bold courage to declare his truth."

Michael pointed toward the sunset, the direction in which the chariot had disappeared. "Elijah has gone to live forever with the God who designed him. The Almighty had a plan for Elijah, and Elijah lived his life to fulfill God's plan. Now that he has completed the work, he will receive his full inheritance from God."

Michael spread his wings and stared down into Seth's eyes. "Remember what you have seen today. It is only a shadow of what the Almighty will do much later. A greater event will occur in future times when God's divine plan to rescue mankind from evil will cause him to pay the greatest price of all. He has told his angels, 'At the right time, he will send one to earth who is greater than Elijah and all the prophets, one greater than all the kings of earth. He will be called the Prince of Peace, Lord of Lords, and King of Kings. He will reign on the throne of David, and he will deliver the children of God to his eternal kingdom.'"

Michael smiled. "It will be even more amazing than how he gathered Elijah to himself today. But, like Elijah, he will gather the people of God in his time, and they will receive their reward and live with God forever in his eternal kingdom."

Seth picked up a tall stick in their path and dragged it through the dirt behind him. Elijah had done so many incredible things and served God with so much boldness and devotion. He doubted he could ever live up to the prophet's example. "Do we have to be like Elijah before we can be taken into heaven?"

Michael laughed. "Ha! That is impossible. No. And you do not have to be like Jehoshaphat either, or anyone else, for that matter. The Prince of Peace will pay the price for your freedom. Just trust him to do it. God has promised that those who look for him will find him. When you trust his promise and turn to him, you will want to do what is right and good, just like Elijah did."

With a last fond look at his young charge, Michael said, "It is time for you to return to your home and family, Seth. Hold all these memories in your heart. Remember and believe what he says is truth. Then, take courage, and live the life the Almighty God has prepared for you. Choose to endure whatever comes your way. Stand with courage against the enemy's tactics. And always remember, Almighty God will never leave your side."

CHAPTER 21

heart of Valor

et up! What are you doing? We have to get this seed in the ground before the day is over."

Seth opened his eyes and looked into the face of his sister. She frowned down at him. Seed spilled from her bag and sprinkled his face. He sat up and brushed the precious nuggets from his cloak.

"Why are you napping?" Rizpah pulled on his sleeve. "Father expects us home soon, and you haven't even finished tilling the field. Are you feeling sick?"

"I don't know. I guess the sunshine made me drowsy." Seth grabbed the walking stick lying on the ground beside him, stuck it in the dirt, and stood up. "Go ahead and seed the furrowed rows. I'll finish this side of the field and help you." He glanced at the midday sun. "We can still get it done before dark." Taking a long drink from the water bag strapped across his body, he headed for the plow. His head was spinning with memories of what he had just experienced.

"Look!" Rizpah jabbed him in the ribs and pointed ahead. "Who is that?"

Seth glanced over his shoulder. A man was stumbling through the clearing near Nod. He staggered several times and fell at the edge of their field. Seth dropped his plow and ran toward the stranger. Rizpah followed quickly.

The man wore torn and dirty clothing. His face was flushed and bruised, and blood oozed from a gash under his right eye. Seth reached the battered man and kneeled beside his wounded body.

He helped him sit up. Seth offered the man his water bag. The stranger's hands shook as he took the bag from Seth and gulped until the liquid flowed down his chin and beard.

The stranger bent over and held his sides. "Thanks. I think they broke my ribs."

Seth had a sickening feeling in the pit of his stomach. "Who did this? What happened?"

In his haste to help the man, Seth hadn't considered the possible danger the stranger could cause. *You don't look like the men of Nod. Are you one of Cain's offspring who followed the river to the southern forests? If so, Father has met your family before and traded skins and tools, amiably.*

The man choked and spit blood on the ground. "I'm not sure which ones they were. I was passing through Nod, trading some leather goods for food. Everything was fine for a while, but that's always been a rough bunch. I decided to move on through the area when four ruffians stopped me by the river. They said I had to pay them for the right to cross their land. I made the mistake of calling them 'young twerps' and tried to push past them. They surrounded me and pushed me around, from one to the others. I dropped my bag of supplies and tools and tore into them. I didn't want to hurt them, but they'd asked for it. I fought with the biggest of the bunch first, but when I had him pinned on the ground, the others started beating me with rocks and heavy tree branches. I passed out, and when I came to my senses, they were gone and so were my goods and tools." He struggled to his feet and grabbed his side. "Agh!"

"Come with us. We'll take you home, and you can rest." Seth took the man's arm to help him up.

"No," he winced. "I've got to go back and get my tools. I can't do my business without them. Besides, those boys have to learn a lesson."

"You may be right, but first you have to be in one piece!" Seth chuckled. He stepped beside the stranger, put his arm under his shoulder, and offered him the walking stick. "Come on, lean on me. It's not far. You are welcome in Adam's home. He is always hospitable to those who respect his name. My mother will clean your wounds and feed you a good dinner." The man put his arm over Seth's shoulder and nodded in agreement.

Seth lowered his voice. "Rizpah, hurry home and tell them we are coming. Father will want you to gather food for a good dinner, and Mother can prepare the herbs and medicines for the man's wounds."

The next morning, Seth woke to the sweet aroma of fresh bread. The air was cool and dry. He opened his eyes and watched his father stoke the wood fire pit before sitting down with his cup of warm broth.

Seth stretched his back and rolled to his knees. His movement brought Storm to his side, tail wagging, nosing Seth for a rubdown. Seth smiled, rubbed his own eyes first, then massaged the dog's ears and nuzzled nose to nose with the lovable creature.

"Hey boy, let's go get some breakfast and see how our visitor is today."

They walked over to the morning fire, where Seth's little brothers were huddled near Adam with a pile of thin sticks. They were taking turns at tossing them into the dancing fire. His mother was offering a bowl of bread and soft eggs to the stranger who called himself Elidad.

Elidad scooped the warm food into his mouth with his hands and chewed with caution. The cuts and bruises around his mouth were still raw, but not bleeding. His head was wrapped and bandaged with a clean cloth.

Seth took a deep breath and smelled the fresh camphor his

mother had used to medicate the man's gashed forehead and cheek. He smiled at the stranger. "You look better. How do you feel today?"

Elidad furrowed his brow and shook his head. "Not so good," he groaned. "But I've got to go back and find my tools."

"You'll have plenty of time for that once you recover," Seth said. "I'll walk back over the trail you made through the clearing and mark the route for you so you can retrace your steps."

"Thank you. That should help me." Elidad nodded and reached for a cup of steaming goat's milk.

Seth helped himself to a bowl of hot porridge and bread. When he finished, he put the wooden bowl into the tub that Rizpah would use to wash the utensils. He stretched and picked up more wood for the fire. Seth nudged one of his brothers, interrupting their game. "Come on, let's get our chores done. We need to bring more logs and kindling for Mother. Her supply is running low."

The smaller boys groaned but followed him to the wooded area beside their home. "Who can gather the biggest armful of sticks?" Seth dashed ahead of them and looked over his shoulder. They squealed, "I will, I will!" and scattered through the small grove of trees, grabbing up twigs as fast as they could. Before long, their arms were piled high with limbs and sticks. They laughed and teased each other, struggling to see over their piles to follow Seth home.

Back at the storage area, they dropped their bounty and restacked the piles by size. "Good job." Seth brushed his hands together. "Now, go see what Mother has for you to do."

He retrieved his walking stick and headed to the field to finish his furrowing. After being certain he had completed his task, he headed into the clearing to mark Elidad's path. Reaching the other side, he made his way through the sparse forest and looked down into the narrow, deep valley below. A slow-moving river cut through the jungle of plants and trees. His heart jumped when he realized that Nod lay on the other side of the river. *I can do this. I'll just mark the path for Elidad. The ground is moist, and it will be easy to track his route from Nod. It won't take long, and I want to help him. If I don't mark the path today, he won't be able to retrace his steps.*

Seth took a deep breath and slowly let it out. *Besides, Michael has shown me that when I face an enemy, I don't have to depend on my own strength. God is with me.*

Seth watched the billowing clouds sprinkled across the blue heavens, wishing he could see angels in their midst. Then, looking again at the valley below, he tied a piece of cloth to a tree branch and started down the hillside.

Twigs crackled and snapped under his feet, and birds fluttered overhead. He walked for several miles, following Elidad's footprints and marking the trees and shrubs with cloth. Finally, Seth stopped and leaned against a tree trunk, pulling a piece of bread from his bag. But before he could take a bite, he froze at the sound of a deep growl ahead of him. He put the bread back in his bag and gripped his stick with both hands, stepping slowly away from the tree.

Before his eyes, he saw a wolf stalking a young boy who whimpered behind a bush. Fear gripped Seth's body. *I've got to do something! God, help me save this boy.* He took several steps to come between the boy and the growling wolf. Then, with a deep voice, he yelled as loud as he could, "Ahhh!" Seth raised the walking stick over his head, stood tall, and swayed back and forth. The wolf showed his teeth and snarled at his challenger.

Seth took a small step forward and again filled his lungs with air. Exhaling, he yelled again, "Yah!"

The wolf stopped in his tracks and stared at Seth. Then the beast let out a short whimper and started to back away. Seth's heart pounded in his chest until the wolf turned and disappeared into the trees. When he was comfortable that they were both safe, he scrambled to the crying boy crouched behind the bush. He reached out and pulled him close. "You're fine. The wolf is gone. The danger is over."

The boy sobbed and shook. Seth took his hand and led him to a fallen tree to sit down. The boy wiped his eyes with his cloak and took the water pouch Seth offered. He sniffled a few times and then took a quick drink.

Seth noticed that the boy clutched a sharp, angular stone knife wrapped with new leather at the handle. "Are you alone? Why are you so far from your home?"

The boy's voice shook as he answered. "I went to throw rocks in the river, and saw the tree had fallen from bank to bank. I knew I could climb over it and cross to this side. I wanted to explore the places my brothers have seen." He sniffed and wiped his nose. "I've never been here before, and I thought I could find some berries or even pomegranates. But I got confused and lost." He looked around a moment and continued, "I couldn't remember the way back to the tree that crosses the river."

Seth felt his stomach plunge to his knees. *This boy is from Nod,* he surmised. *I have to take him back to his family. They must be looking for him already.* Seth bit his bottom lip. *Maybe we won't run into his brothers. Even if we do, I have to take him home. God be with us!*

He had pictured his next meeting with the brothers of Nod many times—but he'd never thought he would be the one to seek *them* out!

"Let's go down to the riverbank and see if we can find your fallen tree," he said. Seth pulled the boy up and looked around. He noticed larger footprints ahead of them, so he tied off another branch, and they followed the prints to the river.

The boy brushed the twigs from his legs and looked up and down the stream. "I don't see the tree."

"I don't either, but we can cross over these large stones. Take my hand and follow me." Seth put his foot on the first rock with caution. Once he determined they wouldn't slip, he reached out to the young boy, who grabbed on with both hands. They wobbled and swayed from rock to rock until they reached the muddy shore on the other side of the river. Seth pulled the boy to the top of the bank and smiled. "We made it, and you're still somewhat dry! Now, let's go find your home."

Seth stopped long enough to tie one of his last leather strips to a tree branch as the boy searched for familiar ground. Seth joined him. *There must be clues that Elidad was here,* he thought. *What looks different or disturbed?* In the distance, he spotted a lone sandal. "This way," he shouted to the boy. When they reached it, he broke a tree branch and left it hanging as a marker, and then he picked up the sandal. "Does this belong to you or your family?"

"No, we use a whole piece of leather, not just straps and soles," replied the boy.

Seth tucked the sandal into his belt and kept walking toward the clearing, occasionally glancing over his shoulder to see that the boy was still behind him. When they reached a small clearing, the boy ran ahead of Seth and pulled himself onto a low branch of a sycamore tree.

"I see our field. Look! There's my brother," cried the boy.

Seth walked ahead and saw the boy's brother standing near an open fire. He was husky, and his tunic barely reached his knees. Beside him were three or four more figures lounging around the smoldering pit. At first he didn't recognize them, but then one of the boys turned in his direction. Seth felt his head spin. His fist tightened around the walking stick and steadied himself. It was them! The brothers of Nod!

He glanced over both shoulders, and blood-freezing fear gripped his chest. These were the brothers who bragged about their strength, who worshiped images made from stone and followed in Cain's violent footsteps. They had teased and tormented Seth's sister and even threatened to kill his family if they got in their way. Seth filled his lungs with air and fought back his fear. *But are they really so strong? What did Michael say? He said, "The truth is what God says about us, not what man says about us. God has promised he will not leave us or abandon us to face the enemy alone."*

Seth felt himself take a step forward as he collected his thoughts. *I'm not going into their territory in just my own strength. I'm going in with the power of God at my side. Elijah faced a king and queen who tried to kill him, and Jehoshaphat faced the vast armies of Syria and the hordes across the great sea. He knew God was at his side. Surely I can face these few bullies with God at my side!*

The boy dropped from the tree and ran through the clearing toward his brothers. He stopped long enough to look back at Seth. "Come on!"

Seth caught up with him, and they raced toward the boy's home. Their panting and laughter alerted the brothers and brought them to their feet. Seth felt a burst of energy mixed with caution when they approached the young men around the fire pit. Two of the brothers stood up and swaggered toward them.

One more phrase came back to Seth's mind: *You fear the enemy too much when you fear God too little.*

Seth smiled down at his young friend and tussled his hair. "We got you home." The young boy grinned up at Seth and ran to his brothers.

The larger of the two brothers kept his eyes on Seth and shoved the boy behind him. "About time you came home." He stretched his large body up and growled at Seth, "What are you doing here? You have no right to be on our land."

Seth waited for his heart to stop pounding and answered, "Your brother was in danger of being attacked by a wolf on the other side of the river. He was lost. I promised him I would help him find his way home."

The older brother turned and grabbed the boy by the arm. "Where did you go? You know you aren't to cross the river." Then he pushed the boy to the ground.

Seth's blood boiled, and he stepped forward to protect the boy. Out of the corner of his eye, near the fire, he saw the leather arti-

cles Elidad the merchant had described. There was the knife with
the carved leather handle and the tools he used for his trade, all
scattered near an opened leather pouch. Seth could feel his stomach lurch into his throat.

"What are you looking at? You came here to spy on us. Get off
our property." The brother raised his fists.

The others stood and moved toward Seth. One brother pulled
a flaming stick out of the fire pit. He waved it in Seth's face. "You
skinny little snake. You heard him, get out of here."

"No!" cried the boy, running toward Seth. "He's my friend!
Leave him alone."

One of the brothers stuck out his arm and held the boy back.
He struggled and tried to get loose, but his brother pushed him to
the ground again.

The leader of the group marched over to Seth and shoved his
shoulder. He looked back at his brothers and snickered. Then he
stared into Seth's eyes and warned, "You're not near Adam's village
anymore. There's no one to protect you here." He shoved Seth
backward.

Seth caught his balance. He heard the glee in the brother's
threat, but he didn't take his eyes off his adversary. "God, help me,"
he mumbled under his breath. Seth stiffened and stepped a foot
closer to the brother. "All I can say is what I know to be true. Your
young brother was in danger and is now safely home."

He pointed with his walking stick toward Elidad's tools. "And
those tools don't belong to you. You attacked a traveling merchant
and left him for dead. Those are his tools, and I'm taking them
back to him along with his merchandise. I'm not leaving without
them."

The three brothers circled around Seth, chuckling. One kicked
dirt at him. Another picked up a jagged rock and tossed it from one
hand to another, snickering and laughing. "Who do you think you
are? You're a little frog of a boy. There's no one here to help you.

You'd better run as fast as you can before we send you home bloody too."

Seth shivered. But he was determined to face his fear this time. *I will not run. I am going to take those tools back to Elidad. Even if they beat me up, I won't run, so help me God!*

He forced his lips to move and with a quiet voice said, "I am not alone." His face flushed. He spoke again, with a stronger voice. "I am not alone. God Almighty and his angels stand with me." His muscles tightened. He knew he needed to go through the brothers and take Elidad's tools. But he couldn't move. He stared at the biggest of the brothers and drew in a deep breath.

And then, suddenly, his attention was broken when a feather fluttered in front of them and rested on the foot of his enemy. His mind raced and filled with thoughts of Michael's great wings and his battles with the demons of Satan. *God, you have heard my prayer! You are here to help me.*

Gathering new strength, Seth stared again into the eyes of his opponents, one by one. Finally, he stepped between the brothers and marched straight to the pile of tools.

At first the brothers only stared at him. "Don't touch those tools, or I'll…I'll…." The leader forced a weak laugh. "I'll break your nose."

Seth narrowed his eyes and stared back at the brother. No one moved. He felt a breeze tickle the back of his neck and heard the flames of the fire crackle and hiss as it shot its jumping embers into the sky. He remembered Elijah and Mount Carmel. *You could send fire from heaven to save me, Lord.* His heart raced, but he stooped and gathered Elidad's tools along with his merchandise. He put the vests, aprons, and bowls into the leather bag along with the tools, and tied it with a cord.

Seth stood and one last time returned his enemies' stares, one by one. Then, without a word, he walked toward home. His heart and head danced with relief and great joy. He had stood against the brothers of Nod. But best of all, he knew that God Almighty had given him the courage he needed, a courage he had never known and a courage he would never forget.

The brothers watched him fade into the woods by the river. They shouted anxious, angry threats, but no one moved to follow him.

The mighty angel crossed his arms and relaxed his stance as he watched Seth walk across the clearing. "Well, Seth," he said, smiling, "you have done it! You are working out the courage God has worked in you. Good! Now he can show you even more."

Then Michael spread his wings and disappeared into the heavens.

These things I have spoken to you,
so that you would know that
in me
you may have peace.
In the world you will have trials.
But take courage. I have overcome the world.

JOHN 16:33, PARAPHRASED

Epilogue

Empty breakfast plates sat in front of the quiet children. Barking dogs and humming lawn mowers could be heard in the distance. Nana was the first to break the silence. She smiled at her grandchildren's attentive faces. "So, God's heroes don't always look like the ones we see in the movies. His heroes are real people who depend on *him* for miraculous provision and strength, and not on themselves. They became heroes when they listen for God's instructions and believe his promises."

Nana poured more juice into Kelly's empty glass. "Sometimes, as we heard in our story, it can be very hard to do the right thing—like disagree with a popular leader or a king! But true heroes know their futures rest with God, not man. So they choose to do what God tells them to do, even when they know it may not please the crowd. And God gives them the courage they need to do what he has asked."

Ryan broke the silence. "Yeah, King Ahab sure chose the wrong power to follow. Look where he ended up…in a downpour, soaking wet! I can't believe he was so stubborn and wouldn't listen to Elijah. And why didn't King Jehoshaphat pay attention to the prophet of God? Look at the mess he got himself and his troops into!"

John snickered. "Yeah, all he had to do was take the advice of the prophet and stay out of King Ahab's war. Things could've sure turned out differently."

"Especially for Ahab! So much for his disguise!" said Ryan.

Nana straightened her shoulders and spread her hands on the breakfast counter. "And do you know that the greatest hero of all time sits at the right hand of our awesome God? He is the King of

Kings and the Lord of Lords that Michael talked about. He chose to be a hero for us before we were even born. He wanted to correct what Adam and Eve had broken: our closeness to God. So he took their judgment for disobeying God, and he took the judgment for us, because we disobey God too. The cost was the highest of all costs. He gave his life, like the sacrificial lamb at the temple."

"He died on a cross outside of Jerusalem, the same Jerusalem that Jehoshaphat lived in and fought for," Grampa chimed in. "And after three days, he came back to life. Then, before long, he went up into heaven as our King of Kings."

Nana rested her back against the counter and opened her arms wide. "Now the gate to God is open forever, and we are free to follow his ways. He defeated Satan for us, and we can use the courage he gives us to stand strong when troubles come along."

Grampa pushed back his stool and began to pick up the dirty dishes. "Many other kings ruled on this earth before and after King Ahab and Jehoshaphat. But only one will ever be called the King of Kings and Lord of Lords." He paused and smiled at his grandchildren. "The next time you visit, we can read more about the other kings. Because God's story isn't finished yet."

Characters

Abraham
Father of the nation of Israel, father of Isaac and grandfather of Jacob

Adam
Seth's father, lived in garden of Eden, first father, father of Cain and Abel

Ahab
King of Israel, son of Omri, reigned twenty-two years (874–853 BC)

Ahaziah
King of Israel, son of Ahab, died young, reigned for two years (853–852)

Angel of the Lord
Most special messenger of God, God himself in physical human form

Baal
Mythical storm god of Queen Jezebel, brought to Israel from Sidon

Ben-Hadad
King of Syria (northeast of Israel), battled with Ahab and Jehoshaphat

Brothers of Nod
Troublemakers from Nod, descendants of Cain, threat to Seth's family

Deceiver
Chief demon warrior for Prince of Darkness

Demander
Demon warrior for Prince of Darkness

Elidad
Merchant, wounded by the brothers of Nod, helped by Seth and his family

Elijah
Prophet of God Almighty, hated by Jezebel, challenged Baal at Mt. Carmel

Elisha
Prophet of God Almighty, Elijah's protégé, asked for double blessing

Gabriel
Important messenger angel of God Almighty

Jehoshaphat
King of Judah, son of Asa, reigned twenty-five years (873–848 BC)

Jehu
Prophet of Almighty God, confronted Jehoshaphat, faithful

Jezebel   Queen of Israel, Ahab's wife, idolatrous, perse-
                      cuted prophets of God

Joshua   Led the Israelites after Moses, took Jericho by
                      marching around the walls

Joshah   Seth and Rizpah's brother, a natural leader

Micaiah   Prophet of God, prophesied victory for Israel
                      against Ben-Hadad

Michael   Archangel of God Almighty, protector of Israel,
                      Seth's protector-guide

Moza   King Jehoshaphat's chief adviser and friend,
                      faithful

Naboth   Owned the vineyard confiscated by King Ahab
                      and Queen Jezebel

Omar   Chief adviser and personal administrator of
                      King Ahab

Omri   Ahab's father, a strong king of Israel, reigned
                      twelve years (885–874 BC)

Prince of Darkness Satan, angel who fell from heaven and led
                      angelic rebellion (see "Satan")

Rizpah   Seth's younger sister, teased by the brothers of
                      Nod

Storm   Family dog of Seth and Rizpah

Satan   Number one spirit enemy of Almighty God,
                      devil, thief, liar, deceiver, murderer (see also
                      "Prince of Darkness")

Seth   Son of Adam and Eve, forefather of the nation
                      of Israel, lived nine hundred and twelve years

Zedekiah   Prophet of Baal, convinced King Ahab and
                      King Jehoshaphat to go to war

Thoughts to Explore

Think about three questions as you consider Seth's adventure:

1. What did a king or Seth *choose to do* in his situation?
2. What did God *do* or *say* about their choice?
3. What would *you* choose to do in a similar situation?

Scriptural Suggestions

CHAPTER 1:   *The Challenge of Faith*
          1 Kings 17:1, 18:1–15

THEME: "Yes, there is an enemy."
          Isaiah 44:6–8;
          Hebrews 13:5b;
          Psalm 10:16;
          Daniel 10:13

CHAPTER 2:   *The King's Choice*
          1 Kings 18:16–21

THEME: "Truth matters."
          Deuteronomy 28:1–2;
          Isaiah 46:11, 54:17;
          Ephesians 6:12

CHAPTER 3:   *The Cry for Courage*
          1 Kings 17:1–24;
          2 Chronicles 15:2–4

THEME: "Trust anyway."

Daniel 3:17;
Psalm 20:7;
Romans 8:28

Chapter 4:   *Crossroads of Chaos*
1Kings 18:20–29

Theme: "Take a stand."
Isaiah 7:9;
James 1:8;
Joshua 24:15;
Psalms 11:4–7, 18:9–17;
Ezekiel 1:25–28;
Isaiah 6:1–3;
Revelation 4:2;
1 Peter 5:8;
Numbers 11:23;
Psalms 37:4, 62:7;
Luke 1:37;
Matthew 6:24;
Galatians 6:7

Chapter 5:   *The Command From Heaven*
1 Kings 18:29–40

Theme: "No middle ground."
Revelation 2:28;
Luke 1:37;
Galatians 6:7

Chapter 6:   *The Cloud of Promise*
1 Kings 18:41–46

Theme: "God will not be mocked."

Matthew 6:24;
Isaiah 40:26–31

CHAPTER 7:   *Road to Revolution*
              Genesis 15:1–7, 17:3–4

THEME: "His plans will succeed."
              Romans 4:18–21;
              Hebrews 13:5b;
              Romans 5:8;
              1 Chronicles 16:9; 1 Peter 5:8

CHAPTER 8:   *A Boastful Breed*

THEME: "Be strong and courageous."
              Psalm 46:10;
              Joshua 1:9;
              Zephaniah 3:15;
              2 Chronicles 15:2–4, 16:9a

CHAPTER 9:   *Besieged*
              1 Kings 20:1–14

THEME: "There is a battle for your mind and heart"
              2 Chronicles 16:1–9;
              Psalms 23, 33:10–12;
              Proverbs 3:5

CHAPTER 10:   *Bedlam in the Barracks*
              1 Kings 20:15–28

THEME: "He wants no one to perish."
              1 Peter 3:9;
              John 3:15–16;

Psalms 1:6, 37:20;
Joshua 24:15;
Proverbs 22:8

CHAPTER 11:   *Ahab's Betrayal*
1 Kings 20:29–34

THEME: "Judging the heart."
Joshua 1:9, 5:13–6:20, 24:15;
Psalm 10:14;
Proverbs 14:15

CHAPTER 12:   *A United Banner*
1 Kings 22:1–28;
2 Chronicles 18:1–27

THEME: "Unequally yoked."
1 Kings 21:15–29;
Galatians 6:7

CHAPTER 13:   *The Last Bastion*
1 Kings 22:29–38;
2 Chronicles 18:28–34

THEME: "He keeps his word."
Proverbs 10:23;
Isaiah 5:20;
Hosea 7:16, 8:17;
Psalms 56:11, 34:15–16

CHAPTER 14:   *Buttress for Courage*
1 Kings 22:41–44, 51–53;
2 Chronicles 19:1–11, 22:1–4

THEME: "He is not finished with us yet."

1 Corinthians 6:14;
Psalms 37:4–5, 139:23–24

CHAPTER 15:   *A King's Folly*
2 Kings 1:1–18

THEME: "A fool says there is no God."
Psalms 28:7, 31:24;
Isaiah 40:31;
Proverbs 14:12;
2 Corinthians 16:9;
Isaiah 33:3;
Galatians 6:7;
Psalm 118:24

CHAPTER 16:   *The Testing*
2 Chronicles 20:1–13

THEME: "Consequences."
Psalms 18:1–19, 103:12, 139:1–4, 23–24;
Numbers 14:18;
James 1:6;
Ephesians 6:13–17

CHAPTER 17:   *The Petition*
2 Chronicles 20:5–13

THEME: "Put on the full armor of God"
1 Peter 3:18;
John 1:29;
Hebrews 9:15, 22–28;
Matthew 19:14

CHAPTER 18:   *The Power of Courage*
2 Chronicles 20:13–18

THEME: "Stand, then."
Ephesians 6:13–17;
Psalms 9:10, 10:14, 20:7;
Ephesians 3:20;
Revelation 19:6;
1 Timothy 6:15;
Isaiah 9:6;
Malachi 3:6;
Hebrews 7:21;
Philippians 2:12;
Proverbs 27:12;
1 John 1:9

CHAPTER 19:   *Battle of the Mind*
1 Kings 19:1–21;
2 Kings 2:1–18

THEME: "Agreeing with the enemy."
Joshua 1:5;
Philippians 4:8;
Psalm 37:24;
Isaiah 41:10;
Lamentations 3:22–23;
Mark 4:15

CHAPTER 20:   *A Prophet's Reward*
2 Kings 2:1–18

THEME: "All things are possible with God."
Deuteronomy 6:5;
Hebrews 13:21;

Job 11:13–15;
James 4:7;
Romans 12:3;
John 1:1;
1 Timothy 10:15;
Isaiah 53:4–10;
Hebrews 1:3;
Isaiah 41:10

Chapter 21:   *Heart of Valor*
Isaiah 41:10

Theme: "Stand firm in the day of evil."
Hebrews 13:5;
Ephesians 6:13–18;
1 Chronicles 5:20b;
2 Chronicles 16:9;
Psalms 28:7, 34:4–8;
Philippians 4:13;
Mark 11:22–25;
2 Corinthians 5:7

References

Anders, Max and Gary Inrig. *Holman Old Testament Commentary, I & II Kings.* Nashville: Broadman and Holman, 2003.

F. F. Bruce. *The International Bible Commentary.* Grand Rapids, MI: Zondervan, 1979.

Douglas, J. D. *New International Bible Dictionary.* Grand Rapids, MI: Zondervan, 1987.

Edersheim, Alfred. *The Bible History of the Old Testament, Vol. 5–7.* Grand Rapids, MI: Eerdmans, 1962.

Edersheim, Alfred. *The Temple Its Ministry and Services, Updated Edition.* Peabody, MA: Hendrickson Publishers, 1995.

Gutzke, Manford George. *Plain Talk about Christian Words.* Grand Rapids, MI: Zondervan, 1964.

Hodgkin, A.M. *Christ in All the Scriptures.* Westwood, NJ: Barbour and Company, 1989.

Holy Bible, Authorized King James Version. Nashville: Thomas Nelson, 1975.

Keller, Werner. *The Bible as History.* Revised Edition. New York: Bantam Books, 1982.

Lockyer, Herbert. *All the Men of the Bible.* Grand Rapids, MI: Zondervan, 1958.

Wiersbe, Warren W. *Bible Commentary Old Testament.* Nashville: Thomas Nelson, 1991.

Whiston, William, A.M. *The Works of Flavius Josephus, Volume III.* Grand Rapids, MI: Baker Book House, 1979.

Wright, Fred H. *Manners & Customs of Bible Lands.* Chicago: Moody Bible Institute, 1953.

Walvoord, John F. & Roy Zuck. *The Bible Knowledge Commentary, Old Testament.* Wheaton, IL: Victor Books, 1985.